Also by Chrissie Manby

Flatmates
Second Prize
Deep Heat
Lizzie Jordan's Secret Life
Running Away From Richard
Getting Personal
Seven Sunny Days
Girl Meets Ape
Ready Or Not?
The Matchbreaker
Marrying for Money
Spa Wars
Crazy in Love
Getting Over Mr Right
Kate's Wedding
Writing for Love (ebook only)

About the author

Chrissie Manby is the author of sixteen romantic novels
and a guide for aspiring writers, *Writing for Love*.
Raised in Gloucester, Chrissie now lives in London.

You can follow her on Twitter @chrissiemanby, or visit
her website to know more: www.chrismanby.co.uk.

CHRISSIE MANBY

What I Did On My Holidays

HODDER

First published in Great Britain in 2012 by Hodder & Stoughton
An Hachette UK company

1

Copyright © Chrissie Manby 2012

A CIP catalogue record for this title is available from the British Library

B format ISBN 978 0 340 99283 8
A format ISBN 978 0 340 99284 5

Typeset in Sabon MT by Palimpsest Book Production Limited,
Falkirk, Stirlingshire

Printed and bound by Clays Ltd, St Ives plc

Hodder & Stoughton policy is to use papers that are natural, renewable and
recyclable products and made from wood grown in sustainable forests.
The logging and manufacturing processes are expected to conform to the
environmental regulations of the country of origin.

Hodder & Stoughton Ltd
338 Euston Road
London NW1 3BH

www.hodder.co.uk

To Isabella Abigail Davis

With thanks as usual to all the team at Hodder and my agents Antony Harwood and James Macdonald Lockhart. Thanks are due also to my family, especially my sister Kate. And finally to Mark, my dearest dear, without whom I'd have to make my own tea. Milk, no sugar.

Chapter One

Back when I was a child, a summer holiday meant three things. It meant loading up the caravan with enough tinned food to see a family of four through a nuclear winter. It meant starting out at six in the morning to spend eight hours in bumper-to-bumper traffic on the motorway to the South Coast. And when we finally got where we were going, it meant rain. Traffic jams, tinned food and torrential downpours. No wonder my sister, Clare, decided to lie when she got back to school the September she turned nine and 'What I Did on My Holidays' was the subject on the board.

Forget a soggy fortnight in Cornwall; my sister claimed we'd spent three weeks in Florida as special guests of the Disney Corporation. She said she'd had an early birthday celebration with Mickey and Minnie. They gave her a special present, she claimed. Alas, she left it on the plane. Everyone in her class was impressed. When the truth came out – another mum on the school run expressed surprise that we had taken such an exotic trip so soon after Dad was made redundant – my sister was sent straight to bed and had to forego her birthday party. 'But holidays are meant to be about fantasy,' said the precocious nine-year-old when Mum asked her why she'd lied. It stuck with me, that thought. Holidays are meant to be about fantasy. And finally, aged 29 and

357 days, I was going on a holiday worth fantasising about.

So how did I end up spending the second day of it nose to nose with a dead mouse? Ugh, you must be thinking. I should have sued the holiday firm for thousands! But the dead mouse was the least of my worries. I hadn't even made it to the luxury hotel I'd chosen oh so carefully all those months before. No, I was inhaling deceased-rodent dust and spider droppings beneath my own bed, in my own little flat in south London, wondering how on earth everything had gone so horribly wrong.

Shall I tell you why everything had gone so horribly wrong?

Callum Dawes, that's why.

My name is Sophie Sturgeon and no one deserved a holiday more than I did. I'd had a stinking few months in the office. Make that a stinking few years. I wasn't a big fan of my job as a PR officer. Sounds wonderful, eh? A career in public relations is pretty glamorous. A career in public relations for a company that makes lifts and escalators? Not so much.

My employer was a company called Stockwell Lifts. They were based, as the name suggests, in Stockwell, south-west London. It was by turns a tough and boring job. Largely boring. There are only so many stories you can persuade the national press to feature on lifts and escalators, and most of them aren't good. My job was to ensure that the public read about our biggest development projects and safety innovations, and not about the people who spent their bank holiday weekend stuck between floors eleven and twelve. I ran a company blog called Going Up and tweeted as @liftlady. I had eleven followers. All of them worked at head office apart from my mum.

It was very dull, but it paid the bills and it paid for me to have a really good time on those few precious weeks off each year. Right then, after yet another wet and miserable June, there was nothing I needed more than a fortnight at a fabulous hotel with an infinity pool and a sea view. I was especially looking forward to this break for several reasons. Firstly, we had been having one of the worst summers I could remember. Everything had been rained off, from Wimbledon to Glastonbury to the swimming gala at my local outdoor pool. It was that bad. Secondly, I could not wait to have fourteen days away from my desk-mate, Hannah – the only other member of the Stockwell Lifts PR team – who had been driving me nuts for months with her wedding-planning woes. Her big day was still a whole year away, yet to judge by the constant state of low-level stress she had induced in herself, and the rest of us, you would have thought that no one in the world had ever got married before. Finally, I was looking forward to spending my thirtieth birthday with my wonderful boyfriend, Callum.

Callum Dawes. The moment our eyes locked across a box of serving-sized UHT-milk cartons in the staff kitchen, I knew that my crush on Daniel Craig was so over. As Callum nodded towards the cartons I was carrying and asked me, 'Can I have one?' his smile lit the room (which had been in a state of perpetual darkness since the fluorescent tube blew some three months earlier). Unfortunately, on that very first meeting, I was sporting a time-of-the-month pimple the size of a ping-pong ball and I was wearing my second-worst suit. It was an unflattering grey number in some cheap synthetic fabric and probably six or seven years old, but I was loath to throw it away, because what was the point of spending my limited wages on work clothes when I worked at a company where 'paunch' was part of the job spec for all the male employees? Or at least it had been up until that moment.

Callum Dawes changed everything when he started work at head office. Here at last was a colleague worth brushing my hair for. I certainly wished I had dabbed on some concealer before I left the flat that morning. Callum seemed to focus right on my spot while he introduced himself as the new operations manager for the north of England. I leaned on the staff microwave and propped my chin on my fist, cunningly hiding my pimple in what I hoped looked like a pose of casual interest in Callum's story. But I didn't feel in the least bit casual. This man was gorgeous. He was much younger than the guy he had replaced – two decades younger, in fact – and much better looking. He was definitely paunch-free. Later that day, someone said he looked a bit like the actor Christian Bale and the nickname stuck. Well, 'Batman' did for a while.

Callum's arrival at the company was like a rainbow at the end of a long, grey summer's day. With his slim-fitting suits (a rumour went round that they were Hugo Boss) and his colourful ties, he was an exotic fish in a tank full of guppies. He caused such excitement. All the girls in my office straightened up when Callum walked down the glass-walled corridor en route to the canteen. Even Hannah couldn't help flicking her care-fully highlighted hair in his direction.

Yes, Callum turned even Hannah's faithful head. He was *that* good-looking. It's true that he didn't have much in the way of competition at Stockwell Lifts' headquarters, but I was pretty sure he could have seen off most of the competition at a male-model agency too. Which was why I was surprised that my in-box was soon fit to burst with jokes that he had forwarded and that he always seemed to appear in the staff kitchen when I was making the tea. It's why I was astonished when we ended up snogging on a fire-exit staircase at the next staff Christmas party. And it's why I was absolutely flabbergasted when that drunken snog turned into an actual date and that actual date became the beginning of a proper *relationship*.

It was such a thrill. At first, we tried to keep things quiet, because we weren't sure how our colleagues would react or even if our budding relationship might have breached some code of conduct that could lead to our dismissal, but I can't tell you how happy I was to go to work during those months when Callum and I were fresh and new and we would try to snatch the odd moment in the stationery cupboard. Such a cliché, I know, but it was the only room in the entire 1970s building that didn't have at least one glass wall.

Callum and I managed to keep our increasing involvement with one another our little secret for almost four months, but eventually we were outed by Alison, the company chairman's PA. She saw us crossing Oxford Street hand in hand one Saturday afternoon. She was almost killed by a bus as she ran across the road to confront us. Callum quickly dropped my hand and pretended to be looking in a shop window, but his evasive action came much too late. Alison was gleeful as she imagined what trouble she could cause. We had been seen looking 'coupley'. We had to fess up.

Telling Alison anything was like making an announcement on Twitter. Even before we got to work the following Monday morning (staggering our arrival by a couple of minutes, as was our habit) the news was out. Our relationship wasn't a sackable offence, thank goodness – we were both single and both grown-ups – but after the story became public, we had to make a special effort to appear professional and that meant no PDAs (public displays of affection) in office time. Not even so much as a friendly glance over the staff kettle. There would definitely be no more sneaking off to the stationery cupboard. That was a shame, but I was glad to be able to tell everyone that Callum was my boyfriend at last. Even if it did raise a little in-house envy.

'If I hadn't seen it with my own eyes,' said Alison to Hannah, when she thought I was out of earshot, 'I never would have believed it. Him and *her*? I would have said he was out of her league, wouldn't you?'

Hannah agreed. 'Right out of her league.' The cow.

If I was honest, however, I couldn't quite believe it myself. Callum was handsome and clever and funny and definitely going up in the world of lifts. (Alison sneaked a copy of his appraisal my way one afternoon.) He probably *was* out of my league, but it didn't seem to matter to him, and eighteen months after Callum and I shared our first kiss at that Christmas party, we were still very much a couple. This long-planned fortnight in Majorca was to be our third holiday together. Since we started going out, we had spent a weekend in Malaga and a week in Crete. I couldn't wait to go to Majorca for my thirtieth birthday celebrations. I just knew it was going to be special.

Chapter Two

I had chosen Majorca on Hannah's recommendation.

Hannah and I had a love-hate sort of relationship . . . What am I talking about? It was much more 'hate-hate' than that. Since we held the same job title in a department that was overstaffed by 100 per cent (and there were always rumbles of redundancy), there was, of course, a certain amount of professional competition, but there was also a horrible degree of personal competition, which naturally focused on our success in relationships. For a brief period after my relationship with Callum came out into the open, I was on top – Callum, the hottest man at Stockwell Lifts, if not the hottest in lift engineering full stop, was considered a serious catch – but then Hannah and her 'sainted Mike', the management consultant, got engaged. 'Fiancé' trumps 'hot boyfriend' every time.

Since that moment, Hannah had taken it upon herself to offer me unsolicited relationship advice at every turn. She was constantly checking the temperature of my relationship with seemingly innocuous questions. Had I met Callum's parents yet? What did my parents think of him? Were we planning to introduce our families to each other? Hannah's reaction to my answers left me in little doubt that she thought we were making slow progress. I tried to ignore her, but eighteen months in, I couldn't help wondering what it was about Hannah that had persuaded Mike to take their relationship to the next stage, while Callum and I still spent important family dates, like Christmas and Easter, apart. I'd met his mother only once and that was accidental: I arrived as she was leaving Callum's flat after a weekend of Christmas shopping. I hadn't met his father at all, or his sister, and she lives inside the M25. I was always offering to cook Sunday lunch for them all, but Callum said it was too much bother. Hannah said she met all of Mike's family in their first three months of going out. That was a sign of his intention, she explained.

It was during one of her relationship pep talks that Hannah *counselled* me to choose Majorca for our next holiday. She said she had never had such a wonderful time as she'd had on that island.

'You've got to go to the north side,' Hannah told me. 'Much classier than the south. You want to try Puerto Bona. There's a great hotel right near the beach.'

It was in Majorca that Hannah's sainted Mike had popped the question. She said he had been so overcome by the beauty of the view from their hotel room that he decided he should propose there and then to capitalise on the perfect setting, despite not yet having asked Hannah's father's permission or bought an engagement ring.

I had been thinking about a fortnight in Tenerife – my mum's best friend had an apartment on the island and we could have stayed there for free – but Hannah soon had me sold on her special resort and I booked two flights to Palma. If a view could move a man to marriage, I wanted Callum to see it. After eighteen months spent shuttling up and down the Northern Line between my flat in Clapham and his flat in Kentish Town, I was keen at least for us to move in together. Callum, on the other hand, didn't seem to be in any kind of hurry to move things forward, despite the fact that it would make good financial sense – we were neither of us loaded, my lease was coming up, and he already spent four nights a week at my place because it was nearer to work.

'You want to start charging him rent,' Hannah suggested.

As our holiday in Majorca drew closer, however, it had been a long time since Callum had spent the night at my flat. He'd been up in Newcastle for the best part of a month, overseeing the installation of six super-long Stockwell Lifts 'Trojan' escalators at a new shopping centre on the outskirts of the city. It was a really big deal for the company, which had been losing out more and more frequently on major projects such as this to cheaper foreign manufacturers. This Newcastle project was the deal that kept Stockwell Lifts from going under during the Credit Crunch. We all owed our jobs to that shopping centre, especially those of us who worked in the overstaffed PR department.

Callum often had to go away for a few nights – he was the north of England manager, after all, and he had clients to visit in all the major cities up there – but the time he had spent on the Newcastle project was the longest we had been apart since we first got together. It was awful for me, and for him too, I assumed. He was working so hard he wasn't even able to come home for the weekends. I missed him terribly during our time apart and was counting the days until our holiday. Though I texted and called several times a day, it wasn't the same as being able to share lunch at his desk or poke my head round his office door whenever I wanted. I had grown used to being around Callum 24/7. I really couldn't wait to see him again.

With the holiday just a couple of days away, I was like a child at the end of term. I was in such high spirits that I happily listened to Hannah witter on about her wedding plans all day long and never once had the urge to stab her with a Biro. Meanwhile, she was more than happy to go over the events of her own holiday in Majorca in real time, reliving Mike's fabulous proposal with a 40-minute monologue that exceeded the duration of the actual event by, oh, 200 per cent, I should imagine. I caught Alison – my office frenemy (everybody's office frenemy, in fact) – smirking when Hannah broke into an unaccompanied and somewhat shaky rendition of James Blunt's 'You're Beautiful', which a live band had been playing in a nearby bar when the sainted Mike was overcome by the view and decided to make his move.

'You are going to love Majorca,' Hannah assured me. 'It really is one of the best places on earth. I can't think of anywhere I would rather be. I've told Mike I want us to retire there. Spanish food, all that sunshine, lovely beaches, friendly people . . . the romance . . . Oh, you have to go to this place too . . .' She scribbled down the name of another club. 'I can't believe I forgot to tell you about the Palacio Blanco. We had mojitos there. Best on the island. I am so jealous of you two going to Majorca on Wednesday. You are going to love it, and I just know that Callum is going to love it too.'

I hoped so. Callum and I definitely needed some quality time. On a couple of occasions when I'd called him that week, he'd seemed a little disinterested in hearing the latest developments in the detailed itinerary I had been putting together with Hannah's eager assistance. I put that down to his feeling tired after a month of non-stop work. He had every right to be exhausted as the Newcastle project drew to a close. I'd been working hard back at head office too. We had earned every day of our trip.

I hoped Callum and I would have at least as good a time as we'd had in Crete the previous year. How magical that holiday had been. The resort was perfect. The weather was perfect. We soon fell into a daily rhythm of long mornings cuddling in bed, afternoons lazing by the pool and evenings spent dancing in the cocktail bar. When we came back from that holiday, so happy and relaxed in each other's company, I felt that we had grown much, much closer. 'It was like we were Siamese twins,' was how I'd heard Callum describing it to one of the lift engineers when I happened upon them in the staff kitchen. Actually, 'bloody Siamese twins' was what he said, but I knew that men sometimes like to play down their feelings in public. Anyway, it had been a mistake to let so much time elapse since then without even so much as a mini-break. I hoped that as soon as Callum got on that plane, he would start to perk up and feel excited again. Unbeknown to him, I was planning for our holiday to start long before we got to the airport.

Chapter Three

I had everything organised to the last detail. Since we were flying from Gatwick, it made more sense for Callum to come and stay in my south London flat rather than spend the night at his own place in Kentish Town. He would catch the train down from Newcastle as soon as he could get away that afternoon, swing by his place to drop off his work gear, pack his suitcase for the holiday and get the Tube to mine for a delicious supper and an early night. We would have to be up at the crack of dawn the following morning to get a minicab to the Gatwick Express at Victoria. Charter flights always seem to leave really early. I had booked the cab two weeks in advance to make sure we didn't get stranded.

Having done my holiday shopping and packing during the lonely weekends while Callum was stuck up there in Newcastle, I had plenty of time to prepare a really special meal for our last night in Inglaterra. (See how well my Spanish was coming along?) I was going to cook something with a Spanish theme, of course. That last day at work, I spent my lunch hour in Sainsbury's, buying everything I needed. To begin with, stuffed olives, chorizo and Manchego cheese, plus four bottles of Spanish beer to wash it down. For a main course, I was going to make chicken rice from a recipe I'd found on a Spanish tourism website. For pudding, a traditional Spanish lemon tart. OK, so I bought a ready-made tart . . .

Back at the office, I spent the afternoon tormenting Hannah with the thought that the following day I would be in her favourite place on earth, while she would be in my least favourite place in the universe, and dealing with my calls to boot.

'Don't forget to send us a postcard,' she said as I prepared to leave at five on the dot without so much as a goodbye tweet from @liftlady.

'You'll be lucky if I have time to send a text,' I said.

I had no intention whatsoever of spending my fort-night away corresponding by postcard, text or otherwise with the people I had been so looking forward to getting away from. As I walked out through the revolving doors, I was a free woman. At least for the next fourteen days. Fourteen days! I didn't even care that when I came home, I would no longer be in my twenties. Two weeks with no work more than made up for that. Two weeks with nothing to do but concentrate on my dearest, darling Callum. It was going to be heaven.

As soon as I got home, I changed into something much more 'holiday-like'. I checked that my passport was in the right place: in the outside pocket of my special black travel holdall, which I'd carefully chosen to fit in an overhead locker. There was no reason why it wouldn't be. It had been there for most of the week.

Next, I went into the kitchen and put on some suit-able music while I prepared our Spanish feast. The Gipsy Kings seemed appropriate. I would only later find out that they were French and not Spanish after all. Anyway, for now their frenetic guitars and catchy rhythms fit the bill. My mood was as high as a helium balloon. I wiggled to the beat as I took the packaging off the cheese and the chorizo and arranged both on a plate as though for a TV cookery show. I danced across the room to put the beer bottles in the fridge. I jigged from foot to foot as I sent Callum another text – my fifth since leaving the office – to find out how he was doing. Was he at King's Cross yet?

'I can't wait for our holiday to begin!' I texted as the CD started from the beginning a second time.

Callum didn't text me back as quickly as I hoped, but I put that down to his perhaps already being on his way. I snuck a piece of cheese while I waited to hear from him. Hmm. The Manchego wasn't quite as exciting as I'd expected. Not much flavour at all considering that one tiny lump had cost as much as a paperback novel. I wouldn't be bothering with that again. Unless Callum really liked it, of course. If Callum liked it, I would definitely buy some more. I had a special shelf in my kitchen for the things that he liked: Doritos, Peperami, beef jerky . . .

Then I went online and looked at various views of our hotel. I had spent a lot of time on that hotel website while Callum was working away, just looking at the pictures and imagining us together by the pool. Adjacent sunbeds. Holding hands. It was going to be so good for us to get some time together alone again. I don't think I had ever looked forward to a holiday more than I was looking forward to our fortnight in Puerto Bona. I could almost feel the sun on my face and the sea breeze in my hair.

Meanwhile, Mum texted to wish us both a happy holiday and me a happy birthday. While wasting time on the Internet, I had already noticed that Mum had changed her Facebook status to 'Can't believe my little girl is going to be thirty next week. Have a very happy holiday, Sophie.' Mum loved her status updates. While many of her contemporaries claimed to find the Internet overwhelming, my mum had moved straight into the fast lane of the information superhighway. She had a Facebook page before I did, and when I told her that I had opened a Twitter account for work, she signed up that very afternoon so she could follow me. Mum tweeted as @hotflushheather and had eighteen followers to my eleven. She updated at least ten times a day and every time Dad made a joke he asked her, 'Are you going to twit that?' Apart from me, Mum followed several yoga gurus and her local weatherman. Apparently, he was rather funny and a good deal more accurate than the BBC.

Anyway, being the type of person who plans ahead, Mum had already sent me my thirtieth birthday present, a silver photo frame, which I'd filled with a picture of Callum and me on Valentine's Day. It was my favourite photo of us together, though the day itself hadn't gone quite as I hoped. When Callum told me he'd booked the restaurant where we had our first date for 14 February, I thought he might be planning something special. Unfortunately, he wasn't, but the chap on the next table (which was less than two inches away – the restaurant was packing 'em in) did choose that night to propose. As we were leaving, I wished the happy couple the very best and offered to take a photo. They reciprocated and it turned out to be the nicest photo of Callum and me ever taken. So I put it in the frame and tried not to think about the argument we'd had later that night. I think it was about where we'd be spending Easter. More importantly, it was about whether we would be spending Easter together, which was what I had very much hoped for. We didn't. Callum said that Easter was an especially sacred time for his family.

I texted Mum back, making sure I added 'I love you', as we always do when any family member is about to fly. A little morbid, I know, but wouldn't you just hate for such things to have gone unsaid? After that, I texted my sister to let her know that I loved her too. Most of the time, it was true.

Chapter Four

Clare was my big sister. She was just over two years older than me and for a long time we had fought like cat and dog. During my teens there were times when I had actively hated her (mostly when she refused to lend me her real black leather jacket or her favourite high-heeled shoes), but now that we were both proper grown-ups and making our way in London, we had become much closer again. The time she pulled the legs off my box-fresh equestrian Barbie was long since forgotten, as was the day I broke her silver charm bracelet. (At least, that incident was only mentioned once every couple of months now.) We had put our childish squabbles behind us and I would say that over the past couple of years Clare had become one of my very best friends.

Clare was living quite close to me. I had a one-bedroom flat in Clapham Old Town. She shared a sweet little terraced house with her fiancé, Evan, an auditor for an insurance company, just two stops down the Northern Line in Balham, though she liked to call it Clapham South. We were always in and out of each other's houses. I had looked after Clare's goldfish, Cheryl Cole, while she and Evan went camping over Easter. (Cheryl Cole's bowl-mate, Ashley, died after making a suicide leap onto the carpet while Clare and Evan were at work. It happened on the day the real

Coles announced their divorce, which seemed prophetic.)
Now Clare was going to return the favour by watering
my house plants while I was away. At least, she would
water them if she remembered. I just had to make sure
she remembered. I knew Clare wouldn't let me down
deliberately, but she could be a bit dreamy.

'Love you. Please don't forget my plants!' I begged
her in my text.

'Of course I won't forget,' she texted back. 'I'll water
them every day, I promise. I love you too.'

Water them every day? I doubted it. But if she
managed once a week, the plants would probably
survive.

So everything was set. My case had been packed and
ready for the best part of a fortnight. My passport was
still where I had put it. The airline tickets and accommodation and car-hire vouchers were with my passport.
I had bought a special pink folder to keep everything
together. It matched the pink leather passport cover,
embossed with my initials in gold, that Clare had given
me for my birthday the year before.

Both my suitcase and my hand luggage were packed
with incredible precision. Prior to packing my case, I
had made tiny drawings of every item of summer
clothing that I owned. I cut these out, like a paper doll's
wardrobe, and mixed and matched until I had worked
out the least possible number of clothes I needed to
pack to make the greatest number of outfits. There
was no room for excess baggage with the budget airline
charging more for an extra suitcase than we had paid
for the flights in the first place.

My hand luggage contained an emergency change
of clothes, should my checked luggage go awry. It also

contained my incredibly flattering new bikini. That was going in my hand luggage because when a girl finds a bikini that she really, really likes, she should take no risks with losing it. A good bikini is as rare as Mr Right.

My carry-on also contained essential toiletries, which I had decanted into airport-security-approved hundred-millilitre bottles and tucked into a clear ziplock bag. I was very proud of my packing indeed. It might have featured in a photo shoot for one of those 'How to Travel Light' articles you get in all the women's magazines every summer.

I knew that Callum would be just as careful with his luggage. Callum was a man who appreciated good clothes – hence he bought his suits at Hugo Boss when all the other guys at the office went for drip-dry M&S. He certainly had the body to make the most of them, especially since he started doing boxercise at the gym on a Saturday morning. Anyway, he was the only man I had ever met who bothered to put layers of tissue paper between his trousers to stop them creasing in the hold. He also had a skincare regime that would have made any girl proud.

'Don't forget your sunblock,' I texted him as the Gipsy Kings struck up for a third time. He didn't really need reminding, I knew – Callum was not the kind of guy who would spend his first few days by the pool looking like a lobster – but I wanted to jog him into letting me know where he was. It was strange that he hadn't texted or called. He generally responded to every sixth text I sent, at least.

However, by eight o'clock I had still heard nothing from Callum and my holiday mood began to waver just a little. Where had he got to? I had been under the impression that his train from Newcastle would get into London at around half past five. It shouldn't have taken more than fifteen minutes for him to get from the train station to his flat in Kentish Town, and it wouldn't take him longer than half an hour to throw some things into a bag. All that meant he could easily have been at my place by eight. But even if he had been delayed, surely he should have let me know?

Had his iPhone run out of battery? He would never have let that happen. Callum would sooner be without his shoes than his iPhone. Ordinarily, he was a slave to its pings and vibrations. We'd once had a spectacular row after he responded to a text while I was giving him a private viewing of some newly bought underwear. There's nothing quite so humiliating as standing in the middle of the living room in nothing but a new bra and thong, while your boyfriend lets his best mate know what time the rugby kicks off . . . So it was not like him to have not responded to *any* of my texts that day and soon the worst-case scenarios began to drift through my mind. I was certain he'd have let me know if he had missed his train or if he'd been delayed, but what if there had been a terrible accident?

I went back online to check, but there was nothing about a train crash on any of the news websites. Mum, however, had tweeted, 'Hope Sophie and Callum are having an early night ahead of their holiday.' Hannah, who was one of Mum's followers because she thought it was 'cute' that I had a tweet-happy mother, had added, 'I hope they make the most of their time in Majorca because I'm left behind and doing all the work!'

Alison also followed Mum. She had tweeted, 'Hear, hear.'

I found it very disconcerting that my mother and colleagues were Twitter-mates, especially when Mum tweeted about her hot flushes. She thought she was striking a blow for menopausal women everywhere and that one day her insights – such as 'Standing in front of the fridge with my blouse open' or 'Have found a natural alternative to KY' – would be collected into a best-selling book. For me, knowing that my colleagues had been treated to the thought of my mother chilling her cleavage was just another reason to dread going into work.

I logged off Twitter and sent Callum another text.

'I thought you would be here by now,' I wrote. 'Is everything OK?'

And then I waited and I waited some more until it was almost nine o'clock. Dinner was certainly ruined. The rice, now overcooked, was as hard and dry as it had been when I poured it out of the packet. My carefully planned schedule had assumed we would be in bed by half past nine. Where the hell was he? I called him and went straight to voicemail.

'Callum,' I said, 'I'm really worried now. You were supposed to be here ages ago. Your dinner is in the oven, but it's completely dried up. The cheese is looking sweaty. The beer is warm. And we're supposed to be in bed in half an hour. You do know what time we've got to get up in the morning, don't you? Please give me a call.'

As soon as I put down the phone, I wondered if my message had sounded too brusque. My mind continued to race with visions of train crashes and car accidents.

Was he stuck underground in a broken-down Tube carriage? There were so many reasons why he might not have called. Alas, there was one worst-case scenario that I hadn't thought of. Worse than train strikes and Tube stoppages, worse than Callum being late to my flat because he couldn't find his passport, worse than just about anything. I mean, why would I have thought of it, given that Callum and I were due to go on a lovely romantic holiday the very next morning? Our future could not have looked brighter.

'I'm not coming over to your place tonight,' Callum texted at last.

Well, at least he was alive.

'Why not?' I texted back. The fuzzy feeling of relief I had felt at seeing his name in my in-box at last was quickly replaced by annoyance. His dinner had been ready for the past two hours and now he was telling me he wasn't coming over? What was he thinking? I guessed that he wanted to spend a night in his own flat. After all, he hadn't spent the night there for a month because of the Newcastle job. But still . . . he was being very selfish having waited so long to let me know. He must have known I would cook for him. I always cooked for him.

'You do know how early we're going to have to set off for the airport?' I added. 'Shall I come to you?' I suggested before he could text me again.

'No. Don't come over. I mean, I don't want to go to Majorca,' was his reply.

Well, I wasn't going to text my response to that one. I called Callum right away.

'Hello.'

He picked up, thank goodness.

'What do you mean, you don't want to go to Majorca?' I asked without preamble.

'I mean, I don't want to go to Majorca,' he said simply.

I was about to ask him if he was anxious about the flight, though he'd never been anxious about flying before, or whether he thought he had too much to do here in London – I knew he must have household admin backing up from his month away – but then he added, 'With you.'

Chapter Five

'With you.'

Those two little words were like a body blow. Before I'd had time to digest them, my stomach was already reacting to the news. He wasn't saying *that*, was he? I sat down on a kitchen chair and waited for clarification. Maybe Callum didn't actually mean what my heart was already mourning.

'I'm really sorry,' he said. 'I really am.'

Oh dear. The downcast tone of his voice confirmed the worst.

Never let it be said that my darling Callum didn't have fabulous timing. On the dance floor, he never missed a beat. When it came to telling a joke, he always knew the exact right amount of time to pause before delivering the killer punchline. But having decided he was going to dump me, he was going to do so the night before our long-awaited two-week holiday in Majorca. My thirtieth-birthday holiday! What kind of timing is that?

Over the course of the next ten minutes, the terrible truth came out.

During the month that we had been apart, Callum had been doing a lot of thinking. He knew that I wanted to settle down eventually, so he thought he had better tell me sooner rather than later that it wasn't going to be with him. We were neither of us getting any younger, he added, reminding me with a jab of my upcoming thirtieth birthday, which would fall smack bang in the middle of our holiday. What a great birthday that would be now. It wasn't that he didn't care for me deeply, he said, or think I wouldn't make someone a wonderful wife. It was just that he didn't think he could give me everything I needed right now – he wasn't ready for that kind of commitment with anybody, he added – and that realisation made him sad. It was best that we didn't take things further. He didn't want to mess me around. That's why he wasn't going to be coming on our trip.

I couldn't believe it. Callum and I had been planning our annual holiday for months. OK, so it's perhaps more accurate to say that *I* had been planning that holiday for months, but I had no reason to believe that Callum was any less enthusiastic about the prospect of going away than I was. He knew it was especially important to me to do something different over my big birthday. I wanted to mark the occasion in style. And yet, with less than ten hours to go, when he was supposed to be at my flat in south London, eating a specially prepared Spanish-themed supper before we got an early night ready for our crack-of-dawn taxi ride to the airport train link, Callum was at his flat in north London, telling me, over the phone, that our eighteen-month relationship was over.

Couldn't he have dumped me after the holiday? That was my first muddled reaction. I asked him. Apparently not. Bless his sensitive little heart, Callum told me next he'd wrestled with the idea of going on the holiday and wielding the axe upon our return, but decided that ultimately I would be more upset if he came on the trip and dumped me as soon as we got back. Likewise, any effort he made to celebrate my birthday with me would only look deceitful in retrospect. Besides, knowing what was coming up would ruin the fortnight for him. How could he enjoy himself when he was already feeling so guilty?

'It wouldn't be honest,' he said. 'Not when I've already made up my mind to break up with you.'

How thoughtful.

I tried to stay calm. Callum and I had forked out the best part of £1,200 each for our flights and accommodation. Was he really going to junk that? If I could just get him to Majorca, I was sure all this nonsense could be sorted out . . .

'You're just tired,' I told him, struggling to keep my voice calm as I brushed off everything he'd said. 'You've been working so hard up there in Newcastle. Let me come over to your place and bring you some dinner. As soon as we're back in the same room you'll remember what it is you like about me,' I added with as much humour as I could muster. Believe me, it wasn't easy as the panic began to rise. 'Please, Callum. You haven't had a day off for a month.'

'I have had a day off,' said Callum. 'I've had every weekend off, in fact.'

'You said you didn't . . .'

'I just didn't want to come back to you.'

'What? Did you come back to London?' I asked.

'A few times. I hid out in my flat,' he confirmed. 'I kept the curtains drawn in case you came round.'

Oh, no. All this honesty was too much. I had been pacing the kitchen as Callum and I talked. Now it was time to sit down again. 'You actually hid from me?' I squeaked.

'I did. I had to. I just couldn't face you. I'm sorry, Soph, but if I'm honest, I've been feeling this way for a lot longer than the past month. Us going out and working together too. There were times I felt like I couldn't breathe. I thought being away from you for a while would make things better. Absence makes the heart grow fonder and all that. But it didn't happen. The longer I went without seeing you, the more I realised that I wasn't really missing you. Not at all. And now I've got a fortnight off, I don't want to spend it pretending things are still OK. I want to spend it on my own.'

'You came to London and you didn't see me?' I was still stuck on that point.

'I wanted some thinking time,' said Callum. 'It's not a nice thing for you to hear, I know, but I wanted to get things straight in my head before I talked to you.'

'And now you've got things straight in your head and we're over?'

'That's pretty much it,' he agreed. 'Yes.' He sounded relieved by my summary.

'Is there someone else?' There had to be someone else. What else could have happened to change his mind in such a short period of time?

'There's no one else,' he promised me.

'Then come to Majorca. We need to see each other right away. We can't talk about this properly on the phone.'

'I know,' said Callum. 'It's not ideal. I really hate to do this to you other than face to face. I feel really bad about it, especially with it being your birthday holiday and all.'

'Then why didn't you come to my flat?'

'Because I didn't want you to persuade me to go to Majorca. Not when I'd made up my mind not to go.'

But at least he didn't expect me to miss out on that well-planned trip because of him.

'We'll see each other when you get back. You should still go,' he continued. 'I know how much you've been looking forward to it.'

'I was looking forward to going with *you*,' I reminded him. 'I wanted to be with you when I turned thirty. How can I go on holiday and have a good time now that I've been dumped?'

'Perhaps it will help you get over me,' Callum suggested. 'Two weeks in the sun. It will change your whole perspective, I bet. I won't expect you to pay back my half of the accommodation, of course,' he added generously. 'Unless, maybe, you can get someone to go with you. If they could pay my half . . . that would be really helpful . . . I've had an expensive month.'

Though obviously not because he'd spent a fortune on a birthday gift for me. 'Who?' I snarled. 'Tell me who can I get to go with me to Majorca with less than eight hours until the taxi arrives to take us to the Gatwick Express?'

'Um . . . you could tweet it,' he said helpfully. 'Someone might know someone with a fortnight off starting tomorrow.'

Now I was angry. 'You've ruined everything!' I yelled.

'There's no need to shout,' he said.

'There is every need to shout,' I told him.

'Look, I'm sorry,' said Callum. 'I'm really sorry.' He said it again and again, but he wasn't going to change his mind. It was obvious to me that while I was sinking into despair, he was feeling happier by the second. The worst was already over for him. He'd done what he had to do. He'd told me we were finished. He'd handed over the baton of pain. I could hear the relief in his voice as the conversation began to wrap up. That tipped me over the edge.

'Fine,' I shrieked. 'Fine. See if I bloody well care.'

'You'll have a great time in Majorca,' he said as he ended the conversation.

Have a great time? What on earth was he thinking?

'Oh, I will,' I assured him. 'I'll have a bloody good time. Just you see if I don't.'

So that was that. I heard nothing more from him that night, and yet as the clock ticked towards midnight, I was strangely certain that when morning came, Callum would have relented. Back in his frankly grotty flat for the night, he would start to see the appeal of two weeks in the sun. And I was sure the thought of all that money potentially lost in a late cancellation would bug him too. So I formulated a strategy of sorts. I couldn't sleep, but I was careful not to bombard him with texts and calls. Every time I had the urge to text, I made a cup of tea. I got through a whole box of tea bags. It was harder than I had ever imagined, but I told myself I just had to trust that if he thought I might be taking him at his word, he would wonder whether he'd made such a good decision.

All was not lost, I promised myself. Our flight wasn't until half past eight. As long as he got to my place by five thirty, we'd be fine. I'd check us in online. We'd just bring hand luggage. It wouldn't take more than twenty minutes to get through security at that time in the morning. But five thirty came round without so much as an SMS from the man I loved. I sat by the door with my suitcase in front of me. I texted him one more time.

'Please come. I can meet you at the airport,' I said. 'We can get separate accommodation. We don't even have to sit next to each other on the plane.'

'Your text woke me up. You've got to go on holiday without me,' Callum replied. 'We've split up. I'm not changing my mind. *Bon voyage.*'

Oh! There was something about that '*bon voyage*' that made me angry again. Angry enough to do something completely out of character. With that flash of rage empowering me, I thought I might just call his bluff. I thought perhaps I really, really could go on holiday without him. That would show him. Why should I miss out on my long-anticipated fortnight away just because he didn't want to go with me? In a matter of hours he'd realise he'd made a terrible mistake. He'd change his mind. He'd probably book another flight and follow me. I would be there in Majorca waiting for him. I could see it now. I would be sitting at a bar by the pool, sipping a cocktail, reading my new Marian Keyes. And when he turned up, I would just say, 'What kept you so long?'

Yes, in my head it would all work out. I was going on my own. I pictured myself striding through Gatwick's South Terminal looking like Cameron Diaz starring in the Hollywood version of my life. I was strong and independent and definitely not the kind of girl who would miss out on her thirtieth-birthday holiday because of some stupid man . . .

But I couldn't hold on to the vision for long enough to make it stick, and by the time the long-booked cab arrived, though I was sitting by the front door with my suitcase between my knees, theoretically all ready to go, my feeble confidence had ebbed right away. The taxi driver honked his horn antisocially. He did it again a minute later. Longer and louder this time. I had to go out to tell him that I wasn't going to Gatwick before he woke the whole street up. I paid him £20 for his trouble, and then I went back indoors and slumped down on the floor like a sack of spuds.

'We're not going on a summer holiday . . .' sang a little voice inside my head.

Chapter Six

What a disaster. Having sent the taxi away, the reality of my situation finally dawned on me. I really wasn't going on holiday. Callum had dumped me. I should have been queuing at the check-in desk at Gatwick. Instead, I was sitting on my doormat, staring into space as though I had been hit on the back of the head with a mallet.

For the time it should have taken me to get to the airport and check in, I remained in a ball of misery just behind the front door. I pulled my knees up to my chest and rested my chin upon them. I placed my iPhone on the floor beside me and stared at that for a while, willing the damn thing to ring, but it didn't ring. At half past seven, an email came through. I leaped to check it, sure for just a moment that Callum would have written to let me know more about his sudden decision, but it was only an email from a company selling cut-price swimwear. They were offering a further 50 per cent off their sale prices. Fat lot of good that was to me now, I snorted. When the email came through a second time, giving my heart another unnecessary jolt, I practically threw my damn phone down the hall.

'Oh, Callum,' I groaned, covering my face with my hands, 'how could you do this to me?'

The sudden change in my circumstances was surreal. Was there another Sophie in a parallel world preparing to board that plane at Gatwick with the man of her dreams still beside her?

Outside my flat, London life continued as normal. The rest of the street was getting ready for the day ahead, for school and for work. My neighbour's children – children I had only ever heard and never actually seen – had a ferocious squabble about who would be taking the Nintendo DS to school. Every word was clear through the paper-thin wall that divided our flats. Their mother intervened at top volume. The DS would be staying home. Later, I heard their front door slam and the noise of squabbling children drifted away down the street. Minutes after that, the guy who lived on the top floor of my building thundered down the communal stairs. Late for work again. It sounded as though he fell down the final four steps. He did quite a bit of swearing at the bottom. In the flat directly above mine, I heard the slower, quieter sounds of the old woman who lived there making her solitary breakfast. I heard her turn on the tap to fill a kettle. I heard the scraping sound of a chair pulled out from beneath the kitchen table. The same routine every day. Would that be me in fifty years' time?

The thought of a solitary old age jolted me into action. Callum and I could *not* be over. Not like this. I knew we had much more to talk about. I dragged myself from my spot in the hall to the kitchen table, and at the moment that our flight would have taken off, I began to draft an email to him, telling him what I thought we had to save. What about all the good times we'd had? We'd been joined at the hip for so long. I worked on that email for an hour and a half. Since both of us had the day off, I suggested, why didn't we get together over lunch and have a proper discussion about it face to face? If I could just persuade him to see me, if I got myself dressed up and did my hair and acted like it didn't really matter, I was sure he would reconsider. I was reading my hopeful entreaty through a final time to make sure it was perfect before sending it when an email from the office came through.

It was from my nemesis Hannah. It was entitled 'WTF'.

To: Sophie Sturgeon
From: Hannah Brown
Re: WTF
6 Jul 2011 10:10

Callum has just walked down the corridor. I thought you guys were supposed to be leaving for Majorca this morning. WTF is going on?

Of course, while I was sitting on the floor feeling sorry for myself, I had considered the horrible prospect of having to tell everyone at the office that Callum and I had split. I'd felt my stomach turn as I thought of Hannah and Alison's snake-eyed sympathies. They wouldn't care about my pain. Far from it. In fact, I wouldn't have been in the least bit surprised if Alison, upon hearing the news, immediately rushed off to offer Callum her bosom to cry upon.

Telling my workmates was always going to be awful. However, it had not occurred to me that the terrible moment would have to come so soon. It had certainly not occurred to me that Callum would decide, since he wasn't going to Majorca, that he wouldn't take his annual leave after all. I felt dizzy as I imagined him going about his daily life as though nothing had happened, putting on his suit and tie and going into work, while I had been sitting at my kitchen table, my life in suspension, writing an email that begged him to reconsider our split.

I was desperate to know what reason he had given for his unexpected reappearance at Stockwell Lifts and how he seemed to feel about it, but at the same time I didn't dare ask Hannah for more information. Luckily, I didn't have to wait long for Hannah to offer up more information herself. Five minutes after the first email came another one.

To: Sophie Sturgeon
From: Hannah Brown
Re: WTF
6 Jul 2011 10:15

OK. So I cornered him over by the coffee machine. I said, 'Aren't you supposed to be on holiday with Sophie?' and he told me that you've gone to Puerto Bona by yourself! Email me at once and tell me why you're in Majorca and your boyfriend is still in this shit-hole.

Where should I start? Evidently, Callum had not told her that we had split up. At least, not yet, but I was only halfway through crafting my reply by the time Hannah emailed me again.

This time, her email was entitled 'WTF!!!' with three exclamation marks.

Callum just told Alison that you two have split up! That is
crazy. Are you telling me you broke up right before you
were setting off on a romantic holiday? What happened?
When? Last night? This is incredible. I thought you two
were heading for the altar.

That last bit dripped insincerity – Hannah had never
said any such thing to me. In fact, she'd often implied
the exact opposite, given Callum's reluctance to introduce me to his family or spend any of the big annual
holidays with me – but once again, I didn't have time
to respond before Hannah continued.

So it was his decision! I went over to his office on the
pretext of borrowing a stapler and asked him if he
wanted to talk about it. He said he didn't think it was
fair on you to say much about the situation, but he did
tell me that it was he who ended it. God, Sophie, you
must be gutted. I know I would be.

Hannah's email was swiftly followed by an email
from Alison, who had been the first to hear the news
from the horse's mouth.

'I am so, so sorry,' she wrote. 'I can't tell you how
bad I feel on your behalf.'

Yeah, right, I thought. I imagined Alison pulling her
blouse over her head and doing a victory lap round my
desk. The idea of her knowing that Callum was single
– however temporary I hoped it would be – made me
very nervous indeed.

Then Mary, who scheduled the lift engineers' site
visits, texted to find out if the rumours were true. She'd
never heard anything so awful as being dumped before

a fortnight away, especially with a big birthday right in the middle of it. And then Candace, Callum's own PA on the Newcastle project, emailed to ask if I was OK, since Alison had telephoned to tell her the whole story. I couldn't believe it. I had been thinking I would have at least two weeks to get used to the worst having happened before I had to tell the witches in the office and already the news of the break-up was spreading like a fire in a tissue-paper factory. Soon, it seemed that every woman who had ever worked for Stockwell Lifts had emailed or texted to offer me her support. My iPhone had never been so busy. Buzz, buzz, buzz every thirty seconds. I imagined Hannah writing a bulletin for the Going Up blog or, God forbid, mentioning the disaster on Twitter. At this rate by twelve o'clock it would be on the BBC news.

'It's the talk of the company,' Alison confirmed. 'Nobody can believe you guys split up right before your fortnight off. Right before your birthday! What an idiot that man is. I'm not going to call him Batman any more. I'm going to call him *Rat*man from now on. I never really thought he looked like Christian Bale anyway.' Though she was the one who had started that particular idea.

'I can't believe that you've gone on holiday on your own!' commented Candace. 'You are one brave girl.'

'It's the best thing you could have done,' said Hannah in an email she copied to all the girls. 'I can tell that Callum is really gutted you went without him. Gutted enough to be regretting his decision if you ask me.'

Hannah continued, 'He told Alison that he dumped you because you aren't independent enough and can't seem to do anything without him and it's been driving

him nuts, but now you're in the Med on your own.
How's that for independent? By the time you get
back,' Hannah concluded, 'Callum will be eating out
of your hand.'

'Yeah,' Alison chipped in. 'He can't believe you went
without him. You've got the Ratman on the back foot
now for sure. You couldn't have made a better move.'

Really? I felt a small flicker of hope.

Chapter Seven

Here was my position: I was totally in love with Callum Dawes. Head over heels. Utterly besotted. I had woven him into every part of my life, and my dreams of the future were nothing without him as the romantic lead. I simply did not know how I would carry on without him as my boyfriend. How would I fill my lonely nights and long weekends? Worse still, how on earth could I be expected to carry on seeing him in the office five days a week, knowing that he didn't want me any more? My heart would break every weekday morning. And then there would be the hell of discovering who had replaced me in his heart, because I would be bound to hear all about it. Hannah and Alison would make sure of that. And what if it was Alison! She'd certainly do her best to persuade him that it should be. The reasons why one should never date a workmate were quickly becoming clear. If I couldn't get Callum back, I would only date long-distance from that moment forward. Preferably someone on death row in a Texas prison who could be guaranteed not to transfer his affections on to one of my office colleagues.

Right then, however, my colleagues seemed to be firmly on my side. They were so enthusiastic in their 'Go, girl!' cheerleading for my decision to holiday alone that it brought tears to my eyes. If only I had warranted their praise. I knew I would have to tell them the truth at some point. What would they say to me then? They'd think I was pathetic. The thought of their pride turning to pity was just awful. I couldn't face it. Not yet. Not while my head was still reeling with the reality of being dumped. So I didn't respond to their emails. Neither did I send Callum that begging email I'd composed so carefully. There didn't seem to be a lot of point. He wouldn't be able to meet for lunch, would he? He was back at work.

Perhaps I was crazy with the shock of being dumped, but though I had started the day with a long sit-down on a hard floor, by five in the afternoon I was feeling almost cheerful. Hannah reported that Callum had been seen 'moping' in the staff kitchen around three o'clock, so she and Alison went in on the pretence of making some tea and talked loudly about the wonders of Majorca until Callum started to go pink with embarrassment. 'He looked like he was going to burst with fury.' When I read that email, I almost liked her.

'In going on holiday alone,' she concluded dramatically, 'you've struck a blow for womankind.'

If only I had. Part of me wished I had taken that flight alone. A much bigger part of me knew I would never have had the guts. If I'd managed to get as far as the airport, I'd almost certainly have ended up sobbing over the check-in desk. That image of me as Cameron Diaz striding through security would for ever be a fantasy. I was a wimp. I always would be.

But at about six o'clock in the evening, I heard a key in the door, jolting me from my moping. Without stopping to think, I fled for the safety of my bedroom. I had forgotten that my sister would be coming to water the plants.

Chapter Eight

Now, there was no doubt in my mind that if I told my sister what had happened over the past twenty-four hours regarding Callum and the cancelled holiday, she would have been firmly on my side, but right then, I just couldn't face the idea of saying out loud I'd been dumped. In my fragile state, I didn't want sympathy and I didn't want sensible solutions (not that Clare had ever really been big on those). I definitely didn't want a talking-to from our mother, which is what would come next if Clare passed the news on. It seemed infinitely easier to say nothing at all for the time being. That is why I hid.

Fortunately, as she walked into my flat, my sister was jabbering away on her phone, which distracted her nicely from any noise I might have made while getting into my hiding place behind the bedroom door. She was totally oblivious to my presence.

Once behind the door, I was pretty sure I would be safe from discovery. Luckily, I had already moved my suitcase from the hallway back to the bedroom. In an effort to make Clare's task of looking after my plants easier, I had, as promised, grouped them all together on the draining board next to the sink in the kitchen, which meant that all Clare had to do was fill the big jug I had left in the sink and go slosh, slosh, slosh from one plant pot to the next. There was no need for her to venture any further into the flat than the kitchen to do what I'd asked of her. In any case, having known my sister for three decades, I doubted she would do any more than the bare minimum. It simply wasn't her style to pay much attention to anything but shoes and hair products. I was 99 per cent sure I was as well hidden as I needed to be.

I had left the bedroom door open just a crack, so that I could peer out and see what she got up to. After the twenty-four hours I'd had, I actually craved the sight of a friendly face, even if I wasn't going to admit to being there. My flat was so small that from where I was standing, I could see pretty much the whole of the kitchen.

When Clare got there, she was still talking on her mobile. She stopped and exhaled loudly. She glanced to her left and right and announced to the person on the other end of the line, 'Well, the door was only on the top lock, which is very strange for Sophie given that she's such a security freak, but I can see the telly from here. It's still there. No burglars.'

The person at the other end said something that made Clare snort.

'Well, if it was a sixty-two-inch screen, they wouldn't be able to get it through the door, would they? OK. If it was a *flat-screen*, then yes, of course they'd be able to get it through the door, but . . . oh, you know what I mean.'

Sixty-two-inch screen. Big tellies were her fiancé Evan's current obsession. She had to be talking to him.

'I am walking into the living room now,' she said. 'Not only is the telly still there, the DVD player is also exactly where I last saw it. As is the silver-framed photograph of me in a Brownie uniform. I wish she'd get rid of it.'

I imagined Clare picking that photograph up. I knew she hated it. She begged me to hide it whenever she came over, but I refused until she reciprocated by taking down a picture of me, aged three and naked in a paddling pool, that she'd fixed using magnets to her fridge door. We'd had a small falling-out when she invited me and Callum over for dinner one night and drew his attention to the unflattering shot.

'I think I can safely say that Sophie hasn't been burgled,' Clare continued. 'Though there is a dirty mug on the coffee table. And some cheese. That isn't like her at all. Either a burglar just dropped in for a snack or she must have left in a real hurry.'

When she passed by my bedroom door on her way to the kitchen again, my sister was carrying that dirty mug, perhaps with the intention of washing it. That wasn't like her at all either. The Clare I knew never washed up until she had run out of mugs or her fiancé demanded it for reasons of health and hygiene.

Evan was issuing instructions now by the sound of Clare's end of the conversation. Evan was a very practical man.

'Yes, yes,' she said. 'Of course I will. And yes, I'll turn a light on so it looks as though she's still here. Of course. Of course. I'm doing it right now. I know what to do, Evan. I am thirty-two years old and I have a degree.'

Evan said something.

'A two-two in comparative literature is still a degree, Evan Jones.'

I heard the tap running.

'Yes, I'll double-lock the door before leaving. I'll be home in half an hour. Bye-bye.'

Clare sounded annoyed as she finished her call. She placed her phone on the kitchen table with quite a clatter; then she let out a very loud sigh.

'Do this . . . do that . . . Anyone would think I was a bloody child. Right, let's see.' She perked up now she was talking to the plants. 'One of you should only have a little bit of water, and one of you likes to be soaked, and I can't for the life of me remember which is which. Never mind. Better to have too much than too little, eh?'

I imagined her drowning my precious jasmine. I could have saved it. I only had to shout, 'Not the jasmine,' but I could not let her know that I was there. I didn't want to. I didn't want to have to explain why I wasn't in Majorca but in my flat. Not yet. Not while I was still digesting what was going on.

I heard the metallic clang of the jug being dropped back into the sink.

'All done,' Clare muttered to herself. 'Now I'd better go and get those dishwasher tablets or . . .'

I heard her open the cupboard beneath the sink. It had a distinctively creaky hinge. Evan said it needed WD-40. Not to be outshone by Evan's handiness around the house, Callum had been promising to have a go at it for months. He never did. Perhaps now he never would.

'Ah-ha! A whole box. Thanks, sis.'

Clare had found what she was looking for. She was nicking my brand-new box of dishwasher tablets! I'd bought them just a couple of days before. They cost me £8.

'I'll pay you back,' she said out loud, as though she knew that I was there.

I let the gap between the door and the frame widen just a little more so that I could see further into the kitchen. As I suspected, Clare was at the kitchen table, tucking my dishwasher tablets into her handbag. So far, so Clare. But just as I thought she was getting ready to leave, she pulled out one of the kitchen chairs and sat down on it heavily. She slumped forward. Then she let out another long sigh and lay her head down on her folded arms.

'Oh God,' she exhaled, 'what am I doing?'

Thunk. She let her forehead drop onto the table. She gently banged her head on the Formica three times before she settled it on the cushion of her folded arms again.

What was she doing? Was she all right? Her shoulders weren't moving up and down as I might have expected had she been crying, but her downcast pose definitely wasn't a normal posture to assume at your sister's kitchen table when you've just popped over to water the plants. Banging your head on the table ain't exactly normal behaviour either. From where I was standing, she looked thoroughly depressed. Had I been able to come out of my hiding place, I would have put my hand on her shoulder and asked if she was OK. Instead, I could only watch anxiously from the crack in my bedroom door. If she showed any signs of acute distress, I told myself, then I would have to confess that I'd been there all along, but if she was simply tired . . . I would have to wait and see.

Clare stayed like that, with her face buried in her arms, for a good long while. Long enough for the kids

46

from next door, who were playing in the street outside, to sing the whole of 'Over the Rainbow'. They were practising for the next set of *Britain's Got Talent* auditions. I'd overheard them saying as much to their mother.

So, for the whole of 'Over the Rainbow', my sister, Clare, who normally went through life like a whirlwind in Chanel No. 5, sat motionless at my kitchen table. Just the slight movement of her shoulders from time to time gave me any proof she was alive at all. Then, when the kids outside had finished playing Dorothy and worked through some Hannah Montana hit instead, just as suddenly as she had collapsed onto the table, Clare sat up again. Her eyes were maybe a little pink, but she didn't really look as though she had been crying. Maybe she was just tired. She smoothed her hair back from her face, slicked on some lip gloss, got to her feet and left with my dishwasher tablets. And a whole packet of biscuits, I would later find out.

After Clare had gone – I waited until I heard her double-lock the door – I crept back out into the kitchen. As I had suspected, she had overwatered my plants. They were drenched. I carefully dabbed my favourite jasmine dry. The plants would survive, but I was oddly disquieted by having seen my sister slumped over the table like that. Was she unwell? I decided I would text her to 'find out' if she had watered the plants and, when she responded, I would ask her if everything was OK, giving her a chance to confess to whatever was bothering her.

Clare beat me to it. She must have texted me on her walk to the Tube station.

'Plants watered,' she wrote. 'Everything looks fine. Nothing's been nicked, but someone must have broken in and left a dirty mug on your coffee table. I can't believe you would have left the flat in such a state.'

'Ha, ha,' I responded. 'Thank you. Are you OK?'

'Of course I'm OK,' she replied. 'How about you? What's the hotel like? Has Callum proposed yet?'

That stung. I had told Clare about Hannah's sainted Mike and the nuptial view. She'd listened politely enough, but I wasn't sure she'd ever rated the chances of lightning striking twice.

'Having a great time,' I texted back without answering her question.

'Good,' texted Clare. 'You deserve it.'

I did deserve a holiday, didn't I? Bloody Callum Dawes had ruined everything. Somehow I was going to make him pay.

Chapter Nine

So I spent the first night of my holiday in my own flat, being disgruntled and angry and sad. Mostly sad. I ate some of the remaining Manchego. A day out of the fridge had not improved its flavour, alas. I ate a little piece of the lemon tart. That tasted OK, but I didn't really have much of an appetite. After that, I logged on and read my colleagues' updates on Twitter. Hannah had tweeted on the completion of the Newcastle project and the inauguration of the second-tallest building in Luxembourg, which also contained three of our lifts. There was nothing about my solo holiday, thank goodness. All utterly professional. Mum meanwhile had tweeted about a great evening at Older Eve, the yoga class for menopausal women. 'Makes me feel much better about being the mother of a nearly thirty-year-old!' she'd added. 'Can't believe Sophie's thirty next week.'

Thanks for reminding me, I thought.

Next, I logged on to Facebook and clicked on Callum's page. I screwed my eyes shut tight while his page loaded, then read his profile through my fingers. There didn't seem to be anything different about it. At least not yet. He hadn't de-friended me. He didn't appear to have any suspicious new 'friends'. Neither had he changed his relationship status. That could have been a good thing, or a bad thing. Either he wasn't so sure that he had done the right thing by breaking up with me and he didn't yet want to announce it to the world or he had moved so seamlessly into a new relationship it hadn't seemed worth changing his status to 'single' in between. I told myself I had to assume the former or I would go mad. My own Facebook profile still bore the status 'Excited about going to Majorca with Callum tomorrow.' I didn't change it. I mean, what was I going to say? I couldn't think of anything that wouldn't sound strange or bitter. Not yet.

Having reassured myself that my humiliation had so far been contained to the offices of Stockwell Lifts and was not yet out there in cyberspace for everyone to read about, I went to bed. I didn't sleep for a long while, no matter how many times I turned my pillow to get the cool side, no matter how many imaginary sheep jumped the fence. I didn't want to sleep. All I really wanted was to know what was going on across the river in Kentish Town.

Why hadn't I seen it coming? Why hadn't I realised that Callum was unhappy? Like a forensic scientist looking for that single hair or flake of paint that will solve a murder mystery, I went over our last few conversations in minute detail. I analysed everything he had said in the break-up speech and then I went through everything he had said on the phone or via email in the month that we'd been apart. Everything I could remember, that was. What hadn't I noticed? Sure, our telephone conversations had been largely one-sided of late, with me chatting about our upcoming holiday and him adding the odd 'Mm-hmm' to show that he was sort of listening, but he'd still texted several times a day. I went through those texts now, searching for the exchange that should have alerted me to how he was really feeling.

There were no clues there.

Thank goodness I didn't have to wait long to hear more. I managed a couple of hours' sleep and as soon as the Stockwell Lifts office opened the next morning, I got more news. Hannah emailed bright and early to inform me that Callum was in the office again.

> When he walked past to the kitchen, Alison said loudly, 'I expect Sophie's on the beach by now. They've got lovely beaches in Majorca. I can't think why anyone would want to be anywhere else.' You should have seen his face, Soph. He was livid.

On the beach . . . What a lovely thought. When I got that email, I was still safely tucked up beneath my duvet in my Laura Ashley flannel pyjamas. I could not have looked less like a beach bunny if I'd tried. Still Hannah's email was enough to give me the encouragement I needed to get up and splash some water on my tear-stained face. I'd made the mistake of looking at some photos of Callum on my iPhone and had a little weep, but I had to stay strong. The story of Callum and me was far from over.

Throughout the day Hannah and Alison sent me more mini-bulletins. Apparently, after Alison's loud observation about my likely holiday routine, Callum was avoiding the staff kitchen, but he had been spotted looking 'fed up' as he exited the stationery cupboard with two reams of A4 paper at around half past two. Candace reported that he definitely hadn't seemed his usual self when she spoke to him on the phone at three o'clock.

'It was such a good move to go to Majorca,' Hannah said again when she emailed me around four o'clock. 'I have no doubt that he thinks he's made a mistake and it serves him right big time.'

Good old Hannah. I'd never much rated the friendship of my workmates before, but now I longed to hear from her. I basked in the warm feelings I got from their emails detailing my ex's woes. They kept me going. Hannah didn't seem to care that she was getting nothing back from me, but then I knew she liked to hold court whether in person or virtually. I was happy to let her do it.

While Callum mooched around the office, looking satisfyingly glum, I spent the day in my pyjamas, eagerly watching my in-box for more emails.

But at six o'clock, I knew that all the girls at the Stockwell Lifts office would be going home and that would be the end of the daily news feed about my lost love. I imagined Callum clocking off too and it crossed my mind that maybe he was only so grumpy during the day because all the girls in the office seemed to be watching his every move. Would he break into a grin as soon as he disappeared into the Tube station at Stockwell? Did he have plans for that evening? I wondered. Plans with a girl?

There had to be someone else. Had he met someone while working up in Newcastle? Though he had told me that there was no one else, it seemed the most likely explanation for what was, to me at least, a very sudden change of heart. I had visited the Newcastle office of Stockwell Lifts and didn't think I had much competition there. Candace, Callum's PA, was a middle-aged mum who played in her local semi-professional darts team and had a figure to match. Building sites were, generally speaking, a very masculine place to work. It was unlikely that Callum and some gorgeous girl had locked eyes over a girder. But of course Newcastle was full of clubs and bars; maybe he had met someone there. Callum had always had a thing for Cheryl Cole. Maybe he'd fallen for someone with her accent.

I tortured myself further by making an inventory of Callum's female friends from school and college. Over the time we'd been together, he'd introduced me to most of them and they'd all been friendly enough, but there was at least one, Shelley, who I knew harboured a crush on him. She'd made drunken passes at him in the past. What about her? Had she finally got her way? I imagined Callum getting as rat-arsed as he normally did on a night out but without me there to make sure he got home OK. He would be a sitting duck for Shelley in that state. Had he seen her in London on those weekends when I thought he was so hard at work?

That was especially tough to take: the thought that he had been actively avoiding me, hiding from me yet all the while pretending that everything was OK. To think that I had felt sorry for him having to work so very hard! What a joke that had turned out to be. I wondered who else was in on that particular secret. He must have seen some of his friends during those weekends when I thought he was in Newcastle. He wouldn't really have spent the whole weekend indoors with the curtains drawn, would he? I couldn't believe it. Callum loved to hang out with his mates. Did he stick to his neighbourhood or venture into the centre of the city? What would he have said if he'd bumped into me while he was supposed to be up north? Had he already prepared his excuses, or would he have told me there and then that he no longer wanted to be with me? I shuddered as I thought of how close by he had been while I went about my business down in south London quite unknowing. I could picture his friends laughing when he told them what was going on. His pretending to be in Newcastle in order to avoid having to see me was the nastiest thing I could imagine anyone doing to me apart from being unfaithful.

By seven o'clock my mood was back at rock bottom. And then I heard the key in the door.

It was Clare again. Crikey, my sister was being diligent about this plant-watering favour. Even though she'd said that she would water my plants every day, I had expected her to manage once a week at the very most, but here she was again already. The plants had not had time to dry out since the previous day. I could only hope she wouldn't drown them. It was quite the opposite problem from the one I had envisaged.

I still didn't want to see her. This time, the moment I heard my sister's key in the door, I knew what was coming and took care to hide properly. I had got away with standing right behind the bedroom door last time, but I would not take any more chances. At some point, if she was taking her job as seriously as she seemed to be, she was bound to come into my bedroom to check that everything was as I had left it, so I quickly scrambled under the bed. The gap beneath the iron frame looked big enough, but getting beneath it was nowhere near so easy a trick as it had been when I last tried to hide under a bed, approximately twenty years earlier. I just about made it out of sight as Clare reached the kitchen door.

Bloody hell, it was horrible under there, face down on the Wilton twist. I had always considered myself to be a fairly good housekeeper, but the carpet under my bed, which was supposed to be a nice bright cream colour, as in the rest of the room, was absolutely grey with dust. There were dust bunnies down there that looked almost as big as the real rabbits my sister and I had kept as children. I tried not to think of the damage all that filth would be doing to my favourite pyjamas. And then I turned my head to the other side and saw the mouse . . .

Chapter Ten

It took everything I had not to scream. As it was, I hit my head on the bed-boards as I instinctively jerked my face away from the tiny eyeless corpse that loomed in front of me. It lay on its back with all four paws stiffly in the air. I inched as far from it as I could without getting out from beneath the bed altogether. This was the worst possible moment for me to discover that rodent. While Clare pottered about in the kitchen, taking her own sweet time about watering my plants, I itched to get out from my filthy hiding place.

My eyes crossed as I tried to focus on a little black thing a couple of inches from my nose that may or may not have been a flea. Please, God, don't let it be a flea, I thought. Had it come off the dead mouse? I had turned away from it, but the thought of that thing behind my head – empty eye sockets staring at my hair – made the skin prickle from my crown to the soles of my feet. How long had it been there? Did it have friends, and where were they hiding? Soon my whole body was overtaken by a crawling sensation. My skin quite literally crept. I thought of dead mice and maggots and other things that inhabit the grave. Still I stayed beneath the bed and silent. I had to stay hidden. I dreaded my sister's pity that much. After Hannah, my sister was the smuggest fiancée I knew.

Out in the kitchen, Clare's mobile phone rang.

'Hi, darling,' she said to the caller. It must have been Evan. 'I'm there right now. Of course I'm safe. I'm just having a cup of tea.'

Tea? Oh, no. I heard her put the kettle on. Damn. I was under the bed with a mouse corpse and she was having a cup of tea?

'I'll see you later. Of course I'll lock up properly as I leave. Bye-bye.'

Clare sighed as she finished the call.

My bedroom door was open, giving me a view of the hall. I craned my neck in an attempt to see what my sister was doing now. She took her tea and walked into the living room. What was this? She seemed to be settling in for the evening. I had expected her to be in and out of the flat in ten minutes – another splash of water for the plants and then off – but I was sure I had just heard the television go on . . .

I had heard the TV go on. Clare turned up the volume. She was watching *Coronation Street*. The one thing that Clare had in common with our mother was an obsession with that soap. She claimed she never missed an episode, so I suppose it made sense that she would watch that day's instalment at my flat, rather than miss it while she travelled home.

Oh God, I thought. If Clare was watching her favourite soap, it meant that I was facing at least another half an hour under the mattress. Another half-hour with Mickey the Corpse. That was assuming that night's episode wasn't one of the super-long editions the *Corrie* producers seemed so keen on. Half an hour with a dead mouse. I was sure that flea was inside my waistband now too. If Callum and I didn't get back together, I was going to find some way to put that dead mouse in his lunch.

There was barely enough room under the bed for me to turn my head from one side to the other – not that I wanted to turn it back towards the mouse. Further down the bed, an errant spring from the mattress kept catching my shoulder blade. I just knew it had put a pull in my favourite pyjama top. I tried to distract myself by listening to *Coronation Street* with my sister, but though she had turned the volume up, she hadn't turned it up so far that I could hear clearly everything that was being said, and even when I did catch the odd sentence, it made no real sense out of context. I only watched *Coronation Street* if I happened to be at Mum and Dad's while an episode was playing. I hadn't seen the show at all since Tracy Barlow came out of prison. Or was she only out on day release? Who knows. I didn't usually care.

The distant hiss of television conversations that meant nothing to me quickly started to drive me mad. I crossed my fingers that Clare would decide to make a break for home during the commercial break. Instead, as the adverts began, I heard my sister pad across to the kitchen and put the kettle on *again*. I could have wept. What I wouldn't have given for a cup of tea myself right then, face down and cramping with a throat full of dust and hair – when had I lost so much hair? – catching God knows what from that dead rodent.

Perhaps I could get out from under the bed and have a stretch while she watched the second half of the soap. She was bound to be absorbed. When the show started up again, I began to move, but the bed springs creaked far more loudly than I had expected. I had to stay put. Just fifteen more minutes, I told myself. Less than that if she left the moment the credits started. Evan would be waiting for her at home. She wouldn't want to hang around. He liked her to come home promptly. She once joked that he would scramble a mountain rescue squad if she took too long coming back from Waitrose. Fifteen more minutes. I just had to approach my confinement with that mouse like a celebrity doing a bushtucker trial. If Kerry Katona could eat kangaroo testicles . . .

But while the closing theme tune played, my sister moved about the flat dreamily and I realised she was still in no hurry to leave. She made herself yet another cup of tea, and the next thing I knew, she had walked into my bedroom.

Chapter Eleven

'One day like this a year . . . la, la, la . . .' Clare sang.

I lay still and silent as a soldier in a trench, taking as few breaths as I dared without passing out. Peeking from beneath the valance that hid me from her sight, I followed Clare's flip-flopped feet as she crossed the room to the window. She opened the curtains I had kept shut all day. It was still light outside.

Clare continued to hum tunelessly as she sat down at my dressing table. I heard the make-up drawer slide open. I heard the rattling of various bottles and compacts as she looked for something interesting. I hoped she wouldn't help herself to my new moisturiser. Then squirt, squirt, squirt. The cheeky mare was trying out my perfume! A cloud of my favourite eau de toilette – Issey Miyake – filled the room and competed with the dust to make me want to sneeze so badly I thought my head would explode.

I must not sneeze, I told myself. Forget the perfume. Forget the mouse. I held my breath. I couldn't even reach up to pinch the bridge of my nose. I almost passed out with the effort of keeping schtum.

'Ugh,' was Clare's comment on my favourite scent.

What? My impending sneeze was somehow dissipated by indignation.

Clare got up from my dressing table and opened my wardrobe doors. Unbelievable. What did she think she was doing now? I could only watch in open-mouthed horror as Clare rootled through my neat and tidy rails as though she were at the Next sale. I saw the hem of my favourite black velvet dress from Agnès B. swishing around her shins. Was she going to make off with it as she had made off with my new box of dishwasher tablets and a packet of Hobnobs? Was she intending to wear it and sneak it back into my wardrobe before I came home from my hols?

'Naaa,' she said to herself. 'Not for me.'

Evidently, she wasn't going to take my dress home. Thank goodness for that. But did she put it away again? Oh, no. That would be too much effort for my sister. She threw it onto the bed instead. And she hadn't finished. A red dress followed. I think it was the one I'd bought from Hobbs for a cousin's wedding. Clare pulled it on over her leggings but stopped when she got it to her knees and I heard the ominous sound of a stretching seam. Then came the blue wrap dress I'd bought from Zara for my last birthday date with Callum. It was as close as I could get to affording something from Diane von Furstenburg. It was smaller than the red dress. I prayed she wouldn't bother trying it on. She'd always said blue wasn't her colour.

Next, Clare drew out one of my most special items, a multi-layered chiffon skirt that was my 'go-to' skirt for a posh night out. Nicole Farhi. Even at 60 per cent off in the sale, it had cost me a small fortune. I loved it. It was a dark charcoal-grey colour, spattered with sequins, which gave it the look of a cloudless night sky glittering with stars. It was obviously expensive, and when I put it on, paired with a simple black top, I felt as though I could go anywhere and mix with anybody.

It was smart enough for dinner somewhere expensive but boho enough for a night in a Clapham bar. I knew that Clare liked it. She had admired it on several occasions. Now she was pulling it on over her leggings and turning this way and that in front of the mirror to see how she looked. The sequins caught the light as she twirled.

'Nope. A little bit too *Strictly Come Dancing*.'

Ow! Obviously, she wasn't impressed.

She pulled the skirt off and threw that too in the direction of the bed. However, her aim was not quite true and the skirt slithered off the silky duvet cover and onto the floor. Silently, I gritted my teeth. Was she going to pick it up? She was going to pick it up, wasn't she? She didn't pick it up. She left it exactly where it had fallen on the dusty, dirty floor. You know, I really had no idea quite how dirty a carpet can get until that evening when I spent an hour face down on it. And now that I knew I had mice to boot . . .

Clare had not yet finished. As I continued to watch, she slipped off her tatty old Havaianas. She stretched up onto her tiptoes and I was afforded a view of her filthy soles and cracked dry heels ingrained with dirt. Not nice at all. She could really use a pedicure. And then I realised why she was on tiptoes. She was reaching for the top shelf of the wardrobe, which was where I kept some of my most treasured possessions. My very best going-out shoes.

Oh, please, no . . .

First out of the wardrobe were my purple satin Kurt Geigers. I remembered the day that I bought them. I had just moved up to London and started my first proper job as PR to a plumbing-supplies manufacturer.

I bought those KGs with my first pay packet. It seemed important to mark such a special moment in my life with a serious treat, especially since my new job was so dull. I'd been admiring those shoes in the window of the shop for months by the time I got my hands on them. Nearly seven years on, I still thought they were gorgeous. Purple had seemed like a daring colour to buy at the time, but they were surprisingly versatile. They looked just as good with a black dress or jeans. I had kept them in perfect condition. And now my sister was shoving her filthy feet into them! I could hardly look.

Thankfully, she didn't like them as much as I did. Soon the KGs were discarded, alongside (but not *in*, I noted with annoyance) their box. My Russell & Bromley pumps came next. They were the footwear equivalent of the perfect little black dress. I'd bought them the previous Christmas. They were a wonderfully flattering shape and made even my fat little feet look elegant and narrow. They had a very slight platform, which gave the impression that they were higher than they really were, and they were made from a black patent leather that was as shiny as the bonnet of a freshly valeted Porsche. They were classics. I was so pleased to have found them. I intended to have them for years to come and was looking after them accordingly.

As my sister hurried to shove her big feet (which were even fatter than mine) into the Russell & Bromley pumps, her ankle turned over. I closed my eyes tightly. Never mind her ankle. Please don't let her have broken the heel. When I dared open my eyes again, Clare had already tossed the pumps in the direction of their purple satin shelf-mates.

'Boring,' was her verdict. The cow.

There was only one pair of shoes left for my sister to find up there. Unfortunately, of all the going-out shoes I had, these were the most precious. They were only a couple of weeks old. I had bought them as a sort of birthday present to myself, having decided that if I wasn't going to be a millionaire by thirty, I should at least have some millionaire's footwear. They were my Jimmy Choos.

Oh, how grown-up I'd felt as I'd walked out of the Choo boutique on Sloane Street with that pale purple carrier bag swinging from my wrist. How sophisticated. The carrier bag itself was so lovely that I had decided to keep it, folded carefully and stashed alongside the shoes in their box.

The carrier bag fell out of the wardrobe as Clare pulled the shoebox down. She merely kicked it to one side. Oh! Then she sat down on the bed, heavily, as she opened the shoebox itself. I could visualise exactly what she would find in there. I had taken so long to choose those shoes. I'd saved so hard. Once I'd decided that I deserved a birthday splurge, I had spent weeks researching the perfect party sandals. I had pored over Louboutins and lusted after several pairs from Gina before I found those perfect water-snake sandals on the Jimmy Choo website. They were a delicate confection of gossamer-fine straps that wound all over the foot and up round the ankle. They were classy and sexy at the same time. They were the sort of shoes that an Oscar-winning actress would wear to walk the red carpet. They were the kind of shoes you might get married in, if you were marrying somewhere chic and metropolitan. That had definitely been in my mind when I bought them at the shop on Sloane Street rather than via the Internet, because if I was shelling out that much money, I wanted the experience of having the snooty sales assistants pay attention to me, even if only for five minutes.

When I got the Choos home, I took them out of their box and just looked at them for a while. I didn't even put them on. They were shoes that demanded freshly scrubbed feet and glossy nail polish. I never felt quite groomed enough. Instead, I arranged them on top of their lilac box and dust bag as if for a shop display and just admired their perfection. Since that day I hadn't actually worn them at all.

I had been saving their first outing for a really special occasion. I had toyed with taking them to Majorca and wearing them on my thirtieth birthday, but even that hadn't seemed quite an occasion enough. Besides, the pictures I had seen of Majorca suggested that there were cobbled streets all over the place and the last thing I wanted was to scuff or even break a heel by getting it stuck between two stones. So I was saving them for a ball or for dinner in a seriously fancy restaurant. I was saving them for a wedding. Preferably my own. Heaven only knew when any of those opportunities might arrive, but it seemed like a good idea to wait.

And now my sister was trying them on! She struggled to get her fat toes through the loop of leather that fitted easily round my own. When it came to doing up the ankle strap, Clare had no chance, but that didn't stop her from huffing and puffing and tugging and pulling as she tried to get buckle and holes to meet. She would not give up. She was stretching them all out of shape. I wanted to reach out and grab her by the foot and tell her to stop it at once.

When she finally managed to close the buckle and got to her feet as unsteadily as a drunk, I could stand it not a moment longer. The creamy leather soles, still clean and unblemished, creaked under her awkward stance. The heels buckled inwards, putting strain on the outside edge where they joined the soles. Why didn't she try to stand up properly? She was going to break my new shoes before I even had a chance to wear the things outdoors.

'That's it!' I yelled from beneath the bed. 'Take my bloody shoes off.'

Chapter Twelve

How I wish I could have seen Clare's face when she heard me bellow from beneath the bed. She was so startled she fell onto the mattress, pressing the springs against my back so that I howled in pain as well as rage. I scrabbled out from under there, mad as a rattle-snake. I couldn't get from beneath that bed quickly enough, both to escape the dead mouse and to rescue my shoes. Mostly to rescue my shoes.

'Go away, go away.' Clare kicked at me with my own best sandals. 'Get away from me.'

I made a grab for her ankle before she could get me in the eye with my own ten-centimetre heel.

'Oh Lord, our father . . .'

I couldn't believe it. Clare had gone nuts. Was she praying? She shut her eyes tightly and started saying the Lord's Prayer. She made the sign of the cross at me.

'Hallowed be Thy name . . .'

Using all my strength to pull her by the legs, I dragged her off the bed. She continued to kick at me from her new place on the floor.

'Clare,' I shouted at her, 'stop kicking me.'

'What are you?' she wailed.

'It's Sophie. It's your sister.'

'Get thee behind me, Satan,' she swore.

'For heaven's sake.'

I had her on her back now and was struggling with

the buckle on the sandal she'd crammed onto her left foot. Clare was still muttering a prayer.

'What are you?' she said again, feeling for my face. 'You must be a vision.'

'Will you just open your bloody eyes?' I asked, as she poked me in the nostril. I grabbed her wrist.

'I'll do anything,' she said. 'Just don't hurt me.'

'I'm not going to hurt you,' I promised her. 'Much. Just take my shoes off, you silly tart.'

Clare opened her eyes at last.

'Sophie? Sophie, is that really you?'

'Yes, it's me. Who on earth did you think it was?'

Clare just stared at me with her jaw hanging slack in surprise.

Giving up on the buckle for the time being, I got to my feet and brushed off the dust. As I had suspected, my pyjamas would need to go straight into the wash. I didn't even want to think about the mouse I would have to deal with later. Instead, I picked up my purple Kurt Geigers from the floor and waved them in front of Clare's face.

'What are you doing trying all my best shoes on?' I asked.

'What are you doing,' she countered, 'hiding under your bed? Aren't you in Majorca?'

'Evidently,' I said, 'I'm *not* in Majorca. Take my shoes off.'

'All right, all right, I'm doing it.' Obediently – she was probably in shock – Clare sat back down on the bed and started to unbuckle them. 'I think this one is stuck,' she said, a note of rising panic in her voice.

'If it is, I'll cut you out of it and you'll have to buy

me a new pair. These are water snake. They're Jimmy
Choos. They cost me a bloody fortune.'

'I didn't know you'd bought them,' she said.

Clare and I generally shared notes about our shopping triumphs, though hers were much less frequent
since she'd met Evan.

'That's because I didn't want you to ask if you could
try them on,' I replied. 'I can't believe you were going
through my wardrobe like that, and dropping all my
clothes on the floor while you were at it. What are you
like?' I shook out my chiffon skirt and hung it back
up. '"A bit too *Strictly*" . . . Have you got no respect?
My bedroom is my private place.'

'Well, you were the one who asked me to look after
your flat while you were on holiday.'

'I asked you to look after my *plants*. You only had
to water the plants and leave. You didn't have to
do anything other than that. You certainly didn't have
to ransack my bedroom like some kind of thief.'

'But I thought there might be someone in here,' she
said. 'I thought I heard a noise and there might have been
a burglar in the wardrobe. See, as it happens, I was
nearly right. There was someone in here after all.'

'I still don't get how that justifies you rifling through
my clothes like it was the first day of a Brora sample
sale. You could have checked for a burglar and left.'

'What can I say? I'm sorry.'

She handed me back my Choos. I snatched them
from her and examined them carefully before I tucked
them up lovingly in their tissue paper and slotted them
into the box.

'Dropping all my stuff on the floor . . .' I muttered.

'I would have put everything back.'

'Yeah, right. Breaking my shoes . . .'

'They're not broken,' Clare pointed out. 'There's no harm done. They didn't suit me anyway . . . But what are you doing here?' she asked, getting back to the really important question. 'Why aren't you in Puerto Bona? Where's Callum?'

'Callum's at his flat, I should imagine. He decided not to go on holiday after all.'

Chapter Thirteen

Having made sure that my statement Choos really were still in almost-never-worn condition, I decided that my sister was temporarily forgiven. I let her make me a cup of tea in the kitchen while I poured out the whole story. I was relieved to be out from that dustbowl beneath the bed, but of course it meant I had to tell her exactly what was going on and, in all probability, receive a lecture on how deluded I'd been ever to think that Callum took our relationship as seriously as I did.

I didn't have to tell Clare how excited I'd been about the fortnight in Majorca. She already knew. I started the story from the special effort I'd made for our last supper in England. A small piece of the Manchego cheese was still on the table, looking unappetisingly slick. Clare popped it into her mouth as I talked.

'That's not bad,' she said.

Then I told her about the text from Callum and all the horror that followed. I'd been doing pretty well since then, keeping the tears in check as I tried to formulate a strategy to get him back, but telling Clare the story brought with it a whole new tsunami of tears. Though her reassuring nods and the weight of her arm round my shoulder were the first physical comfort I had been offered since Callum broke the news of his changed feelings, her sweetness somehow made the whole thing seem so much worse.

'But I thought you were so happy,' Clare pointed out.

'Did you?'

'Well, you *said* you were,' she clarified.

'I was the happiest girl in the world. Unfortunately, he didn't feel the same way.'

'It all seems very sudden. Are you sure he was serious about breaking up?'

'Serious enough to miss out on a holiday.'

Clare had to admit that it didn't sound good. To miss a holiday was one hell of a gesture if he was merely feeling a little bit bored. Especially when it was a holiday that had cost him well over a grand.

'He must have been feeling really desperate . . . and it's your birthday in a few days! I can't believe he would be so cruel. What an arse! I went out with Hugh Barnsley a whole month longer than I wanted to so as not to ruin his eighteenth.'

I remembered Hugh Barnsley. In the end he got an extra three months out of Clare by coming up with more and more special dates he wouldn't survive alone.

'Did he tell you why he changed his mind?' Clare asked.

'He told me that it was getting hard going out and working together, but he actually told Alison at work that it was like I couldn't do anything without him and it's been driving him nuts. He said he's been feeling that way for weeks and he didn't want to come to Majorca and break up with me afterwards because that way I might feel he'd been dishonest. Likewise, he said he thought it would be deceitful for him to celebrate my birthday with me knowing we were going to split up.'

'He thought he'd save some money on your birthday present, more like. What a git. I would like to stick a birthday candle right up his . . .'

I waved the image away.

'But why didn't you call me when all this happened?' Clare asked. 'I'd have come straight over to look after you.'

I didn't tell her that I didn't think I could stand her smug nearly-marriedness.

'Were you here when I came over yesterday?' she asked.

'I was behind the bedroom door,' I confirmed, 'all the time.'

'I knew it,' said Clare, thumping the table in triumph. 'I knew there was something . . . I felt a presence. I'm never wrong.'

I rolled my eyes. Clare was always feeling 'presences'. She liked to think she was quite psychic. She had a bookshelf full of astrological tables and never went a day without checking at least six horoscope sites online. Generally she kept on checking until she got a good one. 'But I still don't understand why you said you'd gone on holiday.'

'I didn't actually say I'd gone away. I didn't say anything to anyone. But when Callum and I last spoke, he told me I should give up trying to change his mind and enjoy the trip I'd booked. He even said it might help me get over him.'

'What a great idea,' Clare sneered. 'Spending your thirtieth birthday on your own in Majorca. You'd have jumped off a balcony.'

'I don't think I would have done that, but what he said made me so angry I said I might go on my own

73

after all and he obviously took that as my intention and thinks, because he hasn't heard otherwise, that I must have followed through.'

'I bet he loved that,' said Clare. 'I bet that was the last thing he expected.'

I blew my nose and carried on.

'Apparently, he's really impressed. He decided not to bother taking holiday since he wasn't going to come away with me. He went into work and Hannah has been keeping me filled in on all the gossip since. According to Alison, now that I've gone away on my own . . .'

'You've shown him that you're a proper independent woman who doesn't need a man to have a good time,' Clare chipped in. 'Excellent. I hope he is impressed. I hope he has had second thoughts about how independent and fantastic you really are. You'll probably have him crawling back to you in no time.' Clare clapped her hands together as if the matter was closed.

'Except that when he finds out the truth, he'll know that I'm no more independent and fantastic than I ever was. Because I'm not on holiday, am I? I've been hiding in my bedroom for two days. I'm going to look a real idiot.'

Clare put on a serious face. We both looked at the teapot on the table between us as the reality of my situation sank in. At last, Clare spoke.

'But why should he find out?' she asked.

'What do you mean?'

'Who's going to tell him you didn't go away if you don't? I won't tell anyone.'

'But I . . .'

'I can keep a secret. Why on earth does anyone but me have to know you're here?'

'Because I can't stay here in my flat all fortnight, can I?'

'Why not?'

It was not what I had expected to hear. I had expected Clare to agree with me that I was going to look a complete idiot if I didn't confess I hadn't gone away soon. Instead, she said she thought maybe I had inadvertently done the right thing by not putting my colleagues straight when it became clear they thought I had gone away without Callum. I hadn't told any lies. They had come to their own conclusions. I was just licking my wounds. I needed space. The last thing I needed was tea and sympathy from the likes of Hannah and Alison. Clare had met both of them at my birthday drinks last year and had very little time for either, pronouncing them to be the type of people who are only kind to other women if there's a chance of social or political gain.

'I bet they are both loving this whole saga. I would not want to be around either of them if I was feeling weak in any way,' Clare concluded. 'Especially Alison. She's always fancied Callum.'

That wasn't much comfort, but Clare continued in an effort to cheer me up.

If I wanted to be on my own in the light of such bad news as this break-up, she told me, then frankly I was entitled to be on my own. I had two weeks' paid holiday to use after all. I wasn't going to be inconveniencing anyone by staying out of the office since they were already prepared for my absence. @liftlady's followers on Twitter could manage for a few days without my exciting updates on the daily pudding menu from the Stockwell Lifts canteen. And if the best way to win myself some time and space was by pretending that I had gone to Majorca, then Clare was right behind me.

'You're suggesting I hide in my flat for a fortnight?'

'You don't have to do it for the whole fortnight. Just the rest of the first week. You get to have some peace and save face.'

'Seriously? Because I think that sounds a bit mad.'

'I think there's a touch of genius to it, actually. Not because it might win Callum back, but because it gives you a chance to get yourself together before you face the world.'

Only Clare could put a sensible spin on it. I chanced a smile.

'But another five days on my own? In the flat? How would I pull that off? Someone might see I'm at home.'

'Sophie, I didn't guess you were in this flat until you grabbed me by the ankle from beneath the bed and I can usually feel a human presence, as you know. How's anyone who isn't as sensitive as me – and most people aren't – going to guess by walking past? People don't really take that much notice. Really they don't. You didn't feel that Callum was in London, did you, when he said he was in Newcastle?'

It was true. I hadn't the faintest idea that he was lying to me. So much for being soul mates.

'If I'm pretending to be in Majorca,' I protested, 'I can't even go out to get groceries.'

'I can get groceries for you,' said Clare at once. 'You can have this lot for a start.'

She indicated the two bags on the table.

'There's enough bread, milk and cheese in there to last you for a few days. I'll get some more for me and Evan on the way home. And if you need anything else, I'll go to the supermarket and bring whatever you want with me when I come to water the plants. Easy?'

'Well, yes,' I agreed. 'But what will I do all day, in here on my own in the dark?'

'What will you do all day? Oh, Sophie,' Clare exclaimed, 'have you no imagination? What I wouldn't give for a *single* day all to myself! You can do whatever you like as long as it's indoors. Heaven knows you're not missing out on the weather. It's going to be terrible at least until the weekend. I've even asked Evan if we can have the heating back on.'

'Can you?' I asked. 'Have the heating back on, that is.'

'You're kidding. No heating from April to October. Them's the rules. We're saving for our retirement,' she added with a roll of her eyes. 'But you can have the heating on whenever you want. You could have it at thirty degrees in here and nobody would argue. And you could read. You could watch a DVD. You could knit. You could even write your Christmas cards! I have got so many books on my bedside table just waiting for me to find a spare minute to pick them up. Sophie, a whole week on your own in this flat sounds like a luxury to me.'

I still wasn't convinced, but then I was comparing the thought of another five days in my dingy little flat with a lost fortnight in sunny Majorca. Clare was complaining about finding it hard to concentrate on a book because her fiancé wanted to watch *Top Gear* at full volume in the same room.

'I've suggested I go and read in the bedroom while he watches TV, but he likes us to be together . . . Oh, just the thought of five days without Jeremy Clarkson. Or without having to come up with something different for Evan's supper every night. Five days without having to ask permission to put the flipping heating on in case the electricity bill has gone over budget. A whole double bed to myself! I would swap places with you in a heartbeat.'

That was when Clare said, 'In fact, it sounds so good I think I might come on holiday with you.'

Chapter Fourteen

'I'm not on holiday,' I pointed out.

'You could be! A holiday at home . . . what bliss.'

Clare was just trying to make me feel better. Much as she complained about Evan, I knew she didn't really think five days in my flat would be better than five days in his company. Surely she hadn't forgotten what it was like to be single, or, worse, recently heartbroken, with no one to snuggle up to at night. No one to warm your cold feet on. Having to watch *Top Gear* seemed like a very small price to pay to me. I would have watched *Top Gear* on continual loop if that were what Callum had wanted me to do. If it were what it would take to get him back, I'd wear a Jeremy Clarkson mask in bed. I would go nuts if I had to spend five days in my flat with no one to talk to. Who wouldn't?

Clare had a rose-tinted view of time spent alone because she had spent so little of her life without a boyfriend. Even at primary school, Clare was inundated with Valentine's cards by boys who had previously only been interested in dropping worms down the back of their female classmates' jumpers. She was beautiful and funny. Truly, she need never worry about being on her own for long.

Though I knew she didn't always believe that.

For most of her twenties, my sister had dated a guy called Jake. They met at university and were joined at the hip from that moment on, moving to London together as soon as they graduated. Within five years they were talking about buying their first flat. It was widely assumed that a wedding would follow, then a dog, then 2.4 children and a happy-ever-after straight out of a romance novel. When Jake announced, the day after his twenty-ninth birthday, that he was too young to settle down and wanted to go travelling instead, Clare was devastated. I knew she had planned their life down to the tiniest detail. Back when she and I weren't really friends, when she had just graduated and I was only in my first year at uni, I had caught her browsing a John Lewis catalogue, making notes for the wedding list she was sure she would have relatively soon.

The break-up was slow and painful. Jake kept changing his mind, but the call of the wild got louder and, two months after he first announced his doubts, Jake was booking a ticket to Australia. He tried briefly to persuade Clare to go with him, but she loved being close to her family and her friends and the job she was in at that moment, all of which tied her to London like a web of golden strings. The thought of living out of a rucksack for a year secretly appalled her. Clare was a girl who felt more secure when surrounded by her stuff. She definitely wasn't going anywhere without her heated rollers. So Jake went off travelling alone.

After breaking up with Jake for good, Clare went a bit berserk on the dating front. For six months or so she seemed to be out on a date almost every night. She signed up to three online dating sites. She asked everyone she knew to hunt out single men for her to meet. She even agreed to a date with Duncan Egerton, the son of one of Mum's old friends, despite the fact that he had been the butt of all our childhood jokes for his slightly eccentric ways. After the date, Clare was able to confirm that the poor unfortunate still covered everyone with spit every time he opened his mouth to speak. Even worse, he had become rather more garrulous than she remembered.

So I was glad for her when those crazy months ended and it seemed as though she might have found someone who measured up to Jake at last. Clare met Evan through one of the dating websites. She said she had a feeling he could be the one the moment she read his profile. At thirty-nine, he was eight years older than Clare (and Jake). He was mature. He was not likely to give up his excellent job to go travelling on a whim. Evan quickly told Clare that he had ticked all the other boxes in his life – he'd seen the world 'at the right time', he assured her, in his early twenties. Since then he'd concentrated on building a career, then he'd bought his own place, and now he was looking for someone to share the neat and tidy life he had created.

'He's exactly what I need,' said Clare, when she first started seeing him. 'Evan is a proper steady bloke.'

We all approved. Evan was the kind of boyfriend every mother and father wishes for their daughter. The first time he came to meet us all, over Sunday lunch, he helped with the washing-up and then spent a jolly hour helping Dad fix the garden fence. Dad was pleased to hand over the care of Clare's car (she'd never learned how to check her own tyre pressure) and he was delighted when Evan revealed that he had arranged to exchange the ancient – and dangerous – MG for a nice new Nissan. Always looking out for Clare's safety, Evan was a man after Dad's heart. Evan won even more brownie points when he fitted a chain to the front door of *my* flat and bought Mum a novelty suction mat for the bottom of the bath when she mentioned having slipped on the Jo Malone bath oil Clare had given her for Christmas.

Evan was thoughtful and serious. He was responsible. It quickly became clear that Evan would never surprise my sister with a bunch of flowers, but neither would he allow her to take to the road with a dangerously low level of screenwash. Evan showed his love in practical ways. He took care of Clare. There was no way he would break my sister's heart. After the trauma of Jake, we were all very pleased she had such certainty in her life.

When Evan proposed, Clare was over the moon – as was I – and they'd seemed happy enough since, but while I made us both another cup of tea, Clare began to elaborate on how she might get a few days away to herself. Or a few days with me, at least. Clare was serious. She had quickly developed her throwaway comment into something resembling a proper plan. Soon – as I might have known she would after a whole childhood of experience – she even managed to make it sound as though her crazy idea was in everybody's best interests.

'Think about it, Sophie. If Mum finds out that you're in Majorca without Callum, she will go nuts with worry. You on your own in a foreign country and nursing a broken heart on your birthday to boot? She wouldn't like that one bit. Before you know it, she'd have Dad on a plane and they'd be on their way out there to bring you straight back. Either that or she'd

phone the British Embassy, causing a full-scale inter-
national incident while they searched the island to bring
you home. You don't want that to happen, do you?'

I certainly did not. But why would it happen? Clare
had just spent ten minutes telling me why it would be
perfectly safe for me to remain alone in the flat without
fearing detection. I didn't have to mention anything to
Mum and Dad.

'Twitter,' was all Clare had to say.

She was right. Hannah or Alison would be bound
to let something slip eventually.

'It would be a disaster,' said Clare, reading the lines
of worry that had appeared on my forehead. 'And I
think the best way to circumvent this disaster would
be for me to take control of the situation for you first.
I'll phone Mum and tell her that you and Callum have
split up but you went abroad anyway because you
thought you were feeling up to holidaying alone.
However, since then, the reality of the break-up has hit
you and now you're feeling terrible. The best possible
thing would be for *me* to fly out to Majorca and bring
you home. After five days in the sun, of course.' Clare
grinned.

'What?'

'Genius, eh? I would be surprised if Mum didn't
suggest it herself. Then I just have to tell Evan what
Mum has requested and bingo . . . He won't want to
get on the wrong side of his future mother-in-law. It's
perfect.'

'Clare . . .' I didn't know where to start. It all
sounded so complicated. I was going to continue to
pretend to be on holiday and she was going to join in
with the charade? It could only end in disaster. Besides

which, I was almost thirty years old. I didn't need a chaperone.

'You know what Mum says. We'll always be her little girls.'

That much was true. Mum had tweeted something along those lines just that afternoon, with reference to my upcoming birthday.

'Do you want her to worry about you?' Clare laid it on thick.

'Of course I don't want her to worry.'

'Then I'm going to call Mum right now.'

Chapter Fifteen

She was actually going to go for it. Listening to Clare as she made her phone call, I couldn't help but be slightly horrified by the way in which she managed to make everything she said about my plight sound so very, very convincing. Though I suppose I shouldn't have been surprised that Clare was a plausible liar. When we were children, Clare had me convinced for the best part of three years that strawberry jelly causes mumps, just so she could get at my share. Likewise, raisins were flies with the wings pulled off. No wonder I became a fussy eater.

'Mum,' she said now, 'I've got some bad news, but I don't want you to worry . . .'

It was a phrase guaranteed to make our mother worry.

'I've just spoken to Sophie. She and Callum have broken up.' She paused. 'They were supposed to be on holiday for her birthday, I know, but Callum pulled out at the last minute and Sophie has gone on her own. She sounded OK,' Clare continued in her serious voice. 'She's being very brave. She told me not to tell you because she didn't want you to be concerned, but I think it would be wrong to keep this from you. She didn't say she needed anyone with her, but I can't help thinking that she might. Especially with her turning thirty on Tuesday.'

Clare nodded and pursed her lips in concern while my mother said something in reply.

'That's what I thought. I'll have to ask Evan first, of course, but as it happens, it wouldn't be too difficult for me right now. My temp contract has just come to an end. I'm sure it won't hurt if I take a few days off before the next one starts. I can probably get an easyJet flight for a hundred quid, and of course I'll stay in Sophie's hotel room, so there won't be any extra expense there.'

Mum said something else.

'Oh, Mum, you really mustn't worry. I promise that everything will be OK. We're grown-ups now. There's no need for you to take the plane out there yourself. I just sensed that Sophie needs a little support to get through this time. I can give her that support with hardly any disruption to my life at all.'

'What did Mum say?' I asked when Clare finished the call.

'She said you've always been a terrible worry to her,' she replied with an annoyingly smug smile.

'I can't believe that—'

Clare stopped me. 'You know she's going to call you right away, of course.'

Clare was right. My phone began to ring less than a second later. I snatched it up.

'UK ringtone?' I said when Mum quizzed me about that. 'That's strange. Perhaps it's because the call has to go through a British exchange first.' People so rarely called these days, preferring to text or email, I hadn't even considered I could be undone by a ringtone. I would have to remember to set my calls to divert as soon as I came off this call. I glared at Clare as I began my grand lie in earnest. No longer was it a simple case of a lie of omission. If I lied to Mum too, there was no turning back. I would have to go through with Clare's crazy fake-holiday idea. I didn't want to do it, but, really, Clare had left me no choice.

'Yes, I'm in the hotel,' I said. 'Yes, it's very lovely. And yes, Callum and I have split up, and yes, it does seem to be for real. I mean, why else would he have refused to come on holiday? I don't think I actually did anything, Mum. I just think he decided he was too young for a proper commitment.'

Clare sat back in her chair with a big grin on her face as I dealt with our worried mother.

I feigned grateful surprise when Mum informed me that my sister was giving up the opportunity of a 'very important' temping job to fly out to Majorca to be with me. Having heard Clare's conversation moments before, of course I knew that to be rubbish, but I suppose Mum wanted me to be grateful for my big sister's thoughtful sacrifice. She finished the conversation by asking me if I was certain that I wouldn't rather she and Dad flew out to look after me. She hated the idea of me being alone and abroad on my birthday, but she wasn't sure it was right for Clare to go away without Evan. Not now they were engaged to be married. And I would always be Mum's little girl. A mother's responsibilities never end. I could hear a sigh in every syllable.

'I promise I'm OK, Mum,' I responded. 'It will be nice to have Clare here, but really I think I'll be over Callum in a couple of days.'

'It's a pity you've split up,' said Mum. 'He sounded like such a nice boy. Look after yourself,' she finished.

'Stay off the Bacardi Breezers. It may seem like a good idea at the time to drown your sorrows, but you don't want to end up in a gutter showing your knickers in one of those Brits-behaving-badly shows. Or worse still in the Mail Online.'

'No, Mum, of course not. Please don't worry. Whatever happens, I'll stay out of the *Daily Mail*.'

'I'll stop worrying once I know that Clare is with you. She's always been the sensible one. Now I'm going to let you go because you're abroad and this phone call must be costing hundreds of pounds.'

'Oh!' I hung up in a fury. 'You're the *sensible* one, apparently. Has she ever *met* you?'

'It's just the way she is,' said Clare. 'Tough love. You've known her long enough. She'd have said exactly the same to me were the situation reversed. But she is right behind my coming to stay with you.'

Clare was gleeful.

'You've still got to see if Evan agrees,' I pointed out.

Clare's tack with Evan was entirely different. I could tell from the look on her face as she dialled him that she knew he was not going to be anywhere near so easily convinced as Mum. Speaking to Mum, Clare had sounded confident and in charge. With Evan, she would have to make more excuses. She told him she wouldn't have considered such a thing as going abroad without him but our mother had been so worried and it didn't seem right to make two *elderly* people (Mum and Dad, who would have hated to hear themselves described that way) trek halfway across the world on my account. Still Evan had all sorts of reasons why Clare should not be going to Majorca to see me.

'I know we said we wouldn't go on holiday this year, but this isn't a real holiday, Evan. I am going to Majorca to look after my baby sister, who has just been dumped by the man that she thought she was going to marry. Heaven knows what she might do.'

I wasn't sure I liked this picture of me as someone prone to doing stupid things. Neither did I like the fact that Evan said – at least I think he said from what I could hear – 'Sophie was dreaming if she ever thought Callum would marry her.'

Clare continued, 'I would be more than happy for you to do the same if the situation were reversed and it was your sister who was on her own in Majorca with nothing but a bottle of Bacardi Breezer to keep her company.'

Evan responded.

'Well, of course *your* sister would never find herself on her own with nothing but a Bacardi Breezer to keep her company. I do know she's not that kind of girl. But hypothetically. If Melanie were ever to do anything out of the ordinary, if her perfectly wonderful, well-organised life were ever to come just the slightest bit unravelled, you can bet that I would be right behind you if you wanted to help her sort things out. Sophie is family, Evan. And pretty soon she will be your family too.'

Clare frowned at his response to that.

'All right. Well, I am very, very sorry, but you can bet that Sophie will be incredibly grateful and I'm certain that she will understand the magnitude of this gesture in our wedding year.'

Evan continued for a couple of minutes before Clare was able to put down the phone. Clare held the phone away from her ear as Evan talked, throwing in the odd 'Yes, dear' for good measure.

'That didn't sound good,' I said when the call was over.

'Well, he wasn't very happy about it, that's for sure. It doesn't fit in with our financial plan. But he has agreed that I can go to Majorca to look after you.' Clare clenched her fists in a gesture of triumph. 'Yes!'

'Do you really think you should do this? If Evan isn't happy.'

'Soph, you know what? After the lecture he's just given me, there's no way I'm *not* going to do this. You have got yourself a holiday companion, starting tomorrow morning!'

Shortly after that, Clare left to go home. She had to 'book her flight' and pack her luggage, after all. She also had to swing by a supermarket and find something to cook that would go some way to making up for the fact that she was going away for five days. Apparently, Evan could usually be placated with a chicken and mushroom pie.

Still, even with a chicken and mushroom pie at her disposal, I fully expected Clare to have to get back to me later that night, telling me that Evan had put his foot down about their budget and the trip was off. I hadn't been able to make out most of their conversation, but the tone had not been encouraging. I was wrong, however. Just an hour after she'd left my flat, Clare texted to confirm that Evan had swallowed her tale hook, line and sinker. She had her 'flight' and would be with me around breakfast time the following day.

Well, it would certainly liven things up a bit.

* * *

Now that I didn't have to pretend I wasn't in the flat when my sister came round to water my plants, I could look after them myself. I spent a few minutes picking off dead leaves. I put my shoes back in the wardrobe and re-hung the favourite skirt that Clare had just tossed onto the floor. I gave my wardrobe a bit of a reshuffle while I was at it, making sure that everything was in colour order. Then I got out the vacuum cleaner. I took the brush off the nozzle and, without looking, I sucked that dead mouse straight into the bag. Ugh. Thank goodness my cleaner was an old model that didn't have a see-through cylinder. With the mouse safely inside the bag, I saw to it that the carpet underneath the bed was every bit as clean as the rest of the room. I would never let it get quite so filthy again. Talking of filthy . . . I wiped some dust from the top of the wardrobe with my index finger.

Perhaps Clare was right. There was plenty to keep me occupied at home. That day I kept myself busy until the wee small hours of the morning, polishing each piece of cutlery in the kitchen drawer one by one. After that, when I couldn't resist for a moment longer, I logged on to Facebook – nothing about Callum's profile had changed, thank God – and then Twitter.

'Thinking about my brave girl on her own in Majorca. What kind of man dumps a woman right before a holiday to celebrate her 30th birthday?' my mother had tweeted. I buried my face in my hands with shame. Couldn't she have been more subtle? Hannah and Alison had tweeted that they were right behind me all the way. Minutes after that, my mother had tweeted about another natural cure for vaginal dryness. Funnily enough, Hannah and Alison had no comments to add on that subject.

When I finally got into bed at around half past three, I was almost tired enough to fall straight to sleep. Once my head hit the pillow, however, I couldn't help thinking about the way Callum and I used to text each other 'goodnight' when we weren't spending the night together. That had been our habit from very early on. Now that habit was broken.

It's such a strange thing, breaking up with someone. When someone has been in your life or at least in your mind every day for any period of time, getting used to their absence takes some doing. Instead, you end up with something approaching phantom-limb syndrome. You know, that sensation that amputees sometimes get that the missing limb is still very much there and in need of a scratch. How long would it be before my heart got used to what my mind already knew and I stopped rolling over in bed and expecting to see the dark shape of Callum's body on his side of the bed?

Alone in my bed for yet another night, I cursed Callum's absent bulk and forced myself to stretch out like a starfish. This was my bed and there was no one in it but me. Why did I always confine myself to one side of it, as though I were sleeping on a park bench? There was enough space for three of me on the mattress. I was going to make the most of it. Limbs akimbo, I shut my eyes and started counting sheep.

I might have fallen asleep like that, but next morning, I woke up in my usual position, curled up in the far right corner with my arms wrapped tight round me to protect me from the big, bad world. The thought of Callum brought a lump to my throat as soon as my brain kicked in. If I'd had to spend another day alone in the flat, it might well have been the day I cracked up. Maybe it was a good thing my sister was coming.

Chapter Sixteen

Clare arrived, as promised, just after seven in the morning. She told me she'd got a taxi to take her all the way to the Gatwick Express entrance at Victoria, where she made a show of going down the escalator to the platform before dashing through the station, avoiding the CCTV cameras – 'Just like that scene in *The Bourne Ultimatum*' – then coming up a different escalator and getting into another taxi to come to my flat via the garage with the mini-supermarket at the end of my road. Her complicated route was intended to put Evan off the scent, she explained. Even though he was, in theory, getting ready for work the whole time Clare was travelling, subterfuge was essential. As was her disguise. She was wearing a pair of huge sunglasses and a brightly coloured silk headscarf wrapped round her curly hair.

'In case anyone sees me,' she said.

'Right. You don't look especially anonymous in those big sunglasses,' I pointed out. 'You look more like someone trying desperately hard to be noticed. A wag, for example.'

'Just help me with these, will you?'

She indicated her two enormous suitcases. The driver had, with a distinct lack of grace, just about deigned to haul them out of the taxi's boot, but he would not bring them even as far as the gate. He told us he couldn't.

'I'm on incapacity benefit,' he said.

I couldn't blame him for being unwilling to take on the challenge of Clare's baggage. I certainly wasn't looking forward to it. 'What on earth have you got in those?' I asked, when I saw Clare's mammoth haul. The larger of the two cases could have contained a whole cow. You wouldn't even have needed to chop the cow up first. 'You're only coming to my house for a few days.'

'That's right,' said Clare, 'but as far as everyone else is concerned, we're in Majorca, aren't we? And Evan would be suspicious if I travelled with less luggage than usual.'

'If Evan saw you take all this through the door, he probably thinks you're running away for ever. Is this what you usually take when you go away?'

'No. If I'm going for anything longer than a weekend, I usually take a bigger wheelie case.'

I goggled. She had a bigger case than the one that could hold a whole Friesian?

'But the handle fell off on the flight back from Ireland. Personally, I think the baggage handlers wrecked it deliberately. They covered it in that "heavy load" tape and it ruined the leatherette.'

'Oh.'

'I hope I haven't forgotten to pack anything important.'

'The kitchen sink?' I suggested.

A micro-expression of panic crossed Clare's face.

'Don't worry. I've got one of those. I really can't imagine you've left anything important behind, but if you have, I'm sure I will have something you can borrow.'

'It's so hard to plan for the so-called summer weather

in England,' Clare said, taking off her sunglasses to peer at the grey sky above. 'One minute the sun's out; next minute you're back to wearing three jumpers and bed socks.'

'Clare, we're staying indoors,' I reminded her. 'There will be no weather where we are going. The flat will be kept at a steady twenty-two degrees. I have no intention of changing out of my pyjamas.'

Clare slapped a hand to her forehead.

'Pyjamas! I forgot my pyjamas. I knew it. There's always something. Do you think I could go back to my place without Evan noticing?'

'No,' I said. 'You can borrow mine.'

I made a grab for the smaller case and wrenched my back in the process. That case could not have been any heavier had it contained nothing but solid gold bullion.

'This weighs a ton!' I complained.

'Sorry,' said Clare. 'I should have said. That one's got my shoes and heated rollers in it. And my travel iron. And my hairdryer.'

Heated rollers? Travel iron? Sheesh.

'You take the bigger one,' she suggested.

It was slightly lighter, but all the same, by the time I got it into the bedroom, I felt like the losing strongman in a competition to see who can pull a lorry for half a mile.

Clare's enormous amount of luggage reduced the floor space in my already tiny flat by 25 per cent. As she unpacked those two huge cases, which could have contained all my worldly goods and then some, I marvelled at the things she had brought for the purpose of spending just under a week in my ground-floor flat in Clapham: five bikinis (one for each day, she

explained); five pairs of shorts; five T-shirts; four
sundresses – three of them mini, one maxi; three cocktail dresses – one white, one black, one red; five pairs
of high-heeled shoes – one to match each cocktail dress,
one silver and one gold, which would go with everything. 'Metallics are fabulous neutrals,' she explained;
four pairs of flat sandals; a pair of cowboy boots; and
some trainers.

'In case we go for a walk.'

'One thing we definitely won't be doing this week
is going for a walk,' I reminded her. 'We're in hiding.'

'I know, but when I was packing my case, Evan said
he'd heard that the walking is really good in Majorca.
I could hardly ignore his tip, could I? That would have
made him suspicious.'

'Do you usually like to go walking?'

'Well, no, but . . . there's a first time for everything.'

In addition to all those clothes, she had enough
toiletries to set up her own counter in the cosmetics
department of John Lewis. There were five bottles of
suntan lotion. That's right – not one but five. They
ranged from SPF5 to SPF30. Then there was aftersun.
There was aftersun with aloe vera. There was aftersun
with added tan extender. I had no idea there were so
many variations of aftersun. Then there was exfoli-
ator. A bottle of St Tropez. Another bigger bottle of
St Tropez.

'In case the weather's no good,' she explained.

'Of course the weather's going to be no good,' I
pointed out. 'We're staying in south London. Indoors.
Is this your entire bathroom cabinet? You've brought
more stuff than I would use on a year away.'

'I know,' she said impatiently, 'but I had to make it

look as though I've really gone abroad. Where can I put these?' She waggled two bottles of suntan lotion.

Clare arranged her toiletries on the shelf above the bathroom basin and all around the edge of the bath. She had also brought an enormous bottle of shampoo and matching conditioner. They were of a brand that claimed to be especially good at washing salt out of beach hair.

'Did you buy this specially?' I asked.

Clare confirmed that she had. 'Well, I'll use it one day. Maybe Evan will take me somewhere nice on honeymoon. If it fits with his five-year plan.'

Having taken over my bathroom, she unpacked her hand luggage. She'd brought six paperback books. She really was intending to get some reading done. I had a look through them.

'*Wolf Hall*.' I picked up the Hilary Mantel monster book. 'This isn't your usual kind of thing. I am impressed.'

'Oh, I'm not going to read it. Look at this.' Clare flicked the book open. 'Evan hollowed it out to make a secret hiding place for my foreign currency.'

'Actually,' I said, 'I'm even more impressed by that.'

Clare piled up her paperbacks on the coffee table.

'Now, I could really kill a cuppa . . . One of the best things about holidaying at home,' she observed, as she made some Earl Grey, 'is that you can have a cup of tea whenever you like. You couldn't get a cup of tea like this in Majorca.'

'You're right,' I agreed. 'I really don't know what I thought was missing.'

At around midday, when she calculated that her 'plane' must have touched down at Palma Airport and its passengers all cleared immigration, Clare turned on her iPhone and straight away set it so that her calls would divert to voicemail without giving her location away with a UK tone. She sent a text to Evan to let him know she'd landed safely. She did the same for Mum, telling her that I had been waiting in the airport arrivals lounge as promised. Mum responded at once with a request to know whether I had been looking after myself since the split. Had I been eating? she asked.

'She looks like she's been stuffing ice cream,' Clare confirmed. 'There, that should shut her up,' she said to me.

'Tell Sophie to stay off the saturated fats,' was Mum's response. 'It will only make things harder when she gets to my time of life. I've just tweeted about a new menopause diet that you girls might want to try.'

'How old are we?' Clare asked me.

When Clare had finished contacting all the people who would want to know that she had arrived safely (our mum, Evan, Evan's mum and her temp controller, Beryl, who had become a good friend over the years Clare had spent avoiding a permanent job), she suggested that perhaps it was time I answered some of my workmates' emails.

'How many have they sent?'

'Must be getting on for a hundred.'

I had still not responded to a single one, but Hannah and the others kept writing and asking for more details about how I was getting on, and it was true that their tone was becoming increasingly concerned. I couldn't hope that they would continue to read only good things into my prolonged silence.

'You don't have to say much. Tell them you're having a wonderful time,' said Clare. 'Tell them your sister has arrived to take care of you and you're looking forward to having a great few days with her.'

'I can't,' I said. I didn't want to lie to them, as we were already lying to our parents and to Evan. It seemed too risky. Mum and Evan . . . well, it appeared they were inclined to believe just about anything. Hannah and Alison were a different story. It was best to give them as little ammunition as possible. But Clare pointed out that I couldn't stay silent for ever, because then someone really would start to worry. And if someone started to worry, then someone might try to track me down at the hotel. All people needed was the odd text or one-line email to let them know I was still alive. They didn't really want any detail. They didn't really care, Clare assured me. In any case, I didn't have to lie much. My sister really *was* with me. I could say just that and be telling the God's own truth if it made me feel any better.

Clare had an answer for everything. She always did. And ultimately the little sister in me couldn't say 'no'.

'OK,' I said. Against my better judgement, I sent an email to Hannah, copying in everyone else at Stockwell Lifts who had wished me well so far, telling them I was especially fine and happy now that my sister had arrived to spend a few days with me and that I would let them know more as it happened.

'Good,' said Clare. 'That's sorted.'

The response was pretty much immediate. Hannah confirmed that the girls at Stockwell Lifts had indeed been starting to worry. She had been thinking about sending a message to my mum via Twitter. Then she asked for more details. How was the hotel? How was weather? Had I met any interesting people? By which she meant 'men', she added, in case I hadn't guessed.

'See.' I showed the email to Clare. 'Now she wants to know even more.'

'It's OK,' said Clare. 'You don't have to respond. You're too busy having a marvellous time. Let Hannah conjure up a picture of you on the beach with Juan Carlos the deckchair attendant. You're drinking mojitos and he's rubbing suntan oil into your shins . . . Let Hannah's imagination run wild.'

'She'll certainly come up with a more interesting scenario than the real one,' I said, as I cleared some of Clare's books and magazines off the sofa so that I could sit down too. 'Five days in my flat. What are we getting ourselves into?'

'An adventure. Are you hungry?' Clare asked.

'You know what?' I found myself saying. 'I am.'

I was surprised to discover that I was feeling properly hungry for the first time since Callum dropped his bombshell.

'What shall we have for our lunch?'

Outside, it was cold and grey again and the dampness seemed to have seeped through the walls into my flat, which was ridiculously chilly for a summer's day. I put the gas fire on in the sitting room; then we made ourselves a lunch of mashed potatoes, frozen fish fingers and baked beans. It was hardly holiday fare, but it did the job. You really can't beat fish fingers.

'I bet you can't get these in Majorca,' said Clare. 'Pass the brown sauce.'

We ate our lunch in front of *Jeremy Kyle*. That day's show was all about warring sisters. One pair traded real, live blows on screen as they argued over a rat-faced man who had been cheating on both of them.

'I hope we don't end up like that by the time I go home,' said Clare, giving me a playful punch on the arm.

'Are you glad you came?' I asked her. 'I mean, do you really think we're going to get through this without going mad and ending up hating each other? A whole five days stuck in my flat?'

'We are going to have a lovely time,' Clare insisted. 'I'm going to make sure of it.'

Chapter Seventeen

Clare did seem determined to have a lovely time. She quickly got into holiday mode. After lunch, she unpacked her suitcase, filling my wardrobe to bursting point, and then changed into a pair of my pyjamas. She chose the newest pair. Then she went back to reading her book with a cup of tea by her side and her iPhone plugged into my speakers, playing the type of music she claimed Evan wouldn't let her listen to at home. (To be honest, I agreed with Evan. Clare's taste in music was pretty bad. Lots of screeching emo and death metal.) Meanwhile, I continued the spring-cleaning frenzy that I had begun the previous night. While there was so little in the freezer, it seemed like the perfect time to defrost it. So when I should have been on a sunbed, I was on my hands and knees chipping ice out of the freezer with a blunt knife.

After fifteen minutes or so, Clare wandered through the kitchen in search of a biscuit and told me that I wasn't exactly helping her to find her holiday mood.

'What do you mean?'

'The sound of that knife against the ice is putting my teeth on edge.'

'This is keeping my mind off Callum,' I told her.

'In that case, feel free to mess with my nerves.'

Of course, the defrosting wasn't really helping to keep my mind off Callum at all, but it kept my hands occupied and away from my iPhone while I waited for the regular bulletins from the office.

'Callum just asked Alison if she had any spare Nurofen,' Hannah wrote at about four o'clock. 'The stress of breaking up with you is really telling, if you ask me.'

The thought that Callum was suffering too gave me enough energy to descale the shower head, which was the chore I had chosen to do next.

'Mum's tweeting!' Clare called from the sofa while I was getting busy with the limescale remover. 'She says she's thinking of both her girls in Majorca and looking forward to this evening's Urban Goddess group.'

'Urban Goddess group?' I echoed.

'Hasn't she told you about it? It's about sitting in a circle, eating biscuits and harnessing the power of your menopause,' Clare informed me.

'There's power in the menopause?'

'Oh, yeah. Dad told me. It's like nuclear PMT . . . You should respond to her tweet.'

'My @liftlady account is for work. I only tweet about Stockwell Lifts-related business.'

'Then tweet that you've been admiring the lifts in your Majorcan hotel.'

'Clare,' I said, 'I'm sure my workmates already feel sorry for me . . . If I tweet about the lifts in the hotel, they'll think I've gone insane.'

'Go back to the defrosting, then. Oh! Mum's just tweeted again.'

'What this time?'

'The perils of HRT. She calls it horror-repression therapy.'

I could safely ignore that one.

* * *

So the first day of Clare's stay in my flat was OK. At least I didn't have to make every cup of tea I drank. But in the evening came the first indication that a holiday at home wasn't going to be quite as easy as I hoped. For most of the day Clare had been quiet and relaxed, reading her book and following our mother's embarrassing outbursts on Twitter, but that wasn't going to be quite enough for her.

'Now you've done all the spring-cleaning, perhaps you could just chill out and get into the spirit of things?' suggested Clare as we washed up after supper.

'The spirit of things?'

'Yes. The holiday spirit. Let your hair down. Let's have a drink.'

'I don't think I'm in the right place to be getting into the spirit of things,' I told her. As the clock ticked past six and night drew in, I was back in limbo. The working day was over and there would be no more news about Callum from my workmates that day. In fact, there might be no more news until the office opened on Monday. A whole sixty-four hours away. 'I'm not really on holiday, Clare. I am staying in my flat with the curtains drawn, thinking about the fact that I have been dumped by the man that I love. There's nothing about that to put me in the holiday mood.'

'That, I accept,' said Clare, 'but really, what good is it going to do if you sit here moping for the rest of week? You should try to have the best time you possibly can.'

'How can I? I'm still trying to digest the fact that Callum has dumped me. It's three days later and he hasn't even texted to see if I'm OK. How is it possible that we were together for eighteen months and now he doesn't even care if I'm dead or alive?'

'Of course he cares if you're dead or alive,' said Clare. 'But don't you see that he doesn't need to text you to find out how you're doing? I'm sure Hannah is giving him a running commentary on your great holiday in Majorca. You don't need to be in touch with him directly. She's doing all the work for you. As far as Callum is concerned, remember, you're having a wonderful time without him. What's he going to do? Text and ask you if you're OK only to have you text back telling him about the beach and remind him what he's missing? He's not on holiday, is he? He's back behind his desk. If you ask me, right now he's worrying more about his own heart than yours.'

It was hard to believe, sitting as I was with my sister in that dingy flat I had so longed to get away from for just a little while. And we had another four days to go, with my birthday at the end. Was I really going to celebrate my thirtieth birthday like this? Behind drawn curtains in Clapham? I asked Clare what I had done to deserve such a blow at such a crucial point in my life. The point at which it would become clear that I was a loser who would never achieve life's milestones: the husband, the mortgage, the kids and the dog. Turning thirty in the midst of a break-up was just about the worst thing I could imagine.

'Come on,' said Clare. 'Don't feel so sorry for yourself. Turning thirty isn't so bad. I've done it three times already,' she added with a wink. 'I know this isn't what you wanted, but it's the best that we can do for now. And it just might work. Every day you can pretend to be in Majorca is a day that Callum will spend agonising over his decision to break up with you. I promise. All you can do in the meantime is try to see the funny side. And have a cocktail or three.'

Clare waggled a bottle of Dooley's in my direction.

'What's that?'

'Toffee vodka. I found it in the cupboard under the stairs.'

'My cupboard?'

'Of course. Don't tell me you didn't know you had it. That's a very bad sign.'

I certainly didn't recall having bought it. Perhaps it was left over from the party I'd had when I first moved into the flat.

Clare poured out a caramel-brown slug for each of us.

'Nightcap?' she suggested. 'A toast to our happy holiday.'

'Just a little one,' I agreed.

'That's better. It'll help you sleep.'

Heaven knows I would need more than a shot of Dooley's to help me to sleep that night. One of the things I had forgotten about my sister in the decade and a half since we last shared a room is that she is what one might call an 'active sleeper'. By day, she sometimes managed to be still and quiet for hours at a time. At least, that's what I always assumed, since she worked as a legal secretary (albeit on a temporary basis. Perhaps that was a clue). Anyway, let's assume that my sister could stay in one spot for more than five minutes. By night, it was a different story. All I remembered from that time twenty years ago, when she and I were last bedmates, was that Clare, who, at two years older, was considerably bigger than me, had stolen all the bedclothes. Her favourite game back in those days was to sing 'Ten in the Bed' and push me onto the floor when it got to the bit about 'They all rolled over and one fell out.' Sometimes she pushed me out of bed twenty-five times in a row, even if I was, theoretically, the 'little one', who should have stayed on the mattress until the end of the song.

Anyway, having investigated all the options available regarding sleeping arrangements in my flat, my sister plumped for sharing my double bed. The sofa was too short and saggy to be comfortable. 'I dread to think what it would do to my back,' she shuddered.

I had a pump-up bed that our father had insisted I take to London after one of his garage clear-outs. Dad was always cleaning out the garage, but he couldn't bear to throw things away. 'You never know when you might need it,' he'd say. In the past four years so far: never. But now that its hour had come, we discovered why it been relegated to the garage in the first place. The stupid thing was full of holes and would only stay inflated while the electric pump was actually running. The moment we turned the pump off, the mattress sank back to the floor in an uncanny impression of my broken heart.

So the only realistic solution was for my sister to bunk down with me. And I was fine with that, at first. When Callum and I started going out, he had insisted I swap the standard double mattress that came with the flat for something bigger. (He was tall and broad-shouldered.) Two relatively skinny girls sharing that same bed, lying head to tail like sardines in a tin, should be easy, right?

Wrong. The moment my sister's head touched the pillow she was asleep. Seconds later, she was kicking my back as her leg muscles twitched involuntarily. Shortly after that, she started snoring so noisily I could only be thankful that her head wasn't right next to mine. I would have perforated an eardrum. I gave her a shove, to try to persuade her to roll over onto her side. She didn't roll over. She stayed fast asleep and gave a loud and indignant snort that suggested she was possessed by the ghost of a wild boar. I sat up and bodily hauled her into the recovery position. Still she snored. How on earth was it possible that my sister could snore in the recovery position? Surely nobody snored when they slept on their side? It seems that my sister was the exception to the rule.

It was no good. Clare wasn't going to stop snoring no matter which position she lay in. In the end, I gave up and took myself back to the living room with the solitary blanket I had managed to pull from my sleeping sister's clutches. When she wasn't kicking like a donkey or making a noise like a stricken Jumbo coming in to land, my sister was busy rolling herself up in the covers like a caterpillar preparing to turn into a moth. I retreated to the sofa, which, since these days I was a good two inches taller than Clare, was no better suited to me than it would have been to her. But, hey, who was I kidding? I wasn't going to be getting any sleep anyway. The cinema of my mind was playing a non-stop marathon screening of the best bits of my relationship with Callum, followed by a special audio presentation of the phone call that finished it all.

What was he doing right now? I wondered. Probably fast asleep and dreaming like a baby. I could only hope that he was on his own. Was there any chance that he was thinking about me? I closed my eyes tightly and tried to wish myself into his dreams.

Chapter Eighteen

The following morning, which was a Saturday, I felt as though I had spent the night on a pub crawl with a victorious women's rugby team. My head hurt so much that part of me wished I had just gone for it and finished off that bottle of Dooley's after all. At least then I would have a damn good reason to be feeling like something that even the cat wouldn't drag in. My eyelids were swollen into slits. My lips were cracked and dry, and I could feel a mouth ulcer coming on, right on the end of my tongue so that it stung with every word I tried to speak. I was definitely not at my best.

Clare, by contrast, looked as though she had slept very well indeed. Destination spa-style well. She came into the kitchen stretching luxuriously, wearing my best silk dressing gown over an entirely different pair of pyjamas to the ones she had gone to bed in. My pyjamas. She'd brought all those clothes with her and she was going to spend the whole time in my PJs. Typical Clare.

'What time did you get up?' she asked.

'I've been here for most of the night,' I said pointedly. She didn't rise to it. Instead, she flopped forward to touch her toes and continued to speak to me from between her knees.

'It is so nice to have a night without Evan. He takes up so much space. We need to get a bigger bed, but he says it's out of the question when we're still paying for the new kitchen. I should have insisted on a bigger bed. I'd rather spend my time in there than at the induction hob.'

Clare straightened up and put the kettle on.

'Tea?'

'Make mine a strong one.'

'Can't get tea like this in Majorca,' she said, raising her mug to me.

'Are you thinking of making that your catchphrase?' I asked her. 'Because I am so not in the mood for catchphrases.'

'I hear ya. Now, what are we going to do today?' Clare went to open the curtains. I stopped her just in time.

'We're not here, remember?'

'Ah, yes.' The curtains remained closed. 'Can we at least turn the lights on?'

The lights *were* on. I explained to Clare that my landlord had replaced all the old bulbs in the house with super-long-life energy-savers that basically saved energy by not giving out any light at all. God, it was dingy in that flat. Still, it was pretty dingy outside too. I peered out through a crack in the curtains and noted the usual grey sky and drizzle so fine you could hardly see it. It was the type of drizzle that could nonetheless soak you to the bones if you stepped out in it. It was faintly heartening to know that we weren't missing much out there. It was even better to know that Callum was spending his weekend under this grey sky too.

'London is miserable,' Clare sighed.

'Tell me about it,' I said. 'But miserable suits me today.'

'Don't be like that,' said Clare. 'We're on holiday.'

'If you're going to say that once more,' I warned her, 'I may not be able to get through the next few days without committing murder.'

We ate toast for breakfast, together with poached eggs (which Clare managed to get all down the front of my dressing gown) and a chaser of All-Bran. We drank the only orange juice Clare had been able to find at her emergency stop-off at the garage en route to my house. It contained just 8 per cent orange juice. Everything else was oil and additives. Oil? I squinted at the small print on the label. Since when did orange juice have oil in it? It was a far cry from the freshly squeezed orange juice the Majorcan hotel had promised on its website. I felt my mood drop another notch as I imagined the people who would have been my fellow holidaymakers enjoying their breakfast in the sun while the light played on the crescent-shaped pool. It really wasn't fair.

'Any news?' I asked as Clare turned on her iPhone. I had been monitoring my own email traffic constantly. There was nothing. Not even from Hannah. But it was a Saturday, so there was really no reason why she should be in touch at all. She wouldn't be seeing Callum. Neither would Alison. Unless . . . I shoved that thought from my head.

'Just Evan,' said Clare, as she checked her phone. She spoke without much excitement. 'He wants to know if I had a good night's sleep,' she said. 'He hopes you're well.'

She texted him back confirming that we were both having a wonderful time, breakfasting on the terrace.

'The terrace! Ha, ha.' I picked at a chip of loose Formica on the kitchen table.

There was a pause of a few minutes while we loaded the dishwasher; then Evan texted again.

Clare frowned as she read this new message.

'What's wrong?'

'Now he wants me to send him a picture of the hotel.'

How on earth were we going to do that?

How easy it must have been to pull off a grand lie such as we hoped to in the days before mobile phones and PDAs existed. Back then, if you'd decided to hide out at home rather than go on holiday, all you had to do was draw the curtains, refuse to answer the landline and claim that the postcard you sent from Magaluf must have got lost in the post.

As we were quickly learning, however, in the twenty-first century you couldn't really be incognito for any length of time without raising suspicions. Information was king. Mum was on Twitter. Dad knew how to text. Even our grandmother had a mobile phone with a built-in camera. She frequently sent me pictures of her ancient smelly Yorkshire terrier wearing some new and hideous knitted dog coat. So of course Evan expected some photographs. In an age where people updated their Facebook pages from delivery rooms and tweeted from freshly dug gravesides, not bothering to post a couple of holiday snaps from your deckchair would have looked a little odd. But we weren't anywhere near a deckchair and Evan's request had sent us into a panic.

'You'll have to tell him the camera on your phone is broken,' I said.

'And have him call up the CEO of Apple and demand that a new one is couriered to our hotel at once?' said

Clare. 'He'd do that. I know he would. Then our cover would be absolutely blown.'

'He wouldn't have a phone sent to the hotel,' I said.

'You don't think so? He once called Clapham Junction to ask someone to find me on the platform and make sure I got into one of the front three coaches of the train to Southampton. He described what I was wearing and everything.'

'Did someone check for you?'

'Of course they didn't. But those are the lengths he would go to. Sometimes I think he believes I'm a total incompetent. In any case, if my phone's broken, he'd expect me to use yours instead.'

'Say they're both broken?'

'What are the chances of that?'

Clare paced the kitchen. She looked at her iPhone as though it might reveal the answer of its own accord. She sent Evan a text to tell him she'd send him a picture later in an attempt to buy us time. She sat back down at the table while we thought some more.

Later Clare switched her phone to camera mode and focused on the back of an All-Bran box while we racked our brains for a solution. As it happened, the back of the All-Bran box featured a photograph of a laughing couple enjoying a healthy All-Bran-based meal on a beautiful sunny terrace. In the background, beyond a colourful row of terracotta tubs overflowing with bountiful geraniums and bougainvillea, the azure sea met an equally bright blue sky. Eat this cereal, said the picture, and you too will have the confidence to wear a red string bikini to breakfast with your handsome, white-toothed lover on your exotic honeymoon. Clare focused in on the man's cheesy grin.

'I hate having to face her in her bikini every morning,' I said, turning the picture away from me. 'Nearly puts me off eating altogether.'

'I know what you mean,' said Clare, as she idly clicked a snap of the overly happy couple. 'Why don't they put jokes on the back or something? Pictures of fluffy animals. Lolcats would be great. Anything but Mr and Mrs Glee and their ridiculously flat stomachs.'

I agreed.

Suddenly, Clare sat up straight. 'Where's your laptop?'

'What do you want it for?'

'I've got an idea. Look at this.' She showed me her photograph of the back of the All-Bran box. 'Pretty good, huh?'

'So?'

'So I think we can work with this picture, or . . .'

Clare fired up my Mac. Soon she had logged on to the website of the hotel where she and I were supposed to be staying. The Hotel Mirabossa. She clicked on the photo that had persuaded me all those weeks ago that this was the hotel where Callum and I would reaffirm our love after our long month apart. It was a great photograph, which claimed to be a view from one of the bedroom windows. Along the top of the balcony was a window box full of bright geraniums just like on the All-Bran box. The pool down below was the perfect summer blue. The sea in the distance was dotted with white sails. Happy days. I sighed just to look at it. It was beautiful.

'What are you going to do now?' I asked, as Clare enlarged the photograph to its maximum size on the screen. 'Are you trying to torture me?'

Placing her elbow on the table to steady her, Clare

held the camera lens of her iPhone very close to the laptop screen and took a picture. She looked at the results and shook her head. She turned off my desklight, which was shining on the screen and causing a reflection, and tried another shot. She closed the bedroom door so that there was no reflection from the hallway either. She turned off the bedroom light. She held the camera lens of her phone so close to the screen it was almost touching. Click.

At last. This time she grinned at her handiwork. She passed the iPhone to me. 'There we are, sis. Our very own sea view, taken from our hotel bedroom window.'

I looked at the photograph on Clare's phone with some astonishment. Clare really hadn't done a bad job. She had taken the photograph from such close proximity that it really did look as though she had just held her phone out of the bedroom window and filled the screen with a real, live view.

'That's great, but it's a little bit grainy and—'

'It's perfect. Now let's send it to Evan.'

'No. You can't. He'll guess . . .'

'Guess what?'

'That it's not a real photograph.'

'He won't know it's not real. You know what he's like. He'll glance at it for all of ten seconds and go back to surfing comparison sites for savings on our gas bill. We should send it to Mum too. You know it will put her mind at rest to know we're in such a lovely place. It does look lovely, doesn't it?'

'Yes,' I said. 'It should do. It's the best hotel on the island. That's why I chose it.'

'Such a shame. Will you get your money back? You could always go there for real later on.'

'I don't think so. We were a late cancellation. The hotel rules are that we have to pay full price. And I don't think there's any provision in my travel insurance for being dumped the night before my fortnight off.'

'Hmm,' said Clare. 'You'd have been far better off if he'd been run over by a bus. I'm pretty sure they pay out if your travelling companion is *dead*.'

That wasn't much consolation. Tears prickled my eyes. Looking at that picture online had reminded me all over again what I was missing. I closed the window down so I wouldn't have to look at those sunny pictures any more. Clare put her arm round my shoulder.

'There will be other summer holidays,' she said. 'I promise. But for now, as far as Evan and Mum are concerned, here is the view.'

'Don't send it, Clare,' I begged her. 'This is going to end in trouble.'

Too late. She'd already pressed 'send'.

I felt especially guilty when Mum texted back to say how wonderful the hotel looked and how proud she was that her two little girls were on holiday together, looking after each other just as she had always hoped they would. It made her feel so much happier to know that I wasn't on my own.

'See,' said Clare. 'She's convinced that we're in Majorca.'

'She was convinced that John Barrowman was straight . . . I bet she was wearing the wrong glasses,' I said.

But Evan, too, seemed to be happy to take the photograph of the 'view from our hotel' at face value. He texted to say he was very jealous of Clare being out there in the sun while he was hard at work, saving money for their wedding, by spending his Saturday afternoon sanding down the paintwork on the banisters all by himself. That last comment made a small cloud pass across Clare's face.

'He's trying to make me feel bad,' she complained.

'Do you think so? I don't think that was his intention.'

'I know he's upset that I'm spending money on a holiday when we've been saying all along that we wouldn't go on holiday until our honeymoon.'

'Then he'll be pleased when he eventually finds out that you didn't go anywhere at all and the money is still in your Egg account,' I pointed out.

'I've been thinking about that,' said Clare, brightening at the idea. 'I thought I might use it to buy a pair of Jimmy Choos for the wedding, given that as far as he's concerned it's already gone. Right?'

'I like your thinking,' I told her.

'I think you should send this photo to the girls at work too,' said Clare then.

'No. That's too risky.'

'Mum didn't twig. Neither did Evan. Why should Hannah and Alison be any different?'

'Because they *are* different. Believe me. Unfortunately for Mum and Evan, they have a great deal of trust in you and me. They wouldn't think for a moment that the photo might be fake, but Hannah has actually been to the Hotel Mirabossa, remember? I wouldn't be in the least bit surprised if she recognised that shot from their website.'

'She won't make the connection. It won't even cross her mind. Why would it?'

This time I didn't let Clare persuade me.

'Hannah and Alison don't need a picture,' I said. 'Not yet.'

'OK,' said Clare. 'But they will need some sort of update soon. Something with a bit of colour. In the meantime, what are we going to do today?'

'I dunno,' I said. 'Read some books?'

But Clare wasn't asking whether we were going to watch an entire boxed set of *Glee* or just read our holiday paperbacks. The balcony-view picture had sparked off a whole new chain of thought. She meant, what were we going to do that day for the purposes of entertaining the people who really believed we were away?

To more effectively keep our secret for the whole week, Clare proposed that we drop small realistic hints about our holiday activities via text, Facebook and Twitter. We didn't have to go into any great detail, but Clare thought it would help if we threw in some place names – just enough to add some authenticity without raising suspicions. With that in mind, she went online again and scanned the Majorcan tourist board's website for ideas that would add fuel to our fiction.

'We should definitely visit Palma,' Clare read aloud. 'The cathedral is a fourteenth-century masterpiece. There are wonderful restaurants in the old town that really should not be missed.'

'OK.'

A visit to the cathedral seemed easy enough to fake. There was plenty of information online and it wasn't long before Clare had lifted a picture from the tourism website. She zoomed in on a detail of masonry.

'Arty, huh?'

I had to agree. It looked very convincing.

'The Caves of Drach in Porto Cristo are unmissable,' she told me a little later.

I knew that. They had been on the itinerary I planned for me and Callum. 'We'll pretend to go there on Monday,' I said. 'That's the day the hotel runs a coach trip.'

'OK,' said Clare. 'Let's do this properly.' She opened up a spreadsheet on Excel and divided it into the days that remained of our holiday. 'This will make it easier for us to keep our story straight when we get back to the real world.'

'Good idea.'

'Let's make tomorrow a pool day.'

'You're on.'

'And there's a market in the old town of Pollensa on a Saturday afternoon,' said Clare. 'Shall we go there right now? We should buy some souvenirs. Presents for Mum and Evan.'

'We can't pretend we've bought presents. What happens when we get back empty-handed?' I asked, making virtual speech marks around the words 'get back'.

'Ah. I've already thought of that. You'll leave our gifts in the overhead locker on the plane,' she suggested in an echo of the Disney story she'd told all those years before, when she claimed that she'd left Mickey's gift to her on the plane so that she wouldn't have to show it to her classmates. 'Mum and Evan will just have to believe we bought them something. It's the thought that counts after all.'

'Why do I have to be the one who leaves stuff in the overhead locker?'

'Because the stress of the break-up has made you forgetful?' Clare suggested.

'You're the forgetful one,' I reminded her. 'Remember that time you left the dog tied up outside the supermarket when Mum sent you to get some bread?'

'We hadn't had him long. And Mum had given me such a long shopping list. Not just bread. Besides, it took the rest of you until bedtime to realise he was missing too.'

'OK. What about the time you left my denim jacket on a bus?'

'I knew you'd bring that up. I think I've already apologised a thousand times. It was just a denim jacket.'

'That was the first thing I ever bought with my Saturday-job money.'

'It didn't suit you.'

'Oh, that makes it all right. And then—'

'Now you're going to mention the time I forgot to watch the chip pan.'

'You set the kitchen on fire.'

'I put the fire out. There was just a bit of smoke. Even Mum has forgiven me by now, almost twenty years after the event. Thank God for my Brownie home-safety badge.'

'But you think I'm the forgetful one?'

'OK, OK. I don't think you're the forgetful one. I was only trying to help. It was just a suggestion. A detail to make our coming back with no presents less suspicious. Do you want to convince Callum you're on holiday without him or not?'

'All right,' I said. 'We'll try your plan. But only if you are the one to leave the presents in the overhead locker.'

'If it makes you feel better,' said Clare.

'It does.'

So having lunched on distinctly un-Mediterranean fare of individual chicken and mushroom pies, we 'went to the market' and bought a new leather purse for Mum and a keyring for Dad. Clare texted Evan to ask if he would like a new wallet. Evan texted back that there was no point her spending money on a new wallet if Evan didn't have money to put in it. They were supposed to be saving for the wedding, remember?

'As if I could forget,' Clare sighed. 'Still, that's one less present to cart back to the airport. And for *me* to leave in the plane . . .'

After the market, Clare sank into an armchair and declared herself to be 'by the pool' for the rest of the afternoon. I should only interrupt her if I came bearing cocktails. I was not going to make her a cocktail, I told her. Not before six o'clock. Instead, I spent a short while Googling natural methods of dealing with rodents – apparently, having seen one mouse meant that I was harbouring its brothers and sisters by the thousand. I ordered a couple of those sticky boxes that seemed to be the most humane method of dealing with them. It only struck me afterwards, as I was cleaning my silver jewellery with bicarbonate of soda (another job long overdue), that I would have to deal with the mice once they'd got themselves stuck by the paws. It wasn't a very nice thought. Didn't they bite?

When I took her a cup of tea – 'Not quite a cocktail, but you can't get tea like this in Majorca' – Clare told me she'd once read that mice were quite psychic and you could often make them leave a house just by asking them nicely to move next door. It didn't surprise me at all that Clare believed you could reason with a rodent. For quite some time in her twenties she thought she had been Lady Jane Grey in a past life. If only we could have asked Evan what the best solution was. Not only would he have known, he would probably have insisted on taking over the execution of it, saving me the onerous task altogether. Clare didn't know how lucky she was to have a fiancé who would do that sort of thing. Barring a fiancé of my own, or even a boyfriend, I made up my mind to call Rentokil when I 'got back' to my flat.

Chapter Nineteen

Clare was very pleased with her plan to check out what was happening in Majorca online before feeding the information back to our friends and relations. We had texted Mum 'from the market'. A few hours later, Mum had tweeted that she was looking forward to seeing what we'd bought. Hannah – who I would have thought had better things to do on a Saturday afternoon – tweeted in response that she had bought a fabulous leather doorstop in the shape of a donkey. Mum texted me to ask if I could find a donkey for her. She would reimburse me. Clare said I should respond, 'No way, on the grounds of taste.'

Minutes later, Hannah texted saying she wondered whether I might find a doorstop donkey for her too.

'It would be great to have a matching pair.'

'They've sold out,' I responded. 'Only elephants left.'

'Not very Spanish,' was Hannah's response.

'Wasn't Hannibal Spanish?' asked Clare. 'Say that.'

'Clare,' I said, 'we should just leave it. I think the level of detail we're putting into our fake break is going to bring us more hassle.'

'But you must at least be reassured that people seem convinced so far?'

'I suppose,' I admitted. I just wasn't as sure as Clare seemed to be that people were really that gullible or that they would remain so after nearly a week of our texts.

That evening, we looked at the list of bars and clubs that Hannah had given me and chose a place called Palacio Blanco, the White Palace, to be the setting for our first virtual evening out. To make our lives easier, we checked that this particular place had a website. Thankfully, it did. Even more usefully, the website had a webcam feature, which streamed live action from the bar itself. At seven thirty in the evening, it wasn't exactly kicking, but Clare and I were able to compose a text to Hannah in which I accurately described the red-and-black frilly shirts of the band who were setting up for the night.

'I remember that band,' Hannah texted back. 'Ask them to play "You're Beautiful" for me.'

After pretending to barf at the thought of James Blunt's ubiquitous song, we assured her that we would.

'Ask them if they remember me and my fiancé.'

I texted Hannah to say that the band leader had told us he could never forget her or her long, blond hair. That was Clare's idea. She thought a bit of flattery might make Hannah more inclined to keep feeding the good news to Callum and make her less likely to question its veracity.

Anyway, we left the Palacio Blanco webpage open so that we could listen to the music while we cooked our supper, which was a very passable paella. It turned out that there was some saffron in the back of one of my cupboards. I couldn't remember ever having bought it, but it did the job with some frozen prawns that were just within their use-by date.

'At least if I text Evan to say we've had paella, I won't be lying,' Clare pointed out.

After dinner, I played solitaire on the coffee table and Clare knitted. How she had managed to squeeze half a fisherman's jumper and three balls of wool into her case along with the rest of her worldly goods, I really don't know. She asked me to turn the music up and clicked her needles in time. And at ten o'clock – eleven o'clock Majorcan time – the band at the Palacio Blanco did play James Blunt's biggest hit. They probably played it at around that time every night, but we texted Hannah at once and told her they had played it just for her. The band's guitarist remembered her and Mike well, we assured her.

'You know,' said Clare, 'I'm really starting to chill out. Are you starting to chill out yet? Another cosmopolitan?'

While I had discovered a thousand small household tasks I'd never got round to, Clare had discovered a thousand things to do with the assorted bottles of spirits in the cupboard under the stairs, which were all left over from the flat-warming party I'd held three years before. I let her make me one more cosmo and then another and by eleven o'clock in the evening we were actually dancing. The band at the Palacio had knocked off for the evening and a DJ was spinning tunes guaranteed to make you want to get off your chair. We watched in delight as the entire female contingent of the bar's clientele got to their feet for 'I Will Survive'.

'Seems apt,' Clare had said. 'We should dance as well.' She pulled me from the cushions.

Exhausted by our whirling round, Clare and I

collapsed onto the sofa with the laptop balanced on our knees and watched the action at that faraway club on the webcam.

'Isn't it strange,' said Clare, 'to think of all that dancing and laughing going on over there in Majorca and we're watching it as it happens. It's almost like being there.'

'Almost, but not quite.' I smiled sadly. 'Cup of tea?'

'Yeah.'

'You can't get a decent cup of tea in Majorca,' Clare and I chorused.

'Callum really is an idiot,' said Clare as I handed her a milky Earl Grey. 'Not only because he's missing out on all that fun in Majorca, but because he's missing out on being with you. You really are the best girl in the world, and I'm not just saying that because you're my sister. In fact, if you think about it, it probably means more because you are my sister, since sisters are far more critical of each other than ordinary friends.'

Clare was right about that. God knows we had been incredibly critical of each other in the past.

'Do you think I'll get him back by doing this?' I asked her.

'Sophie, I don't think the question is whether or not you'll get Callum back,' she said. 'Guys like him always come back eventually. They hate to let anyone go for good.'

That was true of Callum. I had been slightly disconcerted when he told me that all his ex-girlfriends still sent him birthday greetings. Was it because they couldn't let him go, or was it actually the other way round?

'I think the real question is whether you truly want him back anyway. Look.' She pulled me closer to the screen. 'Look at all those people out there at the Palacio Blanco. Look at all those single blokes hoping to meet a single girl. You could have your pick of them.'

'Do you think so?'

'I know so. Seriously, Sophie. Perhaps you should use this break, if it really is a break, to think about what *you* really want. Callum is good-looking, for sure. From time to time, he's quite funny. But what else is there to him? Is he kind? I don't think it was especially kind to dump you before your holiday. Is he generous? When the looks are gone, will you still find him quite so interesting?'

'I'm not just interested in him because of his looks.'

'Maybe I put that wrong, but sometimes I think maybe you're in awe of him because of his attractiveness. I remember, when you two got together, you told me you couldn't believe it had happened, because he was the best-looking bloke at Stockwell Lifts, if not the best-looking bloke you'd ever seen. Why on earth would he be interested in you? was what you asked me. And all I could think was, Why on earth *wouldn't* he be interested in you? You may not be Giselle, but you're hardly like the back end of a bus.'

My sister knew how to phrase a compliment.

'You've got a lovely face and a fabulous figure, but you've got so many other amazing qualities too. You're kind and you're funny and you're generous. Except with your Jimmy Choos,' she reminded me. 'It's bad news to go into a relationship feeling like you should be grateful for whatever reason. It sets up an imbalance and that imbalance means that the partner who feels they have less to offer often becomes all too willing to accept less than they deserve. Take a good look at Callum's behaviour. I always thought he was a bit mean to you after a couple of drinks for a start.'

'He wasn't,' I insisted.

'Well, how about the *way* he dumped you? He may think that dumping you before the holiday was the honourable thing to do, but you've been together for eighteen months. Couldn't he have tried to make it work for just one more fortnight? He should have given it one last shot and made an effort to turn things round. He should have given you a chance to prove him wrong. You might have gone away and had a wonderful time and all his concerns about your relationship might have been answered. Instead, he selfishly ruined your big summer holiday, not to mention your thirtieth birthday.'

I nodded.

'No wonder he's skulking around the office, keeping out of everybody's way. He knows what an idiot he's been. I'm not in the least bit surprised they're all rooting for you. I know I definitely want you to call Callum's bluff and start looking for someone new. We could set up an Internet profile right now. Why wait? You could have a date lined up for the night you get back from Majorca. Mysinglefriend.com? I'll write you a reference.'

I turned down Clare's kind offer, though I did let her persuade me to look at a few examples of what was out there.

'They're not all losers,' said Clare as she clicked through the men who met the criteria she had decided should be my benchmark. 'They're solvent. They're good-looking. They've got their own hair and teeth. Well . . .'

She clicked on the picture of a chap who had either lied about his age or had lived a very hard life indeed. His brave smile revealed some shockingly poor dentistry.

'Perhaps not him.' Clare clicked him goodbye. 'But you see what I mean? There are other people out there. Good people. Interesting, attractive men who are looking for a girl just like you.'

She was probably right, but the thought of casting Callum off and putting myself back in the dating game was not a happy one. No matter how Clare tried to spin it, I wasn't in the least bit excited by the thought of having to put myself out there and find someone new. I could barely bring myself to believe that anyone would ever look at me in that way again. When I met Callum, I thought I had got my pass out of dating hell. I thought I would never again know the agony of waiting for a phone call. Never again would I have to dodge an unwanted slobbery kiss at the end of the night. I couldn't bear the idea that I was back at square one, facing the hell of first dates and broken dates once more.

I turned off my laptop.

'Time for bed, I think.'

'OK,' Clare agreed. 'Just one more row for me.'

She picked up her knitting needles again.

'I am really enjoying this holiday,' she said.

Chapter Twenty

The following morning, I was no closer to being convinced that my split from Callum could ever be for the better, but I did have a headache of post-hen-night proportions, which was not helped by having spent the night on the sofa again.

Clare seemed to have escaped the worst ravages of her own super-strong cosmopolitans. Or perhaps it was that she spent the entire morning in the bathroom, exfoliating and putting on facemasks and generally primping. That Sunday, she had decided she was having a 'spa day'. When she emerged from the bathroom, followed by a cloud of fragrant steam, she told me what a treat it was to wallow in the bath without having Evan knocking at the door asking how long she was going to be.

'He complains that I take much too long,' she said, 'but somehow it's perfectly all right for him to lock himself in there while he reads the entire *Sunday Times* from front to back. Some weekends he is in there all morning.'

'Yeah,' I said, dashing past her. Once again I found myself having some sympathy for Evan. Clare had been in the bathroom for the best part of two hours and I had drunk three cups of tea while waiting for my turn.

Back out of the bathroom, I set to work on a pile of mending jobs I had discovered (or rather rediscovered) while tidying up my wardrobe. I sewed a button on to a skirt that had lost that fastening almost three years earlier. Finally getting the job done made me rather proud of myself. Meanwhile Clare spent the rest of her morning online, looking at the *Daily Mail* and bitching about the people bitching about the poor unfortunate celebrities who had been snapped in their bikinis.

'I can't believe some of the comments people leave,' she said. 'You just know that none of those people is an oil painting and yet they feel free to be so nasty.' Having said that, she crafted a pithy comment of her own to leave at the end of an article about Ashley Cole. For some reason my sister felt an affinity with Cheryl – hence the goldfish – and never missed an opportunity to point out the star's ex-husband's shortcomings.

'According to the *Daily Mail*, Fern Britton is in Majorca,' Clare shouted as I was in the bedroom ironing a duvet cover. 'Shall we pretend we saw her on the beach?'

'No,' was my reply.

'Are you sure? Mum would love it?'

'Mum would *tweet* it,' I reminded her. 'We don't want to find ourselves in a situation where we've claimed to have seen Fern Britton when she's already flown back to the UK to record some charity chat show.'

'Good point,' said Clare. 'No celebrity namedrops.'

So the morning passed quietly, but of course Evan and Mum were not going to be content with one view from our hotel window. And neither was Hannah, who had seen the view because Mum had tweeted it. She told her Twitter followers that she had spent all day learning how to put up a TwitPic just so she could share our virtual postcard with the world.

'She's going to blow our cover,' I wailed.

'Stay calm,' said Clare. 'If Hannah had figured it out, we'd know all about it by now.'

I hoped Clare was right. Anyway, now that we'd set a precedent, everyone in our virtual loop expected to see more photographs. Specifically, Evan wanted to see that there was a decent lock on the inside of the hotel-room door. Clare sent him a text saying he was being ridiculously paranoid and she was not going to indulge him with a photo of the back of the door, but yes, there was a decent lock and yes, of course we used it whenever we were in the room.

'He's such a worrier,' Clare complained.

'I wish someone would worry that much about me.'

Mum wanted a picture of me, to make sure that I really was still alive and not wasting away to nothing in my heartache: 'I won't be able to rest until I see she's OK.'

'You know she won't,' said Clare.

'But how are we going to do it?' I asked.

'Come here.'

Clare took a photograph of me standing against the background of a white door.

'That's not going to work.'

'Why not? Hotels always have white doors,' she said.

'And they always have those fire instructions.'

'Hang on.'

She rifled through my post and chose a bank statement that, when it was turned over so that you could only read the usual Ts & Cs, and slightly blurred by some dodgy photography, looked like a plausible list of hotel rules and instructions.

'Look more institutional to you?' Clare asked.

I agreed. 'It could be a hotel. Send it off.'

It wasn't the most flattering shot, but Mum responded that it would help her to get a decent night's sleep. She said she hadn't stopped worrying for a minute since Clare broke the news that Callum and I had split up. She had even found it impossible to get into the meditation at Urban Goddess. Achieving anything like a state of bliss was but a distant dream.

'I feel bad lying to Mum,' I said.

'Then don't think of it as lying. Think of it as protecting her from unhappiness,' Clare suggested. 'Like the time I told her that school wasn't doing end-of-term reports as part of a paper-saving eco-drive.'

'Was that the year you were caught with vodka in a water bottle?'

'That's the one,' said Clare. 'See, Mum didn't need to know about that, did she? She'd only have worried.'

Hannah's request was not so easy for us to fulfil.

'Send me a photo of you on the beach,' she said, 'and I'll "accidentally" show it to Callum tomorrow morning so he knows exactly what he's missing.'

Did she mean a bikini shot? Now that really was going to be impossible. Not to mention tacky.

'You should do it,' said Clare. 'Send Hannah a picture of you in your bikini to wave under Callum's nose. You spent so much time at the gym in the run-up to this holiday – you know you look amazing.'

Clare was right in some ways. I had made a quite incredible effort to get myself looking my bikini best. I had gone to the gym five nights a week and hadn't so much as looked at a bread roll since Callum was sent up to Newcastle. For a girl who had never knowingly passed up the chance to eat a Greggs' Yum Yum – and there were lots of chances to eat Greggs' Yum

Yums in my part of south London – this was no mean feat. But I had done it. I had done it for Callum, because I loved him and I wanted him to be proud of me and to love me enough in return that he would want to plan the rest of our lives together. So much for that . . . He had no idea that I'd lost half an inch from my waist since he'd last seen me at the beginning of June.

'Come on, Sophie, put your bikini on and get posing.'

'And pose where, exactly?' I asked. 'How am I going to convince Callum to come back to me with a picture of me in my bikini standing against a white door or lazing on this hideous flat carpet?'

'He doesn't know what the carpet in the hotel is like, does he?'

'But he knows what this one looks like.'

'Trust me,' said Clare, 'men do not notice carpet. If the police took Callum into custody right now and questioned him for three hours under a spotlight, he would not be able to tell them the colour of this carpet, or the colour of the wallpaper, or whether you've got one or two armchairs on either side of the sofa. They just don't notice these things. Evan wouldn't even be able to tell you what colour my eyes are. He's always singing "Brown-Eyed Girl" in the shower. When I asked him why, he said it was because it reminded him of my brown eyes.'

My sister's eyes are light blue.

'So I don't think there's any need to worry about Callum recognising the Axminster,' she concluded. 'Let's take some photos. I'll crop it close, and I can PhotoShop in a background.'

I put on a bikini. I chose the one I thought would

be most flattering to my pale skin, but even that made me look sickly, pasty and cold.

'You'd think you'd have a bit of a tan by now,' mused Clare.

'Well, I suppose I would,' I said, 'if I hadn't been indoors for five days. Oh, this is stupid. We cannot send Hannah a picture of me in my bikini. I look like I've been in a sanatorium, not on a Spanish beach.'

'You just need a little bit of colour.'

It was time to get working on the fake tan. The bronzing plan was simple. We should approach our fake tanning as we would have approached getting a real tan. We had to work on it for a little while every day, building it up layer upon layer.

I wasn't a big fan of fake tan, but there was no choice. The sun was not going to shine inside my flat. Hannah was a devotee of the stuff and often gave off that faint yet distinctive whiff of cat's pee when she came into the office. I sometimes marvelled at the amount of money that must have been thrown at the problem of getting fake tan to look at least partway realistic. I wondered if they would ever throw any money at the problem of the smell, which made me think of dying leaves and other sorts of decay. When I read that was exactly how fake tan works, by causing a process similar to the one leaves go through every autumn as they change from green to brown, it started to make more sense.

Still, I had tried it only once and Callum had refused to come near me because of the whiff. He had also insisted that I change the bedsheets, which had been on the bed for just one night, and had complained for days afterwards that he could still smell the horrible stuff. 'It must have seeped into the mattress,' he'd said. So I was a little reluctant.

'What else are you going to do?' Clare asked. 'Pretend you sat under an umbrella all week?'

Callum wouldn't believe that. I was a proper sun worshipper when I got the chance. Perhaps this would work. It has to be said that having someone else help you to put fake tan on makes the whole process rather easier, and we still had plenty of time.

'It has the added advantage of being healthy,' said Clare, as she slathered on the St Tropez. 'No chance of skin cancer from this. Do I smell?' She offered me her forearm.

'A bit,' I said. 'Do I?'

''Fraid so,' said Clare. 'But what does it matter? There's no one around to smell us, is there?'

Chapter Twenty-One

Talking of smelling, the flat must have been getting pretty unpleasant by now. Sometimes, when I came back home after work and the flat had been shut up all day, I noticed a faint whiff of mildew in the air. Something fetid that made me wrinkle my nose in disgust. I'd complained to the landlady about damp but got no joy. I could only imagine how awful the place smelled now that it had been sealed like a time capsule for the best part of a week. Deciding to take a little risk, I opened the kitchen window, which faced out from the back of the house. There was no chance that anyone who knew me might walk by and see it. As I had already established, my neighbours didn't know who I was. They were hardly likely to tweet 'Just saw Sophie Sturgeon at her kitchen window. I thought she was supposed to be on holiday.'

The view outside surprised me. The weather, which had been typical British-summer weather for the past week – cold with thick, grey cloud – was finally beginning to change. I glanced up at the sky. The clouds were broken here and there by patches of pale blue. It was not quite the azure of the Mediterranean sky I had hoped to be basking beneath, but it was getting there.

Clare joined me at the window. She took a deep breath of the air outside, reminding me of the dog we'd shared as children, who would always stick his nose out of the car window and inhale with such joy you couldn't help but laugh at his exuberance. That's how Clare breathed in the fresh air. And then she spluttered. Someone a little further down the street was having a barbecue and with a change in the wind direction, she'd got a lungful of fatty smoke. She gathered herself.

'Gosh, it would be nice to be outside while this fake tan dries.'

'We're in hiding, remember?'

'Yes, but surely we could go out into the backyard for a few minutes. Nobody would see us. Nobody who cares. Unless perhaps the people in that house over there have a webcam and Hannah subscribes to their Clapham Cuties feed.'

Clare had a point. If I was going to open windows at the back of the flat at all, then we might as well go outside.

One of the things that had attracted me to renting my little flat in Clapham was the fact that it had outside space. The estate agent's details had talked about a 'south-facing garden'. The 'south-facing' bit might have been true, but in reality the 'garden' was not much more than a yard. Whoever had overseen the 'refurbishment' of the flat in the 1980s had gone for a truly low-maintenance option and simply poured a layer of rough grey concrete over what might once have been a scrubby patch of lawn. As a result, it was a singularly unappealing kind of space. I kept my bike out there and didn't go into it for months at a time. Though the outside space had been a selling point for me, I didn't often feel short-changed, since the weather hardly ever merited making the effort to dine al fresco. Now, however, after five days indoors, for the first time ever the yard did look rather appealing. And I could see a couple of weeds that needed dealing with. I should pull them up. I'd spent so much time tidying up inside the flat, I was rather in the zone.

'OK,' I said. 'Let's go outside.'

We dragged a couple of kitchen chairs out through the back door and settled down with our legs and arms splayed out to better dry off the fake tan. Whenever the sun found a gap in the clouds, Clare lifted her face towards it and smiled.

'I feel better already,' she said. 'I feel like a flower that's been growing in the dark. Isn't it strange how much more human one feels for a bit of sunshine?'

She was right. In spite of my misgivings, I was starting to feel better too.

While Clare simply soaked up the sun, I busied myself by pulling up the weeds that had bravely pushed through the concrete since I'd last ventured into the yard almost a year before. I hadn't even been out there to fetch my bike, since the back tyre had a puncture and I had yet to get round to fixing it. I was beginning to doubt I ever would, though 'mend bike' was still a permanent fixture on any to-do lists I wrote. Had I a puncture kit, I suppose I would have done the job then, but I didn't have a puncture kit. Callum was always promising to lend me his. Like fixing the creaky kitchen door, he'd never quite got round to it. Evan wouldn't have let Clare's bike get into such a state in the first place.

Still, the weeds were dealt with pretty quickly.

'Almost a pity,' said Clare, as I pulled them up by the roots, making sure to leave nothing behind that might be a new weed in less than a week. 'At least they added a bit of greenery to the place.'

The yard was 100 per cent grey now, apart from some peeling blue paint on the coal-shed door. If clean and tidy, it looked sad and unloved.

'What's in there?' Clare asked of the coal shed. 'Deckchairs? A barbecue?'

'Spiders, more likely,' I replied. I tried to open the shed, but the handle came off in my hand. The wood was rotted through. I had no doubt that my landlady would make a note of that when it came to handing back my deposit.

We weren't the only people who had ventured outside that day. It was Sunday lunchtime. Up and down the street, my neighbours were also making the most of the respite from the long, grey English summer. After all, it might be fleeting. Children played; dogs barked; someone drilled holes and did a lot of swearing.

'You could make this yard really nice,' said my sister. 'You could have some plants out here as well as indoors. You could have terracotta pots of rosemary and lavender in that corner.' She waved to her left. 'It seems to get the sun. You could get some proper garden chairs and a barbecue. Maybe even a parasol.'

'For the two really great days we get a year?'

'Yeah. You could get some of those hurricane lamps and put them along the wall.'

'Hmm,' I replied. 'Seems like a lot of hard work.'

'You're so lazy.'

The truth was, I'd never even considered making the yard my own in that way, because since meeting Callum, I'd been working on the assumption that all this was temporary. This yard. This flat. I had been so sure that it was only a matter of time before we got a place together. It just didn't seem worth expending any effort or money on making my flat any more comfortable. I told Clare my theory. Her face grew serious.

'Well, maybe Callum noticed that,' said Clare, 'and maybe it freaked him out, thinking that you were waiting for him to make a move the whole time.'

I didn't want to think that I might have pushed Callum into breaking up with me by doing nothing.

'It seems to me that the best way to make a man want to share his life with you is by pretending you're perfectly happy to live without him.'

'What do you mean?'

'I mean, perhaps you should have made some effort with the garden. Perhaps you should have decorated inside. Brightened the place up. Made it look as though you were settling down to a very happy single life that he would be hard pressed to pull you away from. Men love a challenge.'

I narrowed my eyes at her to make it clear that she was getting a little close to the mark, but she wasn't looking at me any more. She was still lazing in her chair, eyes closed, enjoying the freak summer sun. I considered responding to her words of wisdom by pointing out that she was advocating a plan of action that she hadn't exactly subscribed to herself. Far from it. She hadn't been living the glorious single life she wanted to push upon me when she met Evan. She had been living back at home with Mum and Dad, having had to give up her flat when she and Jake split up. She couldn't afford the rent alone. There was no challenge for Evan in persuading her to move out of Mum and Dad's house. She couldn't wait to get out from under Mum's feet. I, at least, had taken the step of renting a flat by myself rather than waiting at home for my knight in shining armour like someone out of the 1950s.

I could have said all this, but I didn't feel like arguing. Not right then.

Instead, I seethed as Clare muttered on about the attractiveness of female independence. My mood was not improved by the fact that I had been 'on holiday' for five days now and still I'd heard nothing from Callum at all. Not even a one-line text to check that I was doing OK. I would have expected that from him at least. I knew that he was probably getting all my news from Hannah and Alison, but wouldn't it have been courteous of him to enquire directly as to whether I was all right in Majorca on my own? We had been boyfriend and girlfriend for eighteen months, after all. You can't just cut someone dead like that, can you?

'Perhaps you need to up the momentum of your "Majorca's great" campaign,' Clare suggested when I asked if we could change the subject before I slit my wrists. 'Perhaps you need to suggest that you're having a holiday romance.'

I wouldn't hear of it. Though Hannah had asked several times in her texts whether I had met any interesting men, I would not have told her if I had. While it seemed she had jumped to my defence when Callum and I broke up, I still wasn't entirely convinced that I could trust her. Sure, in her emails, she was firmly on my side, but how did I know that what she said was true? She may have been telling me that she and Alison were having a great time tormenting Callum by talking about what a fabulous holiday I was having, but it was equally likely that Alison was giving Callum access to her famous 'shoulder to cry on' (i.e. her pneumatic cleavage) while Hannah was letting him share her secret supply of Hobnobs in an attempt to pump him for gossip about our relationship that she could use against me at a later date.

I didn't want to give Hannah or Alison any ammunition that might suggest to Callum that I was so over him I wouldn't appreciate any attempts he made to get back into my heart. Therefore, while I was happy to tell Hannah that I was having a good time, I would not pretend there was any romance involved. Or even flirtation. Neither would I let Clare persuade me to send a bikini shot. That was just tacky. I told her so.

That didn't stop Clare trying to persuade me otherwise.

'You look the best you have ever looked,' she said. 'If anything is going to bring Callum round . . .'

She pressed and pressed the matter until we ended up having an argument in which she reminded me, with near-fatal results, that perhaps the reason why Callum had dumped me was that I wasn't adventurous enough and by refusing to attempt to lure him back into my arms by posing in my swimsuit, I was showing everyone that he was right.

Of course, sisterly arguments very rarely remain on topic. There's always too much ammunition. Clare and I had grown up together. We had thirty years' worth of grudges to dredge up at any given moment. Thirty-one, in fact: as Clare had revealed during the course of one extraordinary row we had the year before, I may have only been on the earth for thirty years, but she started hating me while I was still in the womb.

'I fell over at my second birthday party,' she said. 'I cut my head open, but Mum couldn't bend over to pick me up because you made such an enormous bump. I wasn't in the least bit surprised you were the biggest baby on the ward. You looked like a big, fat slug. I hated you before you were born.'

Great.

Now she was picking on my gardening skills, my interior-decorating skills, the clothes that I considered 'sexy'.

'No wonder I couldn't find anything worth pinching in your wardrobe. My dressing gown is sexier than the clothes you would go out in.'

Next, she suggested that my hair needed a restyle.

'And that coming from the only woman I know who's had a perm in the last fifteen years. There's a reason why everyone else stopped having them.'

And then we came back to the Jimmy Choos, which Clare said showed how repressed I was, but which, from my side of the argument, quickly became symbolic of Clare's expectation that she should be able to enjoy whatever was in front of her no matter whether she had earned it.

'You expect everyone else to provide for you all the time. No wonder Evan gets frustrated with the way you waste money.'

And then Clare suggested that the shoes were wasted on me because I was going to turn into Miss whatsit.

'Miss who?'

'The Dickens one who wore her wedding dress until she died. I can see it now. You'll never get over Callum Dawes. You'll be telling everyone you meet that he was the love of your life, even when he's married to Alison and they've got three teenage children.'

'Alison?'

'Oh, come on. He so fancies Alison. He was all over her at your birthday party last year.'

'He was not,' I said, though of course I thought she had a point. If I needed to worry about anyone trying to steal my man, it was Alison.

'You wouldn't have noticed. You were too busy being wet.'

'What do you mean by "wet"?'

Clare did an unflattering impression of me simpering. Now our argument ranged from the way I was around Callum to the way I had been with other boyfriends long since gone, and that segued into the way I was in general. I thought I was sensible and careful. Clare thought sensible and careful equalled sappy. Then I tried to turn my cautious nature into a virtue by reminding Clare that I had held down a single job for almost three years, while she could rarely be found working out of the same office for more than two weeks at a time. I wasn't in the least bit surprised Evan got exasperated with her. Did someone as grown-up and mature as Evan really want to get hitched to such a flake?

'You can't hold down a job.'

'You can't hold down a man.'

'You only hold on to your man by being a doormat.'

'You only hold on to your job because it's so shit that no one else wants to do it. Public relations for a lift company? I've seen your blog. No wonder you got nominated for "Most Boring Blog in the World".'

'Oh!'

I reeled. I had told her about that dubious honour in confidence and she had sworn that she would never use it against me. I still hadn't found out who had put forward the nomination, but I had my suspicion that it was Alison.

'You think you could do better?'

'I know I could. I'd use some imagination.'

'You're telling me. Though what you call imagination, I would call pathological lying. How did you get me into this mess? Hiding at home and lying to Mum.'

'I was trying to help you. You could have refused.'

'What are you doing here anyway? What kind of a marriage are you going to have if you're happy to tell such big lies to your future husband now?'

'You're lying to Callum,' she pointed out.

'I'm lying to Callum to get him back.'

'Well, I'm lying to Evan because . . . because . . . Oh fuck off.'

We stopped short at pulling each other's hair, but only just. Funny how a row between sisters quickly becomes much nastier than a row between friends.

Unable to find a suitable response to my question regarding her lying to Evan, Clare stormed inside, slamming the back door behind her. She slammed the door so hard that a small piece of masonry dropped off the door frame and fell at my feet.

I instinctively looked up to see if our argument had drawn any spectators. Sure enough, the old woman who lived upstairs was peeping out from behind her net curtains. Seeing me spotting her, she darted back inside, leaving the net curtains billowing in the breeze.

'Bloody old busybody,' I swore under my breath.

I followed Clare inside and gave the back door a slam of my own, just for good measure. The glass in one of the four small panes cracked with the impact. That would be yet another £50 off my deposit.

From the bathroom, I heard the sound of Clare sobbing and then blowing her nose loudly. I felt like crying too.

I took myself into the sitting room to calm down, but because I was still covered in fake tan, I couldn't sit on the chairs or the sofa, which were upholstered in cream-coloured canvas. I tried sitting on a plastic bag, but after three minutes, I knew that wasn't going to be fun for very much longer. I had to wash the damn stuff off.

'Clare' – I knocked on the bathroom door – 'open up.'

'Go away. You're an absolute cow.'

'Come on. Come out of the bathroom.'

'I'm staying here until I've calmed down. It may be some time.'

'Then I'll sit outside the door,' I said.

'You can sit wherever you want. I'm not coming out.'

'You've got to come out.'

'Why?'

I looked at my hands, which were covered in sticky brown gunk. What was the deal with this fake-tan stuff? I felt sure I was getting streakier by the second, but I decided against telling Clare that in case it meant she kept me waiting even longer deliberately. I wouldn't put it past her to keep me out of the bathroom until I looked like a freshly creosoted fence. I would have to bite the bullet and apologise.

'I just wanted to say I'm sorry.'

Chapter Twenty-Two

That didn't work.

'I'm *really* sorry,' I said again. And again. And again. 'And I need to wash off the St Tropez.'

'Ah, there's the real reason!'

Clare sounded gleeful as she kept the door firmly shut against me.

'Clare, be fair. I'm sorry anyway. I'm sorry even if you make me stand here with this stuff on all day.'

'You called me a pathological liar.'

'You said I was a sap.'

'You *are* a sap.'

'Well, you're a liar.'

'I'm only lying to keep everyone happy.' I heard Clare's voice catch and couldn't help but feel empathy for her pain, even though I was the one who had been dumped and she was the loon who'd suggested this stressful solution.

I looked at my hands again. They were going orange, I was sure. This was no time to take the moral high ground.

'I'm sorry. I was being unfair,' I said. 'I know you've been trying to help me.'

'Do you mean it?'

'Of course I mean it.'

Clare slowly opened the bathroom door and confirmed that she was sorry too. She had already had a shower, I noticed at once.

'I guess it's just the pressure of being with each other twenty-four seven,' I said.

Clare agreed.

'We haven't spent so much time together since we were children, and we used to argue all the time then,' I added.

'That's true.'

'Only you used to pinch me then too. You were horribly violent for a seven-year-old girl . . .'

'Hang on,' said Clare. 'You deserved it. What about the time you rugby-tackled me so that I caught my head on the corner of the television? I've still got a scar.'

'I didn't rugby-tackle you. I was four months old. Mum put me on the floor. You tripped over me. And if we're talking about scars . . .'

I only had to gesture towards my knee, which still, despite the fake tan, bore a thin silver line to show where Clare had once hit me with a garden spade when she lost a game of Swingball.

'You were asking for it. You taunted me with that six-nil win.'

'You're my big sister. You were supposed to know better!'

Clare started to shut the door in my face. I couldn't let that happen. I was still covered in fake tan.

'This is ridiculous,' I said. 'I forgive you for my knee if you'll forgive me for your head. We're grown-ups now. And if I don't get this fake tan off quickly, I'll end up looking like a conker.'

Clare smirked. 'That might suit you.'

'It doesn't suit me. Let me have a shower and I'll make you a cup of tea,' I suggested.

'Of course.' Clare accepted my Earl Grey-flavoured olive branch. 'Can't get nice tea in Majorca.'

It was a good job we were both ready to apologise. There was, after all, no way out of our situation for now. Clare and I were stuck together until Wednesday at the very earliest – three more nights – unless we wanted to blow our cover and reveal that we had been in the flat all along. And we didn't want to do that. We had come so far. We only needed to hide out for a few more days before we could 'return home' without losing any face at all.

Whatever happened with Callum, whether my holiday without him persuaded him that there was more to me than he remembered or not, I did not want him ever to find out that we had faked our holiday. It wasn't only Callum that I was desperate to keep on deceiving. The girls at the office would have a field day. And if Mum found out that we hadn't really been to the Med, then she would have our guts for garters. We would never hear the end of it. Never! I could already hear her long-suffering sigh. She would blame me, of course, since to Mum's mind it just wasn't possible that her lovely, sensible Clare could have come up with something so stupid. If Mum found out, I would probably have to leave the country for real. Maybe even go into a witness-protection programme. As for Evan . . . if he found out that Clare hadn't gone to Majorca but had spent five days just two Tube stops away from him, heaven only knew what his reaction would be. Evan was a sweet, kind guy. I think I felt most guilty about the idea of lying to him. What would he do? He might question their upcoming marriage. He would be well within his rights, Clare agreed.

No, as irritated as I was with my beloved sister, I knew we had no choice but to stay put for the sake of her engagement, my relationship, family peace and my reputation at Stockwell Lifts. We swore a vow of silence on the events of this week.

'We will never reveal our secret,' said Clare. 'Not even when one of us dies.'

That thought made me shudder, but we made a solemn pact to keep the secret for ever, sealed with a handshake that involved only our little fingers. We'd developed that special handshake when we were, respectively, seven and nine years old. I was surprised that either of us could remember it, with its complicated twiddles and nods. But we did. It took me right back.

'Whoever tells smells,' Clare concluded.

Chapter Twenty-Three

Next morning, for the first time since she had arrived at my place, Clare beat me to the kitchen. I was still half asleep on the sofa when she pressed a mug of tea into my hand.

'I need to use your laptop,' she told me. 'It's urgent. I'm looking for your birthday present.'

Naturally, I told her she could help herself and settled back for another twenty minutes beneath the duvet. I was in no hurry to get up for another day in the confines of my flat and its bare, grey yard. I was beginning to envy real prisoners. At least they had exercise yards you could actually walk around in. I could take only six steps before I had to turn round again. My last day as a twenty-something should not have looked like this. But at least Clare was going to buy me a present.

What I didn't know was that my sister was not going to use my laptop to log on to Amazon, or Play, or any of those websites where you might ordinarily expect to find a suitable birthday present for a woman about to turn thirty. Oh, no. She was after something much more exotic. By the time I had dragged myself from the shower, she had just finished her mission. She clicked the open page shut before I could see what she'd bought.

'Let me see,' I said.

'It's a surprise,' said Clare. 'But trust me, I did find

exactly what you need and it will be here by half eleven.'

Flowers, then, I thought. Or maybe one of those freshly baked muffin baskets. Now that I didn't have to worry about being seen in a bikini, I would have been very happy with one of those. Or maybe, in my wildest dreams, she had ordered a pair of shiny Louboutins from Net-à-Porter to make up for having shoved her filthy feet into my pristine Jimmy Choos without my permission. It was more likely to be the flowers, of course – Evan went through their bank statements with a red pen, highlighting unnecessary expenditure that should have been diverted into their mortgage – but I had a couple of hours of feeling quite excited about the surprise ahead.

When the doorbell rang at half eleven, I leaped to answer it, but Clare insisted that I stay put in the sitting room.

'You're not to move until I've got everything in place.'

'OK,' I said. Everything in place? What on earth could she be doing? I stayed on the sofa for a couple of minutes as Clare talked to the delivery guy in the hall, but of course I couldn't help tuning in to their conversation.

'Where do you want it?' he asked.

'Straight through to the kitchen,' she said. 'There's quite a bit of it, isn't there.'

'Eight sacks,' said the guy. 'Just like you ordered.'

Sacks?

'I know,' said Clare, 'but I didn't expect the sacks to be so big. Could you take some back if we don't need them?'

'Sure, but once you've emptied them out,' said the

delivery guy, 'you'll be quite surprised. You may even decide you need a couple more. Jase!' he shouted back to his mate. 'Start getting the pallet down.'

The pallet?

What on earth was coming in a pallet? I couldn't hold out any longer. I had to see what was coming into the flat. I parted the curtains, expecting to see . . . Well, I don't know what I was expecting to see, but I was certainly not expecting to see one of those huge builder's merchant's lorries with its very own crane on the back. On the pavement was the loaded pallet.

I raced out into the hallway. The delivery men were already hauling the first two sacks in.

'What's going on?'

'I told you not to come out here until we've finished,' said Clare.

'I had to see what you were doing. Where are they going with that? What is it?'

'It's your birthday present.'

'My birthday present is eight sacks of *sand*?'

Two burly guys were bringing eight sacks of the type of sand you use for playground sandpits into my hallway. Two guys wearing filthy overalls and hobnailed boots. They bumped against the walls on their way in, leaving marks on the reasonably pristine paintwork. I was far from impressed. My landlady would not be impressed either.

'Get that stuff out of here,' I said, as calmly as I could manage.

'I told you to stay in there until I called you,' said Clare again, as she tried to muscle me back into the living room. 'Now you've totally ruined the surprise.' Trust Clare to somehow make it my fault.

'You call that a surprise? Eight sacks of *sand*?'

'That's what it looks like at the moment, yes, but when it's finished . . .'

'It'll be what?'

'It will be your birthday beach.'

'What?'

'A beach, in the yard. I had the idea last night. It'll be fantastic.'

'You mean you're building a sandpit?'

'I mean a *beach*.'

I pointed at the dirty footprints on the hall carpet. 'They're ruining my flat.'

'I will clean it up, I swear.' Clare turned back to the builders, who were hesitating in the doorway. 'Take no notice of her. She's just a bit surprised. She'll love it when it's done.'

'No, I won't. They're getting sand on the carpet!'

'Through there?' The older guy nodded to the yard.

'Yes, please,' said my sister. 'Er . . .'

'Ted,' he said, 'and this is Jason.'

'Well, hello, Ted and Jason.'

Jason paused to push his fringe back from his eyes and threw a greeting over his shoulder as he went to fetch another sack.

'I think I just heard "The Hallelujah Chorus",' said my sister. 'That man is *hot*.'

She wasn't wrong. Jason was around our age, I guessed. He was good-looking in a Jordan's pet cage-fighter sort of way. His nose looked as though it might have been broken a couple of times, but that was not unattractive. He was deliciously masculine. He was wearing a T-shirt so tight I could almost see the hair on his chest. The short sleeves were rolled up to show his biceps to best effect. And crikey, what biceps they were. Though she was engaged to be married, my big sister could not stop herself from raising her eyebrows at me suggestively when Jason hefted another bag of sand onto his shoulder and asked, 'Where do you want it?'

I blushed crimson.

'The sand,' Jason added.

'Gosh. Sorry. I don't know,' I blustered.

Clare was altogether more relaxed around this Adonis. Flirtatious even.

'In the yard. You're making that look like very light work,' she said, touching him gently on the arm.

Clare seemed to have forgotten that I was not exactly pleased about the sand coming into my flat. My objections had been overruled. At Ted's request, I gave in and put the kettle on. Hauling sand was thirsty work.

'What do you want all this sand for anyway?' Ted was the one brave enough to ask.

'I know it sounds nuts,' said Clare, 'but we're recreating a beach scene for an art-school project.'

'Art?'

I was surprised, but Clare continued seamlessly. 'Yes. It's about bringing the natural world into the city.'

There were moments when my sister amazed me. Where had she come up with that idea? Who on earth did she think would believe it?

'My daughter wants to go to art school,' said Ted, who had seemed oddly unfazed by Clare's explanation. Now I understood that it probably wasn't the most ridiculous thing he'd ever heard after all. He confirmed my hunch.

'She built a nine-foot-high wall made of toilet rolls

for her A-level exhibition. Had to be Andrex. Cost me a fortune. At least I could have got her a couple of bags of sand for nothing.'

'I don't get modern art,' said Jason.

'It's all about hidden meanings,' Ted explained to him. 'Cherry's toilet-roll wall was about the traps we have built for ourselves in Western society. We've separated ourselves from the animal kingdom with our indoor plumbing. We've raped the rainforest to wipe our backsides. The cute little Andrex puppy is another construct that separates us from the truth of our existence. Puppies are cute, but they grow into dogs that bite, yeah? Nature red in tooth and claw.'

'Sounds interesting,' said Clare.

'Oh, she's very clever, my little girl,' said Ted, glowing with pride. 'I always said she's going to win the Turner Prize one day. What does your project mean, then?'

'I suppose it's something similar,' Clare ad-libbed. 'About the separation that exists between man and nature. Nature and man. I'm trying to make a statement about nature reclaiming the land that's been sacrificed to human development. We can keep trying to hold back the tide, but eventually all this will be under the sea again, unless we can tackle global warming and climate change. Nothing but barren sand and the sea.'

'Quite right,' said Ted, as he hauled another bag into place. 'Do you want us to help you arrange it? These bags are heavy even when they're half empty.'

'Would you? Yes, please,' said Clare.

I could only watch and bite my lip anxiously as Ted and Jason tipped the first bag out into the yard. There was no going back. They had been right about the quantities. Though those bags were incredibly heavy, once the sand was tipped out, it didn't look like such a big amount after all. Hardly enough to make a decent sandcastle. Ted and Jason emptied out seven more sacks in quick succession.

'What do you think?' asked Ted.

'Perhaps if we heaped a little bit more here?' Jason suggested.

Clare continued to play art director. As Ted and Jason smoothed the sand out with their big gloved hands, she watched appraisingly. 'I can see some of the concrete there,' she complained.

They did their best to cover the bald spot.

'Now it looks a bit skimpy over there.'

Jason got down on his knees and moved the stuff about effortlessly.

When at last she was satisfied, Clare picked up my lovely clean beach towel and shook it so that it unfurled like a flag before it fluttered down into place.

'Perfect,' she and the builders breathed in unison.

'And here comes the sun,' said Jason.

The sun peeped out from behind the clouds.

'That's right effective, that is,' said Ted. 'Do you mind if I take a photo with my phone to show my daughter? I know she'd be interested.'

'Feel free,' said Clare.

Ted texted the picture to his daughter, who responded that she thought the concept was reminiscent of the work of some unpronounceable Icelandic artist. (Ted showed us the text, but none of us could make a stab at pronouncing the word therein.) Still, it lent some legitimacy to our lunacy. At least these guys from a builder's yard wouldn't think we were flat out mad. We were mad in the cause of creativity and artistic truth, though why that mattered . . .

'So what do you do now?' asked Ted.

'I'm going to take some photographs. My sister here is going to pretend to be on holiday.' She turned to Jason. 'I wonder if you would mind pretending to be a holidaymaker, hanging out on the sand too. Just for a couple of frames.'

Jason looked at Ted. Ted grinned.

'I wouldn't ask,' said Clare, 'but I imagine that you're quite photogenic.' She made a frame with her fingers, closed one eye and peered through at his face, as though focusing a lens. 'Has anyone ever told you that you should be a model?'

This time Jason blushed.

'I bet she says that to all the boys,' Ted cackled.

'You *should* be a model. I don't mean it in a sleazy way,' Clare continued. 'I have been studying classical proportions and you know what? Your face fits those proportions exactly. Like Michaelangelo's *David*. The statue . . .'

'I know about Michaelangelo's *David*,' said Jason. Of course he did, sharing a cab with Ted. And it seemed that the comparison had flattered him.

'What exactly would I have to do?' he asked.

'Just sit on the sand,' said Clare. 'With your top off.'

I bit down hard on my knuckle to stop myself from laughing out loud. Had my sister really just asked a total stranger to take his top off for her? Jason smiled nervously, as though he was waiting to be let in on a joke.

'Go on.' Ted nudged him. 'I would, if I were twenty years younger.'

'OK.'

Jason peeled off his overly tight T-shirt. I looked away. My sister giggled. I snuck a peek. Jason had clearly put a lot of work into his physique.

'Sit there,' she said, pointing to the beach towel.

Jason arranged himself and settled into pouting with remarkable alacrity and talent. He was a natural. As was Clare when it came to pretending to be a photographer. It was all I could do not to snort with laughter as she pretended to frame another shot with her fingers.

'Will you send me some of the pictures?' asked Jason.

'Of course,' replied my sister.

I could only bite my knuckle until it nearly bled.

After they'd gone, it was time to freak out.

'You've covered my yard with sand!'

'Looks dead effective, don't you think?'

'You asked a builder to take his top off!'

'He's cute. I thought it would be a laugh.'

'To take pictures of a half-naked man? You're engaged.'

'It's only an art project.'

'What *art project*? They think we're insane.'

'I don't think Ted did,' said Clare. 'He understands art.'

'Where did you get all that claptrap from?' I asked. 'Art project?'

'Maybe it isn't claptrap. I have been doing an evening course,' she said defensively. 'I've been thinking about trying to get on a degree course.'

This was news to me.

'Since when?'

'Since I decided that I was bored out of my mind with being a temporary secretary and I need a new direction in life.'

I was astonished by Clare's revelation.

'Does Evan know?'

'He wouldn't understand.'

'Have you asked him?'

'I will, I will,' she said, waving the question away. 'I just need to see if anyone would actually have me first. Prove I'm not just a pretty face.'

'No. You're a pretty face hiding a horribly broken brain. Art project? I have sand in my backyard and you just persuaded a builder to take his top off. You're evil, that's what you are.'

'But wasn't it fun? And I got you a phone number,' said Clare. 'You could text him for a date.'

'You're not just evil. You're insane.'

Ten minutes after Ted and Jason left, there was another knock at the door. This time, a B&Q van was blocking the pavement outside.

'Deckchairs and a windbreak.' Clare clapped her hands. 'The finishing touch.'

She arranged the deckchairs on the sand and I had to admit they looked rather attractive with their brightly coloured stripes. If I had ever been in the market for deckchairs, I might have gone for the same type myself. She'd chosen pretty well. Likewise, the windbreak was very festive. Unfortunately, the guy from B&Q was not a patch on Jason and Clare decided against asking him to take his top off too. She just signed the paperwork and got rid of him pronto. There was more fun to be had in the backyard.

I looked out at the scene from the kitchen window. It was surreal.

'Are you coming to sit on the beach?' Clare asked me.

The sun was shining. The chairs looked inviting. The sand was out of the bags. There was little point resisting.

'Oh, all right, then,' I said. 'Why not?'

Chapter Twenty-Four

I'd started my week's holiday hiding under a bed. Now I was in my backyard but pretending to be at the seaside. It was an improvement on sharing the dirty carpet with a dead mouse, I supposed. But really, what were we doing? Had confinement driven us both insane?

'Take off your shoes and close your eyes,' said Clare. 'Feel that sand. We could totally be in Majorca.'

'Sort of,' I said. Apart from the sound of the planes turning over Clapham Common, and horns beeping in the street outside, and the dulcet tones of a taxi driver (it had to be a taxi driver) shouting, 'You fackin' fack,' in his traditional *Landan* accent, I thought. Still, this make-believe was Clare's idea of a birthday present. I tried to be gracious to her face, while inwardly I was already thinking about how I might have my revenge when her birthday rolled around. Fill her bath with pond water and get her a couple of ducks, perhaps? No. That wouldn't work. There was a very strong chance that she would keep the ducks and I would end up having to look after them whenever she and Evan were away.

'There is nothing like the feel of sand between your toes,' Clare continued. 'And at least since it's our own sand, there's no chance of thrusting your pinkies in with gay abandon only to unearth a fresh dog turd. What's more, we're just six feet from the kitchen, so we can have a cup of tea whenever we want one. That's the main advantage.'

'Can't get tea like this in Majorca,' I chimed in duly. 'Though perhaps you can,' I added after taking a sip. 'We'll never know.'

'One day we might. Be positive. I have a feeling that Majorca is still in our destiny. Seriously, I can imagine that island so clearly it has to be in our very near future.'

'Don't go all woo-woo on me,' I warned.

'There's nothing woo-woo about visualisation techniques. Last night, I imagined a beach. This afternoon, we're on it.'

Using her camera, Clare took a snap of her toes. They were freshly pedicured – one of the tasks she'd set to on her spa day – and looked a damn sight better than they had done when she shoved them into my Choos.

'What do you think? I'll send this to Evan,' she said. 'He likes my toes.'

'Very nice,' I said. I looked at my own toes. I wondered if Callum had even had an opinion on them. He certainly hadn't mentioned it. I tried to remember if he had ever said he especially liked a particular part of me.

Evan texted back that Clare's toes had brightened his day after the disappointment of a very large gas bill.

'He's trying to make me feel guilty again,' Clare began.

'He said that you'd brightened his day,' I pointed out. Clare seemed so quick to assume the worst where Evan was concerned.

'Whatever. Shall we have some music?' Clare asked.

'Quietly,' I said. 'We don't want to disturb the neighbours.'

'No one will be around at this time. They're all at work or school.'

They weren't.

'What are you doing?' asked someone from the other side of the fence moments later.

We were being observed. I'd had the sense that we were being watched for some time but had not mentioned it to Clare for fear that she might give me one of her speeches about 'presences'. There was, however, no spirit-world mystery here. Two very real small faces peered over the top of the fence at us. It was my neighbour's children, the ones who fought every morning over the DS or some other toy. The children I had never seen but often heard. Now they scrabbled to get a good view of me and my sister. I wondered what they were standing on. The fence was pretty high.

'That's a big sandpit,' said one.

'It is.' Clare grinned. 'What do you think?'

'It's excellent. I don't think I've ever seen a sandpit that big. Except in the park.'

'Can we come and play in it?' asked the smaller child.

'Of course,' said Clare, before I had the chance to raise an objection.

'You'll have to ask your mother first,' I piped up.

'It's OK,' came an adult voice from the other side of the fence. 'You can keep them for as long as you like. I'll bring them to the front door if you're serious.'

'I'll get my spade!' shrieked the little one with such joy that if we weren't serious before, we had to be now. How could we disappoint a couple of children?

Less than a minute later, we heard the doorbell ring and, for the first time since I had moved into the flat almost three years before, I found myself face to face with my neighbour.

'Rosie,' she said, holding out her hand. 'And this is Sally.' She indicated the smaller child, a poppet with her hair in cornrows. 'And this is Dex.'

'Short for Dexter,' he told us proudly. 'Did you know that?'

'Of course,' said Clare.

Clare waved them in. Rosie came too. I thought that was for the best since I did not want to be left in charge of two children I had known for less than a minute. As we walked through, Rosie murmured politely about the pictures on the walls.

'Have you lived here long?' she asked.

'Three years,' I said, more than a little embarrassed.

'Me too. But people don't talk to their neighbours much in London, eh? I'm sorry we haven't been intro-duced before and now my children are all over your . . .'

'Beach,' said Clare to save her searching for the word. 'It's Sophie's birthday beach.'

'It's your birthday?' Sally's head popped up. The magic 'b' word never fails to attract a child's attention.

'Tomorrow,' I said.

'Are you having a cake?' Sally asked.

'If someone makes it.'

'I'm no good at cooking.' Clare shrugged. 'Are you? Maybe you could make a sand cake instead?'

'That's a good idea,' said Dexter.

Clare was already welcoming the children onto the sand. They threw themselves into the task of building a sandcastle with glee.

'This is like being on holiday!' Sally cried out in delight. 'Except there's no sea. We've got a paddling pool next door. Can we bring it over? Can we, please?'

'It's got a hole in it,' Rosie reminded her.

'I'm sure we can fix that,' said Clare.

'All right,' said Rosie. 'If you're sure.'

Clare looked at me. Alongside her, Sally and Dex adopted puppy-dog expressions. Really, what choice did I have?

While I made sure the children didn't get squashed, Clare and Rosie heaved the paddling pool over the fence. Unfolded, it took up what tiny space remained in the backyard, squashed right up against the wall, and filling it took for ever. There were more leaks in the rubber than we had suspected and we used up a whole roll of duct tape patching it up, but eventually it was watertight and had about two inches of water in the bottom. The children were delighted. I had to admit that it looked pretty authentic when the sunlight shone on the pool, accentuating the bright Mediterranean blue. Just the sight of it gave me more of a jolt of energy than I would have imagined possible. It was as though that blue awakened some part of my brain that had been asleep since the trip to Crete.

Sally and Dexter provided the perfect holiday soundtrack with their shouts of glee and the splashing of water. Around one o'clock, Rosie popped back next door for half an hour and returned with a fabulous picnic, which was extremely welcome after our week on bread and cheese and a variety of frozen foods. All the tastes of summer were there: cucumber and fresh tomatoes from Rosie's garden, strawberries and raspberries, sprigs of fresh mint pulled from a pot on her kitchen windowsill.

'We need something to go with this,' said Clare. She completed the holiday taste-track with a jug of sangria, using up the last bottle of rough Italian red from the cupboard beneath the stairs.

'Weak sangria. Very weak,' she lied. I could tell from the first sip that it was a headache in the making. It tasted great, though.

We three adults lay back on the sand. The yard was a suntrap and looking up at the sun, with the sound of the children and the scent of cucumber, strawberries and sangria, we really might have been somewhere much more exciting than Clapham.

'This is so kind of you,' said Rosie, 'but tell me, why did you guys decide to put sand in the back garden, instead of, you know, potted plants and stuff like that?'

I looked at Clare.

'It's Sophie's birthday present but it's also an art project,' she said, sticking to her story. 'I'm planning to do a degree in art and I need to create an installation for my portfolio.'

'Ah.'

She gave Rosie the speech she had given the guys from the builder's merchants earlier that day.

'I studied art,' she said, 'and I think your urban beach is a really nice idea. You'll wow the admissions tutors. I don't know why more people don't have them.'

Clare beamed at the confirmation that someone else believed she should give art a try. How little I knew about my sister, I thought, as she outlined to Rosie the steps she had already taken to change the direction of her life. I recalled her having been quite good at drawing when we were children, but I had no idea that she had wanted to take an art course upon leaving school but had been discouraged by her teachers and steered towards a more sensible option.

'That's ended up with me doing a job I hate for the money,' she sighed.

'But one day you might be recreating this beach in the Tate Modern,' said Rosie.

Rosie had plenty of advice for my sister and the more she talked, the more I regretted not having made her acquaintance before. This must happen all over London, I thought, people with so much in common living next door to one another but never knowing, sitting indoors chatting to virtual friends when a real friend is really so close. I liked Rosie enormously, and the children I had only known as tantrums heard through a thin wall were in reality so sweet and delightful it didn't seem possible they were the same kids. That day, both children were at home because their school was closed for a teacher-training day. Rosie looked tired. I had guessed from the sounds that came through the wall that Rosie and the children were on their own. She confirmed that their father was living on the other side of town.

'Oh, he left when Sally was three months old,' she said.

That put my dumping in perspective a little. At least Callum had only left me with a couple of unused plane tickets.

'I don't think I could cope in your situation,' I said.

'You just do. You'd be surprised. You just keep getting up in the morning and eventually it doesn't feel so bad.'

Was it really as simple as that?

Sally drew a picture of me in my pink beach kaftan.

She gave me a triangular body with the points in all the wrong places, but I was delighted. My legs, which were two straight lines, looked great.

Clare took a photograph of Rosie and her children sitting on the sand with my bright birthday windbreak behind them to hide the grey fence.

'I wonder . . . It's a bit cheeky of me to ask,' said Rosie, 'but the thing is, I'm not going to be able to take the children away this summer. I wonder if I could sometimes bring them to your beach while you're out at work. I could maybe plant some herbs for you in return. They'd do well. You get lots of sun on that back wall.'

How could I refuse?

'That sounds like a great idea,' I said.

Sally and Dexter cheered.

For a couple of hours I managed not to think about Callum at all.

Chapter Twenty-Five

Later, with the children gone indoors to do their home-work, accompanied by much grumbling, Clare and I lay back in our deckchairs and watched a few fluffy little clouds drift across the sky. We tried to work out where the planes that flew overhead were coming from or going to.

'Las Vegas,' Clare claimed a Jumbo.

'Edinburgh,' I claimed a smaller plane heading north.

'Tokyo,' Clare murmured. 'I've always wanted to go to Tokyo. It looks so interesting.'

'You could go on your honeymoon,' I suggested.

'Fat chance. Not in the budget. We'll be in a tent in Wales if we go anywhere at all. Evan's austerity meas-ures make the government look spendthrift.'

'Doesn't sound like much fun.'

'It isn't. Every penny has to be accounted for.'

'Well, I suppose it's good that Evan takes charge of the finances. You were never that hot on figures.' I stopped short of reminding Clare of the times I'd subbed her in the past.

'He won't give me a chance to find out if I've improved.'

I could only imagine what he would say when he saw the sand and the deckchairs on Clare's credit-card state-ment. When they first started going out, Clare had seemed pleased that Evan helped her work out a plan to repay the enormous debt she had built up while buying herself out of the post-Jake doldrums with weekly visits to Harvey Nics. Now she was debt-free and the part-owner of a house. She couldn't have done it without Evan's thrifty approach. Still, I suppose it was dull to have to justify every little expenditure. I nodded along to Clare's lament that she hadn't bought a new pair of shoes in three months. I wondered if she would ever find enough time to wear the shoes she already had.

For the rest of the afternoon we chatted and dreamed and dozed. Mostly dozed. Clare's 'really weak' sangria had gone to both our heads. In fact, I was asleep when Clare squeezed my arm and asked, 'Is that smoke coming out of that window?'

'Hmm?' I couldn't see anything.

'Up there?' She pointed to the open window on the floor above my own kitchen window. 'That's definitely smoke.'

Clare wasn't imagining things. When I focused at last on the right window, a breeze pulled the net curtains out through the opening, sucking with them a black cloud almost as big as the jolly white ones we had been watching.

'Oh my God.' I sat up.

'Who lives up there?'

'An old lady.'

'*An old lady?*'

'I have no idea who she is,' I had to admit.

'Well, whoever it is, her flat is on fire.'

'Maybe she's just burned something in the kitchen.'

'She must be a very bad cook.'

I just stared, dopey from the alcohol. Clare, however, scrambled for her phone and was quickly dialling 999.

There was, she had realised, no time to lose, and even as she was talking to the fire service, she was filling the buckets the children had left behind with sand. She strode through my kitchen, looking impressively competent, and barked at me to soak a couple of tea towels as I followed her. Then she was out of my front door and on her way up the stairs.

As soon as we got into the hallway, the smell of burning was unmistakable. Reaching the first-floor landing at warp speed, Clare hammered on the door. There was no answer. She rattled the handle. No give. The door was locked. I suggested it was possible that there was no one inside. Maybe the old woman had left a slice of bread in the toaster and gone shopping. Old people could be forgetful, couldn't they? In truth, as I watched the smoke that was now curling under the door, I was feeling scared by what we might find. I wanted the whole thing to be a bad dream.

'It might be safer,' I suggested, 'to wait for the professionals.'

'Are you kidding?' said Clare. 'God knows when they'll get here. And every second we leave it is a second closer to your flat catching fire too.'

Maybe it was adrenaline. Maybe it was the sangria. Maybe it was the thought of potentially losing all her copious luggage. Clare would not be diverted. Next thing I knew, she had kicked a hole in the bottom panel. The door gave way as though it were made of polystyrene. Clare snaked her hand up through the gap she had made and pulled down the interior handle. The door swung open easily.

'We could have a career as burglars,' Clare found a second to joke.

What a way to meet your neighbours, I thought, hoping we hadn't just busted our way into a crack den where the residents were perfectly happy with their black smoke, thank you very much. There was an awful lot of black smoke. I put my hand across my mouth. What next? We couldn't actually go in there, could we?

Clare didn't hesitate. She pressed one of the damp tea towels to her face and ventured inside. If she could do it . . . I took a deep breath and followed suit.

Clare was right. The old lady who lived in the flat was inside. She lay on the floor in the kitchen. On the stove top was the cause of all the smoke. A chip pan burned like an oil tanker. Without really thinking, I threw my wet tea towel over it, smothering the flames. Who would have thought that a trick our mother had made us learn twenty years earlier – after Clare's kitchen disaster at our parents' house – would ever come in handy again? Who would have thought that people still used chip pans? Clare turned her attention to the net curtains, which had been blown inwards from the open window and caught alight. I had no idea what to do with those. Clare, thank goodness, did. Shoving her hand into an oven glove, she ripped the curtains down and threw them onto the tiled floor. She smothered the flames in the sand from my birthday beach and stamped on top of the whole mess until she was sure the fire was out.

Thank God, the fire was all smoke and no real damage – it had spread no further than the curtains – but there was still a casualty to deal with. My neighbour – to whom I had failed to introduce myself so many times – was unconscious, but age and ill health had left her as light as a dried rose. I tucked my hands under her armpits, while Clare took her feet. We weren't sure we should move her at all, but the smoke in the kitchen was acrid and choking, so we carried her into the living room and lay her in the recovery position on a shag-pile rug that was the colour of an old Labrador. She showed no sign of consciousness as we moved her.

'Is she breathing?' I asked.

Clare put her ear near the old woman's mouth. 'Just about,' she said.

'Do you think she was overcome by the smoke?'

'I think she probably passed out beforehand, leaving the chips to catch light. There would have been more damage the other way round.'

'What should we do?'

'I don't know now. The ambulance is coming.'

Clare and I sat at either end of the woman's body, anxiously watching the rise and fall of her birdlike chest. Satisfied that she was at least still breathing, my gaze drifted around her flat. There were framed photographs everywhere, mainly of school-age children with haircuts that suggested the 1980s. I wondered where they were now that they had grown up. Clare studied the photographs too.

'That one looks familiar,' she said, pointing at the picture of a young boy with red hair and no front teeth. 'He looks like that weatherman. That one Mum follows on Twitter.'

I peered at the photograph. I didn't risk picking it up, in case my poor neighbour woke up to find herself in the recovery position while two strange young women went through her belongings, but, yes, I agreed with my sister, he looked very much like the chap who presented the weather on the regional station where we had grown up. He was one of Mum's unlikeliest crushes. Dad said that he blamed the menopause. Prior to that, she'd had sensible crushes, like George Clooney.

'There's a claim to fame,' said Clare. 'Living downstairs from the weatherman's relative.'

'Assuming she makes it,' I said.

Clare put a finger to her lips. 'Sophie, have some tact. She might be able to hear. She's going to make it.'

Out loud, I agreed, but I didn't think that either of us was particularly convinced. Still we gave each other the thumbs-up over the woman's sleeping body. The effects of the sangria were long gone. I had never felt quite so sober in my life as I did right then.

The fire brigade arrived a long, anxious minute or so later, sirens blaring. They were quickly followed by the paramedics. I let them into the house. Half the road had come out to watch the show.

Clare and I drifted into the background as the paramedics got to work, briskly and professionally. They didn't seem overly worried. They'd seen it all before. They clamped an oxygen mask to my neighbour's face and strapped her onto a stretcher for the trip downstairs.

'She should be fine,' one of the paramedics assured me.

'How about you, ladies?' asked his good-looking companion. 'Do you think you inhaled any smoke?'

'I don't think so, but you could check my chest,' said Clare with a grin that turned me crimson with shame.

Chapter Twenty-Six

How strange London life is. The sound of the sirens had brought almost everyone who lived on the street out onto the pavement. Here were the people who lived and ate and slept just feet away from me, yet I knew not a single one of them except for Rosie and her children, and I had known them for only an afternoon. I learned, as my neighbour was carried to the ambulance by the two paramedics, that she was called Emma Kenman.

'Kenman!' said Clare triumphantly. 'That's the weatherman's name. Maybe he's her grandson.'

An old man who lived across the street, whose name was Jim, said he knew Mrs Kenman from a local senior citizens' club. He confirmed that she was indeed the proud grandmother of a TV weatherman. Her other grandson was a solicitor down in Southampton. Her granddaughter was a doctor. Jim's recently deceased ex-wife had known her better, he said. Jim hadn't seen Emma Kenman in three months. Jim didn't get out much these days. Not much to get out for since his wife was gone.

'I've never heard such nonsense! You must come to us for your dinner,' said Nelly, a Ukrainian woman who lived next door to Jim with her husband and teenaged son. This was the first time Nelly had spoken to Jim, though her family had lived on the street for almost a year. She said she was embarrassed that she had not introduced herself already. She blamed pressure of work. She and her husband were setting up a catering company. I had seen their van, painted with the legend 'Nelly's Nibbles – weddings, christenings, funerals'. Perhaps I ought to say something about the off-putting nature of 'funerals'.

'Where I come from,' she said now, 'nobody has to spend all their time alone.'

'Thank you,' said Jim, 'but—'

'No buts,' said Nelly. 'You can come too,' she told me. 'You live on your own, I know. I have seen you walking home looking lonely lots of times.'

Really? Even when I was supposed to be loved up with Callum?

'No one should have to be all by themselves. People aren't meant to be alone.'

'I only wish I *could* get some time to myself,' said her son, earning himself a gentle clip round the ear.

'This is Terence,' said Nelly. 'He should be inside doing his coursework. Second World War. The Blitz.'

'I can tell you a thing or two about the Blitz,' said Jim.

'All the more reason for you to come for supper,' said Nelly. 'Let me know when is convenient for you. Tomorrow? Or Thursday? Are you vegetarian?'

'No, but I don't eat much red meat these days,' Jim told her.

'Good man. Very bad for you. You' – she pointed at me – 'you look like a vegetarian.'

I guessed that it was meant to be an insult this time.

'I will feed you up,' she said, looking me up and down. 'Give you a bust.'

My sister roared with laughter.

In the space of half an hour after the departure of the ambulance, I had learned more about the street I lived in and its inhabitants than I had in the previous three years. All that time I had assumed that my neighbours wanted to keep themselves to themselves, to the extent that I would cross the road to give them space rather than offer a friendly nod as I passed. The thought that I had been so wrong made me quite reflective. Now it seemed that everyone was scrabbling to connect. Nelly was introducing Jim to the people who lived on the opposite side of her house, like an expert hostess putting guests at ease at the beginning of a party.

'This is Zach and Gilda. They're working in a West End show. Aren't they a lovely young couple?'

Couple? I had a feeling that the only thing about glamorous Gilda that interested the equally exotic Zach was her shoe collection, but I nodded at Nelly's observation, and Zach looked happy enough too.

My sister, meanwhile, was enjoying her new status as heroine of the day, recounting the story of how she had spotted the smoke and we'd gone inside and put out the fire, with just a few embellishments. She started from the beginning for two newcomers, Henry and Tabby, who lived in the building on the opposite side. Tabby and Henry were two guys in their early twenties. They worked in the City. I had seen them staggering home from the pub some evenings and staggering out to work on the odd morning. I had cursed them the evening of an England rugby victory, when they woke the whole street with their singing on the way home.

'So, we were sitting on our beach—' said Clare.

'Beach?' Tabby asked.

'Yes, our beach.'

'You've got a beach?'

'In our back garden. You should come over.'

'This I have to see,' said Henry.

'It's just a pile of sand,' I said.

'And a paddling pool,' Sally pointed out.

'With deckchairs,' said Dexter. The children had been allowed back out to see the fire engine. There was no keeping them inside.

'Come now. It's a beautiful evening,' said Clare. 'And we've got sangria.'

'I think we've got some beers we could spare,' said Tabby. 'We were planning a barbecue.'

'So were we,' said Nelly. 'I am experimenting with some recipes for our company.'

'Bring them over,' said Clare. 'We can help you do a taste test.'

'You're on.'

As our new friends disappeared into their homes to prepare for the impromptu evening ahead, I stared at Clare, open-mouthed.

'I can't believe you just invited everyone round. We're supposed to be in hiding, remember? Keeping a low profile.'

'I think our low profile is well and truly blown,' said Clare. 'At least among your neighbours. But who cares? They don't know Callum or Evan. Hopefully, none of them follows Mum's menopause advice online. And there's something to celebrate,' she reminded me. 'Talk about a silver lining. If you'd gone to Majorca, if we hadn't been sitting in the garden, the entire building might have burned down. That lady upstairs – the weatherman's gran – might have been killed. If you can't celebrate something like that . . .'

It wasn't that I didn't think it was worth celebrating. It was more that I was embarrassed at the thought that these people who had been strangers so recently were going to see what Clare and I had created in the backyard. The kids from next door might have thought it was a great idea to have a giant sandpit, but what would this bunch of metropolitan grown-ups think? They would think we were nuts, I was sure.

But it seemed that everyone was prepared to be more open-minded about my birthday beach than I might have hoped. When Tabby and Henry returned to our house with enough sausages to feed 101 Dalmatians, they had changed out of their work clothes and into Hawaiian shirts and shorts. Tabby set to work getting the barbecue lit, while Henry showed Clare how to make his own version of sangria, which contained three times the copious amount of brandy she usually added.

Nelly and her teenage son, Terry, arrived soon afterwards, carrying two dishes covered in foil containing the kind of carefully marinated meat you only ever see on cookery programmes. Terry then went back across the street to fetch their grill, to give us extra space to cook. Nelly also brought a delicious potato salad, made to her mother's recipe, which had been handed down to her by half a dozen grandmothers before, and a whole tray full of canapés.

'I made them for a wedding on Saturday. It was cancelled. Turns out the groom tried to seduce the bride's sister at a lap-dancing club on his stag night.'

I raised an eyebrow.

'He didn't know the bride's sister worked in the club. Neither did her parents.'

'How awful.'

'Oh, I could tell you some stories that would make your eyes pop out. I had a funeral cancelled once when it turned out that the body in the coffin had been misidentified. That turned into a murder inquiry.'

Nelly was turning out to be very good value indeed.

When Jim didn't appear within half an hour of her arrival, it was Nelly who insisted on heading back over the street to make sure he knew he really was invited and there was no need to be shy. She duly returned with Jim on her arm. He wore a jacket and tie, and had brought with him his Jack Russell terrier, Alfred, who was a huge hit with Sally and Dexter. The children were up way later than they should have been, but after the excitement of the fire, Rosie knew she had no chance of getting those two to go back to bed.

Nelly's son provided the music. Clare approved. There was plenty of emo, at least until Nelly insisted on swapping her son's mix for some nice Michael Bublé. Rosie brought lights in the form of a couple of hurricane lamps from her own garden. Clare dug out some old Christmas lights from a box of random 'useful' bits and pieces that Dad had foisted on me during one of his clear-outs and strung them around one end of the backyard, plugging them in through the kitchen window. Jim spent twenty minutes tweaking all the loose bulbs and eventually they worked.

The other occupant of my building – the guy who lived on the top floor and tumbled down the stairs every morning – got home at half past eight. Astonished to smell the smoke and see Mrs Kenman's door with an enormous hole in it, he came downstairs to find out what had been going on. His name was Charles. He joined the festivities, as did his girlfriend, Suze, who generously allowed the chicken she had bought for their supper to be jointed, rolled in Nelly's special mix of spices and added to the barbecue.

Charles and Suze were followed by Jason from the builder's yard, who came bearing Malibu.

'Well, hell-oooo,' said Clare, in an embarrassing parody of that chap from the *Carry On* films.

'I thought it would be just us three,' he said to me and my sister upon seeing the crowd. Apparently, Clare had sent him a text telling him to drop by to look at the results of her photo shoot.

'We've had a very exciting evening,' Clare explained. 'Lots to celebrate.'

Jason agreed to stay and, upon hearing that Mrs Kenman's door needed a small repair, went out to his van and returned with everything he needed to patch the hole up. Clare took him a few glasses of sangria while he worked.

'I can't believe you texted the guy from the builder's yard,' I hissed at her as we passed in the hallway.

'I invited him for *you*,' she said.

'I'm not on the market.'

'You should be.'

Thankfully, we were interrupted by Sally, in search of the bathroom, before we could have a disagreement.

The food – when Henry and Tabby finally managed to get the barbecue started – was great. The sangria was lethal. But the party really picked up when Clare announced the good news, which arrived via a text from one of the paramedics, that Mrs Kenman was already awake and feeling much better and would be home within a couple of days. That prompted a toast from Jim, both to Mrs Kenman's health and to our brave rescue attempt.

Clare joined Jim in a little dance of celebration around the paddling pool. Tabby pulled Nelly to her feet and followed suit. Rosie bumped hips with Tabby and Henry. The children were making the most of their late-night freedom. The party dissolved into laughter as a tango across the sand ended up with Tabby on his backside in the paddling pool.

But there was one more guest to come.

'I hope I'm not too late,' he said.

I almost didn't recognise the paramedic now that he had changed out of his overalls and into a Hawaiian shirt. I must have looked less friendly than I felt because his face took on a nervous expression and he said, 'Your sister invited me.'

'She did?'

'I did.'

Clare was already behind us in the corridor. She took the paramedic by the sleeve and dragged him in.

'Don't just stand there. Come in. Gosh, don't you look different in your real clothes? Very nice. Glad you could make it. This is Tom,' she said to the assembled party-goers in the yard. 'He's the paramedic who carried Mrs Kenman all the way down the stairs.'

'He could give me a fireman's lift anytime,' Rosie whispered in my ear. She had a point. I hadn't taken very much notice earlier, but now that I had a proper chance to look at him, he was like a paramedic imagined by central casting. Clean-cut and friendly-looking.

'Nice hair,' Nelly murmured. 'You should find out if he has a girlfriend.'

Jim proposed another toast to the brave gentlemen of the ambulance service. At least, we all assumed that was what he proposed. He was getting quietly sloshed.

'Nice shorts,' said Tabby.

They had clearly been shopping in the same place. Tom's shorts were a red version of Tabby's green pair.

'Welcome to our beach party,' said Clare, sweeping her arm around the yard, which, with its twinkling lights and smiling people on the sand, could not have looked more different than the dismal grey square I had lived with for three years. All that was missing was the sound of crashing waves.

'Come on, everybody,' said Clare. 'I need to take a group picture.'

She motioned everyone into the centre of the sand. She balanced her camera on the top of the old coal shed so that she could put it on timer, then rushed back into the middle of the group. Tom stood beside me.

'Your sister is really something,' he said.

She was. She had pulled a party out of thin air and it was one of the best I had ever seen.

The dancing continued. Clare bounced around taking snaps. Tom and I were leaning against the coal shed in companionable silence, but Clare insisted we take to the floor too. She pulled me by the hand. Tom gamely jigged from foot to foot. Though I'd had enough sangria to kill an elephant, dancing next to him made me suddenly shy. He had a lovely face, a friendly smile.

But where there's alcohol, there's always, eventually, male nudity. Tabby and Henry took their shirts off. They both had baby beer bellies but seemed very happy to let it all hang out. Nelly and Rosie catcalled. Jason had the moves of someone who took his clothes off for a living, which, it turned out, he did. When he wasn't delivering building supplies, he moonlighted as a stripper for hen nights. Even Jim got to his feet and provocatively loosened his tie.

'Come on, Tom,' said Clare. 'Let's see what you've got underneath those flowers.'

Rosie and Clare whooped as, without unbuttoning the shirt first, Tom pulled it off over his head, revealing the kind of torso that would have made Michelangelo's David want to put on a T-shirt and hide. Nelly gave an ear-splitting whistle.

Rosie and I found ourselves in the middle of a triple-decker man sandwich. Clare clapped and cheered and took more photos.

'I hope none of these are going on Facebook,' said Rosie, as she collapsed giggling onto a deckchair.

'*All* of these are going on Facebook,' said Clare. 'These boys are too gorgeous not to share. Shake that booty, Jason. Give me something worth putting on YouTube.'

Clare seemed to be getting on very well with Jason. The monosyllabic truck driver turned out to be a very different creature after dark. Changed out of his work gear, he looked like an Italian playboy and he had the same kind of charm. He took my sister's hand and pulled her into the middle of the sand, where they danced barefoot. Clare threw back her head and laughed. She looked absolutely beautiful. In her element, really. Her face had taken on a look that I hadn't seen in a long while – carefree and much, much younger than the girl who had come to water my plants and had slumped at the kitchen table just a few days ago. She was having a whale of a time.

And then it was midnight.

'Ladies and gentlemen,' said Clare, 'may I interrupt proceedings for just a moment to propose a toast? It's turned midnight and that means that my darling little sister has just turned thirty!'

Sally and Dexter insisted on singing 'Happy Birthday' to me. I was showered with hugs and kisses. It was hard to keep from bursting into tears, especially when Rosie presented me with the cake that her children had insisted on making for me.

'We could only find seven candles,' said Sally, 'but we know you're *much* older than that.'

So much for my plan to keep quiet and well hidden during my staycation. The noise from our party could probably have been heard halfway across London. But I found I didn't much care if anyone found out I wasn't in Majorca that night. My sister and I had saved a life and made a whole bunch of new friends in the process. It was almost worth being dumped for. Almost. I blew the candles out.

Chapter Twenty-Seven

Not long after Clare announced that I was officially old, people started to drift away. It was way past Sally and Dexter's bedtime. Sally protested that she wanted to stay up all night – just this once. She'd be good for ever – but Dexter had already fallen asleep on his mother's lap and had to be carried next door with the help of Nelly's son. Nelly herself saw Jim and his dog back across the road. Henry and Tabby staggered down the road to their place, taking the last of the burnt sausages with them.

'For the perfect hangover breakfast,' Henry explained.

I had a feeling he would need it. Henry had sunk more sangria than a hen party in Magaluf, despite the fact it was a school night. Tabby, too, was cross-eyed with inebriation, but he promised he would be back the following weekend to mend the puncture in my bicycle tyre.

'I think he likes you,' said Charles's girlfriend, Suze, conspiratorially. Suze, Nelly, my sister . . . it seemed that everyone was keen to set me up with someone.

I went inside to start the washing-up while Tom, Clare and Jason set about tidying up the yard. It wasn't long before Tom came inside. He joined me at the kitchen sink, where I was dealing with those things that wouldn't fit into the dishwasher.

'I'll help you wash up,' he said.

'No need,' I told him. 'It's almost done. Besides, you've got an early start tomorrow.'

'That's true,' he said, 'but it's my last day before I go on holiday for a fortnight, so I'm not too worried about being tired. Anyway, I'd like to help you wash up. I enjoy washing up. Really.'

'OK.'

I let him help me. He could dry the bigger dishes. Nelly had left behind one huge, heavy glass salad bowl that I was terrified of dropping on the tiled floor. It looked expensive. With his big hands, Tom could handle that with ease.

As we worked, he told me some more about his job. It had its downsides, obviously, such as when he was called out to help the victim of a drunken gang fight outside a nightclub and got set upon himself as he tried to save the guy's life.

'Fortunately, I do a lot of martial arts. Taekwondo. Still, that was one night I would not want to repeat.'

But for the most part, he assured me, he loved what he did for a living.

'We see a lot of happy stuff too,' he said. 'I've delivered eleven babies – two of them were named after me – and ninety-nine times out of a hundred, at some point during the day I will be reminded of everything that's good about the human race. Most people want to help. Like tonight. You girls and your quick thinking saved a life and brought a street together. It could have been a tragedy. It turned into a party. This will go down as one of the best results ever. One day like this in a decade makes all the bad stuff worthwhile. Thank you.'

'Thank you. Our first-aid knowledge isn't as good as our epic firefighting skills.'

The last of the plates had been dried up.

'And thank you for helping to wash up,' I added.

'You missed a bit.' He handed back a plate that wasn't quite clean.

'Clearly my washing-up skills aren't as good as my firefighting either.'

'Do you share this flat with you sister?' Tom asked.

'No. She's just here for a few days while . . . while her flat is decorated,' I lied, but of course I couldn't help thinking about the real reason.

'You look a little sad,' Tom observed as I put the dirty plate through another rinse.

'Do I?'

'Yes. You know, it can hit you like that, later on. At the time, you're swept along by adrenaline, but afterwards, when everything goes quiet, the reality of what happened sinks in and you start to wonder what it means for the rest of your life. A brush with mortality really puts things in perspective. It makes you realise how little time there is and you ask yourself whether you're making the most of what's left.'

I turned towards him.

'You did a really brave thing today.' He was talking about Mrs Kenman and the chip-pan fire. 'A lot of people would have waited for the fire brigade to turn up and sort things out. If you'd left it that long, your neighbour might well have died. You saved her life by taking the decision to act.'

'Oh, it was Clare really. I probably would have waited downstairs. She's the reckless heroine in the family.'

'That isn't how she tells it.'

'Really?'

'Really. She says she wouldn't have done it without you. Having you beside her made her brave.'

'Having her beside me makes me brave too.' I realised it was true as I said it. 'She definitely makes life more exciting.'

The conversation petered out.

'Well, I suppose I'd better go,' said Tom after all the plates were stacked and the tea towels were folded. 'Got to get some beauty sleep.'

'Me too. God knows I need all I can get now I'm thirty.'

'I wouldn't have said that.' Tom grinned at me.

'Did you bring a coat?' I asked to change the subject.

I knew Tom hadn't brought a coat. I walked him to the door.

'I've had a really lovely evening,' he said. 'I hope you enjoy the rest of your birthday. Perhaps I could give you a birthday kiss.'

I proffered my cheek. Tom lightly pressed a kiss upon it, but he didn't step away right afterwards. He seemed to be waiting for something. I nervously wiped my hands, damp from the washing-up, on the front of my jeans.

'I'll see you around, I expect,' he said. 'I don't live far from here. We'll probably bump into each other in one of the bars or something.'

'Yes,' I said. 'Enjoy your holiday, won't you?'

'Can't wait.'

'Where are you going?' I asked.

'Majorca,' he said. 'Ever been there?'

'No,' I said. After a moment's hesitation, I added, 'Though my colleague was there last year and I hear it's great.' There was no point getting into my own Majorca story.

'I hope so. I need a holiday.'

'I'm sure you do.'

'I'll send you a postcard,' he said. 'I know the address. What's your surname?'

'Sturgeon,' I said. 'Sophie Sturgeon, like the fish. You can imagine what that was like at school.'

'Oh, yes,' said Tom. 'My surname's Sandwich. I know exactly what that must have been like.'

And then he left, backing away down the path and waving until he was out of sight.

I went back into the kitchen. The party was almost over. There was just one more guest to leave. My sister and Jason from the builder's yard had stayed outside and smoked cigarettes while Tom and I did the washing-up. I didn't know that my sister smoked, but evidently she did and with some aplomb. She held her cigarette like a silent movie star and blew rings that suggested years of practice.

Jason and Clare were still outside. I could hear their whispered voices through the open window. I wasn't able to make out the words, but something my sister said made Jason laugh out loud. His laughter was followed by much shushing on Clare's part. She reminded him that the children next door were asleep.

I was more than ready to go to bed, but didn't especially want to change into my PJs and tuck myself up on the sofa if Jason was going to wander through at any minute. I thought I would give my sister a little hint that it was time to bring the busy night to a close by gently shutting the kitchen window. I had to lean over the sink to do it. And while I was leaning forward, I caught sight of my sister and Jason silhouetted in the light from the last burning hurricane lamp.

No wonder they had gone quiet at last.

They were kissing.

I didn't dare look too closely. I decided against closing the window right then. The sound of the window shutting would have drawn attention to the fact that I had seen Clare and Jason mid-snog and I wasn't sure that I wanted them to know. What would I say? Instead, I slipped back and stepped away from the open window without making a sound. I went into my bedroom and got into my bed for the first time since Clare's arrival. She could definitely sleep on the sofa tonight.

It was at least another hour before Jason left. I lay awake for the whole of that time, occasionally hearing the sound of my sister's laughter drift into the flat, wondering what to say to Clare once he was gone or if I should say anything at all. Clare was engaged to be married. She should not have been kissing some other guy. Evan would be devastated if he found out. He had every right to be. On the other hand, it was just a kiss. A kiss at the end of a long and exciting day that had culminated with far too much sangria. It probably didn't mean anything. In which case, there was no point mentioning it, was there? No point turning a little indiscretion into something that could break Evan's heart. And possibly my sister's too. Evan was such a lovely man. To lose him over a drunken lapse of judgement . . .

In the end, I decided that I would say nothing. That was the only way. What I had seen would have to remain my secret until the day I died. Still, when Clare crept into the room and asked me if I was awake, I pretended that I was fast asleep because I didn't have a clue what I could say without making it obvious that I was shocked and a little bit disappointed.

Chapter Twenty-Eight

Unsurprisingly, my thirtieth birthday began in earnest with a killer hangover. Evil elves wearing four-inch-high Louboutins stalked up and down my brain. They were relentless. From time to time they did a spot of dancing. I woke with a desperate thirst and reached for a glass on the bedside table, only to discover that the water in that glass must have been there for several days and was covered in a thin film of London dust. The shock made me gag. Thanks, Clare, I thought. I had to get up and find something to take away the taste. Clare was already in the kitchen, groaning to herself over a big mug of coffee. She definitely deserved a headache.

'Happy birthday,' she said, coming round the table to give me a squeeze.

'Careful,' I said. 'I feel queasy.'

'Then you won't want a cooked breakfast?'

She indicated some sausages, left over from the night before. I could barely look at them, sitting there in a pool of congealed grease.

'I can think of nothing worse,' I assured her.

'Me neither. You got some cards.'

She had arranged the post in a small pile on the kitchen table. It didn't look too exciting. There were four cards addressed to me, from various aunts and uncles and my godparents. I recognised the writing;

plus hardly anyone in our generation sent real cards any more. Though I was turning thirty, Auntie Mel sent me a card decorated with a kitten. She'd been sending kitten cards since the day I turned four. Never mind that I had developed a lifelong fear of cats, having been mauled by her enormous grey Maine coon when I was three.

Still, I suppose it is the thought that counts and, twenty-seven years after that awful afternoon, I didn't always have to cross the road when I saw a moggy.

Clare arranged the open cards on the mantelpiece while I logged on to check first the weather in Majorca and then Twitter, where I found that Mum had tweeted birthday greetings and accompanied them with a TwitPic of me on my very first birthday. In this particular picture, I was sitting in a tin bath in the garden of our grandmother's house. I was sharing the bath with the West Highland terrier that was Grandma's pet at the time. I was, appropriately, wearing nothing but my birthday suit. The dog, whose name I seemed to remember was Adonis, was looking at me with barely concealed disgust. And barely concealed teeth. It was a wonder that shared bath hadn't become another terrible incident that scarred me for life.

Hannah and Alison assured me by email that they had been thinking about me too. They sent their very best wishes and commiserations about the photo my mother had posted on Twitter.

'Very cute, though,' wrote Hannah. 'And makes a change from her tweeting about the menopause.'

They also promised that they would take me out for a birthday drink just as soon as I got back from my fortnight away. Alison suggested we go to some new place in Clapham that was 'rammed with hot blokes' on a Saturday night. She and Hannah would have me fixed up with a new man in no time. Their joint email did not mention Callum that morning. They did, however, ask how I had felt as the clock ticked over midnight and I hit the big 3-0. They were both still twenty-nine. Was I OK with my new advanced age, or was I feeling sad? What was I doing when it happened?

'I spent the evening at a beach barbecue,' I said.

'Ooooh! Send pictures!' Hannah texted.

'We could,' said Clare when I told her. 'I've got some.'

'No,' I said firmly.

There were plenty of other birthday texts and emails from friends old and new. Someone sent me an e-card in which a man asks a woman to show him her tits and she lifts up her skirt to show him exactly how far her bosom has sagged. That made Clare roar with laughter. I was not quite so thrilled by the implication. Thirty may have been the new twenty-one, but my correspondence that morning didn't suggest it. Everything was about HRT and getting a cat. If being a woman meant twenty years of HRT jokes before you got there, then no wonder my mother was so determined to tweet her way through her menopause.

'It's OK,' said Clare. 'You've got nearly two years before you're really over the hill like me. You still look great. Not a day over twenty-nine. Look at this.'

Clare showed me the screen on her camera. She was scrolling through the pictures she had taken the previous day. She landed on a photo of me and Rosie lazing on deckchairs in the afternoon, a couple of hours before Mrs Kenman's fire and the excitement that followed. We didn't look half bad. Clare had an eye for a good angle. The photos of Jason had also come out very well.

'Pretty good, eh? Mind if I upload them to your laptop? You should have a record of the moment you turned thirty.'

I let her go ahead.

I couldn't help but be impressed by the results Clare had managed to get from her camera and a pile of builder's sand. Clare's pictures really did make it seem as though we had been by the sea. She paused on a photograph of me sitting next to Tom. I didn't remember her having taken it. I didn't remember sitting next to Tom like that. Well, I remembered sharing a beach towel for the time it took me to eat a sausage in a bun, but I didn't remember him being so close to me, or looking at me quite like that.

'Nice,' said Clare. 'You know what? You should post this one on Facebook.'

'No way. If Callum sees that—'

'Soph, that's the whole point.'

Clare enlarged another one of the images on the screen. 'It's so realistic. He does look as though he's very happy there, sitting on the sand with you in Majorca. And look at that,' said Clare, as she found a third pic of Tom and me together. 'He really fancies you!'

I shook my head. 'He'd had a lot of sangria,' I reminded her. I had to admit, though, it did look very cosy. In fact, I looked hot and bothered. Had Tom noticed I looked that hot and bothered? I wondered now. How embarrassing if he had.

'If I didn't know better,' Clare continued, 'I would say that you were just about to embark on a holiday romance.'

'Instead, this morning he'll be attending some road-traffic accident in Tooting while I am trying to work out how I'm going to get rid of all that sand.'

'Hmm.' Clare had forgotten about that. 'Do you have to get rid of it? I mean, it isn't doing anyone any harm. And you've got the children coming over.'

'Imagine it in the winter. Wet and cold.'

'It isn't winter yet,' said Clare. 'The summer has only just begun.'

I took another look at those photographs. There was one in which Tom was looking at me intently, while I grinned for all I was worth. If I didn't know better – if I didn't know that I had spent the evening being as entertaining as a wet fish – the expression in Tom's eyes suggested I had just said something that made him want to hug me. I wondered, had Callum ever looked at me like that? He must have done at some point, but certainly not lately. Even the photograph from last Valentine's Day, the one I had put into the frame Mum bought for my birthday, did not suggest the same degree of closeness. Callum was smiling, sure, but his eyes told another story and his arm, though round my shoulder, seemed stiff and uncomfortable. It was as though he had been asked to put his arm round someone he hardly knew. Looking at it now, I saw that we weren't leaning together but leaning ever so slightly apart. If a picture was worth a thousand words, what was that photograph saying? Had Callum been on his way out even then?

Though I had denied it vehemently when Callum suggested that things might not be as good as they had been, as the days in our hideout ticked by, I looked at the last few months of our relationship with a more critical eye. Had I let things slip? Had I worn my grey tracksuit bottoms once too often? Had I left it slightly too long between bikini-wax appointments? Was Callum hankering for the days when I bought a new set of lingerie for every night we spent together? That period of our relationship had cost me an absolute fortune, and half the lingerie I'd bought had only been worn once or twice. It was all too uncomfortable. When it came down to it, I preferred wearing my plain black knickers from John Lewis, under those grey trackie pants.

Could we change all that? If this time apart had made Callum reconsider, could we both agree to make an effort and get our relationship back to what it had been before? Or is it simply the case that once the novelty has worn off, you can never get it back? It doesn't matter how much time you're prepared to spend in the gym or at the beauty salon. It doesn't matter if you grow your hair here and wax it off there and never let yourself be seen without lipstick. It doesn't matter if you rack up a four-figure overdraft in La Perla. Once a man has become accustomed to a woman, no matter how beautiful she is to everyone else, perhaps he never really sees her any more. It doesn't matter if you wear tartan shirts and trackie bottoms or nothing but pearl earrings and a smile. He can't see the real you any more. The next shiny thing he sees will attract his attention and pull him away.

My iPhone was busy all morning with birthday greetings, but the one name I wanted to see did not appear. There was nothing from Callum. Not so much as a text. Though I told Clare that I didn't expect to hear from my errant ex, and she had agreed it was for the best, of course I had been hoping, assuming even, that he would send a birthday greeting. I didn't think our having 'split up' would have kept him from doing that. It was flat out cold, his decision not to acknowledge my birthday – such a significant birthday – in any way. Not even with two words. Had he forgotten we were supposed to be spending my birthday in Majorca? Did he feel embarrassed about acknowledging my birthday when he had effectively ruined it? It took the edge off every other kind wish I received that day.

Anyway, the sun was still shining, so I went back outside to my birthday beach. I left Clare inside. Having started the day with a great deal more enthusiasm than me, she claimed that her hangover was at last catching up with her. She said that the sun was too bright for her while her head was in such a fragile state.

So I kicked back in a deckchair and flicked through some of Clare's magazines. I tried not to dwell on the lack of correspondence from Callum or get too upset when Hannah wrote to say that 'Callum looks OK today. I think he has a new suit on.' What new suit? Had I ever seen it? The fact was that if Callum didn't change his mind, there were soon going to be an awful lot of aspects to his life that I knew nothing about. I'd never cuddle up with him inside a changing room again, getting a quick fumble while the shop assistant outside asked whether he needed another size. Though I was trying to put a brave face on it, I was sure that day I felt more distant from him than ever.

And with that thought, it was impossible to chill out for a moment longer. I went inside and brought out the vacuum cleaner that had dealt so effectively with the dead mouse. I should try to get rid of some of the sand in the hallway before all the carpets in the flat were ruined for ever.

'Is it OK if I switch the vacuum cleaner on?' I asked my sister. She had been cloistered away for some time now.

'It's fine,' said Clare. 'I'm just lying on the bed, nursing my hangover.'

So I vacuumed the hallway and the kitchen. I was as careful as I could be not to bump the walls and make any more noise than I needed to. But one lesson I should have learned as a small child was that when Clare had been quiet for a while, it was not usually a good sign. There was the afternoon when she painted my favourite baby doll's face with nail varnish. 'I was just giving her some make-up,' she said. There was the day she carefully copied my handwriting to create a love letter for the boy down the road. One that got me into a great deal of trouble with the boy's girlfriend. 'I swear I thought they'd split up,' Clare lied. Or how about the time she hacked into my homework file on Dad's computer, opened an essay on ducks and changed the first letter from 'd' to 'f' all the way through? When Clare was quiet, it was bad news. Indeed, that was the case right then. While I thought she was languishing in the bedroom, with a packet of frozen peas held to her throbbing fore-head, Clare had broken into my Facebook account. I caught her red-handed when, out of the goodness of my heart, I went inside to ask her whether she fancied a cup of tea.

'Absolutely,' she said. 'Can't get a decent cup of tea in Majorca.'

She was at my desk. She twisted awkwardly to speak to me. She was trying to keep the screen hidden, which of course made me immediately curious about what she was looking at. I dodged past her very weak defences.

'That's my Facebook page!' I cried out, seeing my profile.

Clare didn't have a Facebook account of her own, because Evan was convinced that Facebook was a portal to all sorts of viruses that could clean out your bank account.

'How did you do that?'

'I tried three passwords,' she told me. 'Audrey.'

My middle name.

'Eglantine.'

Clare's middle name. Our mother thought it was important to balance the sensibleness of Clare with something exotic. 'Just in case Clare ever wanted to be an exotic dancer,' was our maternal grandmother's response.

'And Callum.'

That was the one, of course.

'But why?'

Clare leaned back so that I could get a better look. 'Ta-da!'

The deed had been done. Despite my earlier protestations, the photographs of me and Tom 'on the beach' had been uploaded for all to see.

'Are you mad? Take them down before somebody sees them. Somebody is going to work out that they're not for real.'

'It's a bit too late,' said Clare.

And then I got the first Facebook alert.

'Hannah Brown has commented on your photo.'

'OMG!' she wrote. 'Who is that handsome man on the beach? Looks like Callum is already history. Serves him right. You go, girl!'

In less than five minutes, three other female Facebook friends had commented in the same vein. Within quarter of an hour of putting those photos up, fifteen of my friends had made comments and still none of them wanted to know anything more than the name of my new holiday acquaintance. There was no hint whatsoever that anyone thought anything about those photographs was odd. They all seemed to believe that they were looking at genuine photographs of me on a Majorcan beach.

'See,' said Clare. 'I told you it would be fine. Nobody's looking at the background. They're just looking at the guy.'

She was pleased with her handiwork.

'Do you think Callum has seen them?' I asked.

'I'm sure he has,' said Clare. 'That was the whole idea.'

'This is a disaster.'

'What do you mean? It'll just make him realise what he's been missing.'

'It'll make him think I'm a slut.'

'This isn't the eighteenth century. You're allowed to talk to whoever you like. Besides you're officially a single woman. You've broken up. He has no right whatsoever to complain if you go off with someone else. It's perfect. Callum will drive himself nuts thinking about you getting all that male attention. He dumped you.'

'Only a week ago. We've only been broken up for a

week and you've posted photographs of me with some other bloke. He'll think that I posted them. He'll think that I'm over him. He'll think I moved on so quickly that I was never into him to begin with.'

'He dumped you. You don't owe him a thing. You're perfectly entitled to hook up with someone else if you want to. Anyway, if anything will get him back, it's the thought of some other man fancying you, I promise you.'

'It looks like I'm all over Tom. How can I maintain the moral high ground over our break-up when you've made it look like I barely dried my eyes before I went looking for someone new? You have almost certainly ruined any chance I had of getting back together with him.'

'Don't be so stupid. These pictures are no big deal. You and Tom are both fully clothed. If anything, they will pique Callum's interest. Men like competition. As soon as he thinks he's got some competition, he will break cover to find out if it's serious.'

'He won't. Callum isn't like that. He always said if I wanted to go off with someone else, he wouldn't stop me. And I look so . . .'

'Comfortable?' Clare suggested. 'Like you're having a good time? You do, don't you? You can't deny that.'

'I'm not denying that, but that's not the point. You actually hacked into my Facebook account to post pictures that will convince Callum he was right to break up with me. I have got to take them down.' I elbowed Clare out of the way and started frantically deleting photos even as the 'Go, girl' messages kept coming in. Clare sat on my bed and watched, tutting at my attempts to save my reputation. She told me I was nuts.

Callum hadn't even texted me to say happy birthday. That was how much he cared.

'He's made up his mind,' was Clare's opinion. 'But even if he hasn't, if this puts Callum off trying again, then I will eat my wedding dress.'

'Your wedding dress? I'm not sure you should bother buying one,' I said.

'What does that mean?' Clare asked.

'I mean, why don't you try sorting your own life out before you make a complete pig's ear out of mine? I don't need your love-life advice any more, Clare. Especially when it's so clear that you don't even know how to run your own life.'

'What are you talking about?'

'I saw you last night.'

'Saw what?'

'I saw you kissing Jason when you thought I'd gone to bed.'

Clare blushed crimson. She didn't even bother to deny it.

'You saw us?'

'Yes, I saw you. You were out there snogging while I was doing the washing-up. I was going to shut the kitchen window when I caught sight of you. So please don't give me any lectures about how I should go about running my love life while you cheated on your fiancé with some random bloke from the building-supplies firm.'

'It was just a kiss,' said Clare. 'It's not cheating.'

'I'm not sure Evan will see it that way.'

'You don't understand,' said Clare.

'I think I understand everything,' I said. 'You're just a hypocrite. You want to have your cake and eat it.'

'You're wrong.' Clare surprised me with a sob. 'It's more the case that I don't want to have my cake. My wedding cake, that is. I don't want Jason, but I don't think I want to get married any more either,' she finally admitted.

Chapter Twenty-Nine

At last the truth was out. Clare's ridiculous decision to come and spend five days in hiding with me in my flat had nothing to do with feeling sorry for me and wanting to keep me company. Neither did it have to do with wanting a holiday but being unable to afford one. It had nothing to do with wanting time off from *Top Gear* either. It had everything to do with her not being sure as to whether or not she still wanted to be with Evan in the long run. These five days were her attempt at a trial separation.

Her anguish was clear. Up until that moment, Clare had been her usual, and at times annoyingly, perky self. Now the façade quickly crumbled and soon her face was wet with tears and her pretty mouth ugly with howling.

'What's wrong? What's wrong?' I put my arms round her. 'Tell me what's going on. Why are you so unhappy?'

She did not look anything like a happy bride-to-be, that was for sure.

'What has he done to you?'

Thank goodness, we quickly established that Clare had none of the usual, big-ticket reasons for wanting out of her wedding day. Evan had not beaten her up. He had not been unfaithful. He certainly hadn't emptied their joint account and made a break for Vegas. He wasn't physically, psychologically or verbally abusive. He hadn't even held her head under the duvet after farting in bed. It was nothing that obvious. He had never been anything but the perfect fiancé. And yet Clare was in pieces.

'All I wanted,' Clare told me, 'was to be part of a couple. When Jake left, I didn't think anyone would ever love me again and it became so important to prove that was wrong. Even more so after everyone else started getting married. I was being dropped left, right and centre. Hardly any of my girlfriends from university called any more and I'm sure it was because I was single. As soon as I got that ring on my finger, I was being invited everywhere again.'

Clare suddenly dropped her face into her hands.

'Soph,' she sobbed, 'I think I've made a terrible mistake. I said "yes" to Evan too quickly. I just wanted to be part of the gang again. I thought Evan being so solid and steady was wonderful, but in reality it's bloody boring. I rushed into marriage so that I would be invited out to dinner to talk about washing machines and cholesterol tests instead of having to stay home on my own. Now I feel like I'm being squashed into a middle-aged, middle-class box way before my time and I don't know what to do except call the whole thing off.'

This was serious.

'I think about it every day,' she continued. 'I wake up and the moment my brain comes to life, I'm thinking about how I can get out of it. I just lie there thinking about another dull day of temping ahead, listening to Evan snoring, imagining myself getting halfway up the aisle, then turning on my heel and running right out of the church. I just can't stop thinking of how I can escape the whole shebang. And believe me, I have thought of some crazy ways to get out of it without upsetting anybody. I thought about driving off and pretending I'd been kidnapped like that girl in the States.'

'Didn't she cause a manhunt? That's insane.'

'That's not the half of it. I've thought about trying to get arrested the night before the ceremony so that I have to spend my wedding day in jail, but I know that Evan would get me out on bail for just about anything except murder. And trust me, I've considered that too. I could just push someone off the Tube platform. I've even thought about faking my own death.'

'Clare!' I exclaimed.

'Seriously, Sophie. It would be the best way. No one would be able to try to persuade me to change my mind and Evan wouldn't have to wonder what went wrong. I'd just be dead. He may be boring, but he is a nice bloke. I know he loves me. I don't want him to be embarrassed. If he just thought that I had taken a walk on the beach, for example, and got washed out to sea by a freak wave, he wouldn't have to put up with any awful speculation about what went wrong. Everyone would rally round him as the widower, or whatever it is you become if your fiancée dies before you have a chance to get married. He doesn't deserve to be with a crazy woman like me. And I must be crazy, wanting to walk away from the last chance I'll ever get to be someone's missus. Because it is my last chance, isn't it?'

I didn't know what to say.

'Evan is offering me the chance of a future that most women would die for. He would always look after me. I know that. I would never have to worry about financial security. I'd never have to worry about putting oil in the car or bleeding the radiators or servicing the boiler. He's steadfast and faithful. Yes. He's very, very steady.

'I should buckle down and be grateful, but . . . oh God, I just can't do it, Soph. I want excitement more than I want steady. I want surprise flowers. I want dancing. I want to stay up all night talking about our hopes and dreams. I want our hopes and dreams to be about more than affording an American-style refrigerator. I want out, Sophie. Every single cell in my body wants to sabotage this wedding. That's why I ended up kissing Jason.'

'Is it just the wedding?' I asked. 'I mean, a wedding is one hell of a thing to organise. I can only imagine how much pressure you must be under from Mum. And the peer pressure too. Maybe you're feeling anxious about the logistics and once everything is in place, you'll be able to concentrate on being loved up again?'

'I don't know.'

'Seriously.' I suggested to Clare that maybe engagements and weddings are supposed to be a testing ground. They are, after all, in most cases the first joint endeavour a couple has undertaken. They encompass all sorts of areas of potential conflict that could arise in married life. Money, family, friends, even your taste in music. I told Clare that I'd heard about one bride who asked for an annulment before she and her husband even made it as far as the honeymoon because her groom chose 'Blue is the Colour', the Chelsea FC song, for their first dance. It wasn't just the song that bothered her. Apparently, the fixture list had been an important influence on the choice of wedding date too.

The wedding certainly wasn't helping Clare to feel

more certain about her impending marriage. Clare admitted she was finding out that she and Evan disagreed on a great many things that she held dear. She had always wanted a big wedding. Evan had tutted at every cost she lay before him, presenting her with a budget that would mean they had to hold their wedding reception at Nando's in order to be able to afford to accommodate all the friends she wanted to be there.

'He says he doesn't see why he should pay to feed people he doesn't really know. I sort of understand where he's coming from. He works hard for what he's got. But what that also says to me is that he has no intention of ever getting to know the people I love. I imagined that when I got married, I would be merging my life with my husband's, that my friends would become his friends. I imagined my world expanding.'

She continued, 'I had this fantasy of a big kitchen table that would be permanently surrounded by friendly faces. I wanted our door always to be open. There would always be something good to eat. Some nice wine. Music playing. And dancing. Spontaneous dancing. Evan never wants to dance.'

I knew dancing was a big deal to Clare. She'd got everybody to their feet at our beach party. But Evan wasn't a party sort of guy. He'd never pretended otherwise. At the end of the day, all he wanted was to spend the evening alone with his fiancée. Preferably in front of *Top Gear*. He got frustrated if people dropped in unannounced. Even me. There was little chance that he would throw another handful of pasta into the pot and invite the unexpected guest to stay for dinner. On the other hand, I said to her, I was certain that Evan was one person who could be relied on to extend an offer of hospitality to anyone who really found themselves in need.

'I know. I know that, but . . .'

The thought of a lifetime of dinner on the sofa followed by the ten o'clock news had sent Clare into a decline.

'I just feel as though my world is contracting,' she said. 'I don't know if marriage to Evan is enough any more.'

'Oh, Clare . . .'

'But it should be enough,' Clare sobbed. 'Shouldn't it? I am engaged to a wonderful man. There are women up and down this country living with total shits, men who couldn't hold down a job to save a life, who would step over my dead body to walk up the aisle with a man like Evan Jones. So why do I feel so unhappy?'

I put my arm round her again.

'I still miss Jake,' she said. 'Well, maybe I don't miss him, but I miss the person I was when he was around. I don't have any fun any more.'

'You're still the same person,' I pointed out. 'You're still the girl who can turn any gathering into a party. Look at last night. You threw a party no one on this street will ever forget.'

'But when did I last throw a proper party? Not since I met Evan. I've been pretending that I've grown up and I don't need excitement any more. Well, it turns out I do. I'm thirty-two years old, Sophie. I'm not fifty. And even if I were fifty, I would still want to go out and see my friends.'

'Have you told Evan that?'

'Not really. And of course I know he'd never say that I couldn't do exactly what I wanted, but he doesn't have to say anything. Evan can make his disapproval blindingly obvious with nothing more than a raised eyebrow. He doesn't even have to raise an eyebrow,' she elaborated. 'He doesn't have to move his face. He can make his disapproval known by contracting his pupils. I just know he won't understand.'

'How can he understand if you won't give him a chance? You've got to tell him what's bothering you.'

'Shouldn't he just know, if he's really the right man for me?'

'That's magical thinking,' I said.

Poor Clare. And poor Evan. I wondered if he had any clue just how unhappy she'd become.

'I've got to tell him I want to call the wedding off.'

'Maybe just postpone it?' I suggested.

Clare nodded in a tired sort of way. She buried her face in her hands again; then she sat up, exhaling powerfully, and tried to rearrange her features so that they looked borderline cheerful. It wasn't especially effective. What a pair we were. Clare sighed. I sighed. We both stared into space.

'Sophie,' Clare broke the silence, 'weren't you supposed to be going on holiday for two weeks?'

'I was,' I said. 'Two whole weeks in the sun . . . Fourteen days away from the office, fourteen wonderful days of—'

She stopped me. 'But that's perfect. I'll call Evan and tell him that we're going to stay out for the whole of the time you guys originally booked. It'll give me chance to think.'

'What? And have both of us spend another week looking at these four walls?' I said. 'No, you can't. I'm coming home.'

Clare was disappointed. 'But—'

'No buts. Much as I enjoy your company, I am going absolutely nuts stuck in this flat all the time. I want to get back to my real life. Even if it means confronting the reality that Callum's gone for good. Besides, it sounds like you've got some reality confronting to do yourself. With Evan.'

Clare looked pained.

'But if you decide to go ahead and call the engagement off, you know you can come back here and stay for as long as you like. I think we make pretty good flatmates.'

Clare nodded. 'I think you're right about that.'

'I promise you, whatever happens, it'll be OK,' I said. 'Isn't that what you're always telling me?'

Chapter Thirty

After Clare's tearful revelations about the state of her relationship, we spent the rest of the day being very careful around each other. What she'd shared with me was very serious indeed. I promised that what had happened between her and Jason would be my secret. For her part, Clare promised she would never again give me love-life advice unless I asked for it. She would definitely stay away from my Facebook account. She also made me about a dozen cups of tea. It was as though she spent the day anticipating my wishes, like a genie. Anything to keep me on her side.

Of course I was on her side, but I made her promise that she would think carefully about her commitment to Evan. She had to work out what she really wanted. I neither wanted her to throw away something good – and I did think that Evan was a great guy – or lock herself into a relationship that made her unhappy. The wedding date might have been booked, but, I reminded her, she would be able to say, 'I don't,' right up until the minute she said, 'I do.' Nevertheless, I didn't envy her the choice that lay ahead of her. I especially didn't envy her having to tell our parents if she decided not to go ahead. What would our mother tweet about that?

And then it was Wednesday, the last day of our holiday at home. I woke up first and went through our usual holiday routine, logging on to the official Majorcan tourist-board website to see what the weather was set to be like that day. Sunny and twenty-six degrees in the shade. Just another day in paradise, I thought, as I opened the kitchen curtains just a crack to see that outside my flat was a typical British summer's day. Overcast. Cold as November again. The brief heatwave we had enjoyed on our private beach was already over. The weather guy on the radio blamed the unusually low jet stream, which was going to bring rain for the rest of the week. Maybe even for the rest of the summer, he joked with the morning DJ.

So far so gloomy. Yet I couldn't wait to be 'home' again. I couldn't wait until the following afternoon, when I could officially fling open the front door and take a proper walk under that leaden sky without worrying who I might bump into. I needed to stretch my legs properly. Maybe even go to the gym. We were running out of food. We had long since run out of old *Sex and the City* DVDs to watch. I needed to open all the windows and let the air blow through the flat. It smelled as though something had died under the kitchen sink and I was finding it just a little hard to cope with my sister's disinterest in keeping things tidy. The draining board was cluttered with glasses and mugs. Clare got through more mugs of tea in a day than a whole team of builders.

I was a little worried about having to talk about my holiday when I got back to the office, but Clare assured me that it wouldn't be so hard. The thing to remember was that no one is really interested in other people's holidays, she said. Any questions would be rhetorical and polite. No one would be in the least bit bothered if all I said was, 'It was great,' then changed the subject back to the office gossip I had missed in the meantime. Even if the office gossip at that moment was all about me and Callum.

'They'll be thrilled to get on to that,' said Clare.

'Hannah will ask questions about the hotel,' I said.

'Only to introduce the subject of her own holiday on the Golden Isle. You can just let her get on with it.'

I nodded. That was exactly what would happen. Hannah never talked about anyone else if she could bring the subject round to herself. But she would be bound to ask me about Tom, I was certain. What could I say about him?

I found myself looking at the photographs Clare had taken again. Tom was very photogenic. He had a kind face that reflected the nice bloke he so obviously was. You had to admire him for his dedication to what had to be a very difficult job. I couldn't help feeling envious of him, heading off on his real holiday that very day. And I couldn't help feeling envious of the girls he might meet while he was there. He would be bound to have a holiday romance. There was no chance that a man as friendly and good-looking as him ever had to spend a night alone at the weekends. I had wondered what it would be like to kiss him, of course. While we were washing up together, there had been a moment when I misheard something he said, I turned towards him to ask him to repeat himself, and suddenly our lips were no more than an inch apart. It would have been very easy to kiss him then. Our proximity had certainly raised my heartbeat. I held back. Just as Tom had held back when he kissed me goodnight. But I hadn't imagined the tension, had I?

I shouldn't be disappointed about that, I told myself. I still had unfinished business with Callum. I still hadn't entirely given up hope of reconciliation. That was all I needed to know. As the time for me to pretend to return from our holiday and subsequently go back to the office grew nearer, I was definitely becoming nervous at the thought of our first face-to-face meeting in such a long time. What would it be like? Would we bump into each other in the corridor, and if we didn't, should I go to his office and say 'hi'? Hannah had stopped reporting that Callum was looking fed up around the office. Did that mean that he had got used to the idea of our break-up and would not want to alter the status quo?

As I boiled the kettle to make some more tea, I imagined our first post-break-up encounter. I had the outfit planned, of course. I would top up my fake tan at some point that day. Clare had suggested that I streak some lemon juice through my hair for the sunkissed look. I would wear a white shirt to set off my tan and the navy-blue pencil skirt that Evan once said made me look like an extra from *Mad Men*. If Evan liked it, then maybe Callum did too. Perhaps I could get Clare to help me add the finishing touches with a killer blow-dry. She was great at doing hair.

If I didn't see Callum before I got to my desk, then of course I should search him out to say 'hi'. It was all about seeming nonchalant. It was all about convincing him that I didn't care whether he came back to me or not. I was perfectly happy as I was. My life would go on. I would carry on working hard at Stockwell Lifts, moving up through the ranks.

Except, of course, that there was nowhere to go at

Stockwell Lifts, and if Callum and I were no longer together, then my job would have lost a big part of its appeal. Without Callum to retain my interest, I might have left Stockwell Lifts within eighteen months of starting there. I knew I wouldn't be able to stand being in such close proximity to Callum if my plan had not paid off. I would have to look for something else. What a rotten time to have to do that, when all over the country people were losing their jobs. Would I be able to sign on if I made myself voluntarily redundant? Perhaps I could persuade my boss to cut his PR budget and my job with it.

Perhaps I didn't want to come back from my make-believe break after all. I had a few pretty awful weeks ahead of me.

How long would it be before Alison decided it was safe to start flirting with Callum again? How long would it be before he thought it was safe to transfer his affections on to my colleague and her infamous cleavage? I knew that the day would come all too soon when Alison considered it no longer necessary to protect my feelings and went all out on her own offensive to win Callum's heart.

But right then, my iPhone buzzed on the kitchen table. I snatched it up. The impossible had finally happened.

Callum had sent me a text.

Chapter Thirty-One

After a week with no contact whatsoever, I had started to grow used to the daily disappointment of Callum's continued silence. Even on my birthday. In fact, it had almost become a comfort to me when another day passed without word from the man I had loved so very much. At least if I hadn't heard from him, then things were no worse than they had been when I woke up without him by my side. As time passed, I had come to think it was so very unlikely he would call to tell me he'd changed his mind that any contact would be, by definition, disappointing.

I have never been one of those people who says of bad news that they would rather 'just know' so that they can get on with the business of reacting to the changed situation. On the contrary, I am the kind of person who likes to live in denial until the last possible moment. I am the sort of person who covers her eyes during horror movies and peels plasters off ever so slowly, wincing with every painful millimetre gained. I know it's better to get some things over with quickly. I know that having all the requisite information makes it easier to plan your reaction, but I really don't think I'm up to shocks.

So when my phone buzzed to tell me that Callum had sent me a message, my first reaction was to feel a little sick. Then a lot sick. That man had so much power over my emotions, it was frightening.

'Open it,' said Clare.

I told her I couldn't. What if Callum was writing to tell me that he had seen the photographs on Facebook of me with my new 'friend' and he never, ever wanted to talk to me again as a result? I would never, ever talk to Clare again as a result of that. Worse, what if he was writing to tell me that he was glad I had found somebody new so quickly because now he could come clean about the real reason for our break-up and her name was . . .

I explained my apprehension to Clare.

'What if he's saying neither of those things?' she said reasonably.

'Just let me have this moment,' I begged. 'This moment where he might still be texting to beg my forgiveness. This moment in a parallel universe where he still loves me and there's still some hope that we'll get back together.'

'Here, you sap. Give it to me.'

I didn't have to give Clare my phone. She just snatched it out of my hand and opened the text before I could get the word 'no' out. I watched her face anxiously for any sign that would betray the nature of the text's contents.

'Well, that's all very boring,' she said, as she handed the phone to me so that I could read the news for myself.

'Sounds like you're having a good time out there in Majorca,' he wrote. 'I'm really glad you had the courage to go on your own. Perhaps we could get together to talk about it when you get back?'

So far, so mundane, but it was as though a real ray of sunshine had broken through the closed curtains of my flat. Callum had reached out to me at last. And he said that he wanted to talk! I danced around the flat with almost as much enthusiasm as I had fandangoed around the kitchen to the Gipsy Kings over a week ago in the moments before he texted to tell me that he wouldn't be coming on holiday.

I showed my sister the message again. She nodded wisely.

'Of course he wants to talk about it,' she said.

'Do you think it'd be too eager to ask to see him the very day we get back? I want him to know he has a second chance.'

'But does he deserve a second chance? He needs to make an effort for you, Soph. Don't let him just slip back into your life like he didn't ruin your holiday.'

'I understand. But the funny thing is,' I told her, 'he really didn't ruin my holiday. I've had a wonderful time these past few days. Just you and me.'

She gave me a high five.

'I've had a great time too,' she said. 'You know what? One of these days, we should go on holiday together for real. In fact, let's promise to do it every single year. At least get away for a couple of days. No matter who we may or may not get married to.'

'Definitely. That sounds like a family tradition that will be easy to keep. Now what should I text back?'

'You're texting back already?'

I nodded. 'Of course.'

'No, you're not,' said Clare. 'Not yet. You're too busy having fun.'

But I couldn't leave it like that. No way. I was willing to accept Clare's argument that my continued silence would make Callum sweat, but I was worried that too long a silence would discourage him from trying for a second chance altogether. What if he thought I was really over him and, as a result, he went out clubbing with his mates that night, drank to drown his sorrows and ended up in the arms of another girl?

Callum's text had arrived at ten in the morning. I managed to hold off replying until four in the afternoon. Mostly because Clare confiscated my phone and sat on it while she knitted the arms of a sweater she had promised her goddaughter.

'I hope you remembered to switch it from vibrate,' I told her.

While Clare knitted, I paced the room, grinding more sand from the backyard into the carpet as I did so. My landlady was going to have a fit. Never mind. Callum wanted to talk to me. Who cared about anything else? I composed a novel's worth of responses to Callum's text in my head. I agonised over each and every word. Should my tone be chilly, warm or neutral? Should I write, 'I'm having a great holiday. No thanks to you,' or should I take the moral high road and not refer to our break-up at all? What would I have written in response to Callum's text were he just a friend and not my ex-lover?

I did practically nothing but compose that silly little text in my head for a whole six hours, so that when Clare finally told me I could have my phone back, I typed up and sent my final edited version in under thirty seconds. I did not let Clare see it before it went, but when I finally told her what I had written, which was, 'Thanks for your text. Having a lovely time. Weather great. Sophie' (no kiss), she said that she approved.

'It's perfectly neutral,' was her verdict. 'No suggestion of anger, desperation or bitterness whatsoever.'

'You think so?' I was very relieved.

'I think you've hit exactly the right note. The fact that you responded at all gives him the opportunity to take it further, but he will have to be the one who goes out on a limb and puts some emotion in his next move.'

But how long would I have to wait until Callum made his next move? The following forty-five minutes made the previous six hours during which I had done nothing but pace the room seem to have passed by in a flash. How could forty-five minutes seem so long? It passed like Pilates time, when an hour in the gym seems like three hours' worth of real time because you just want to be out of that press-up position and eating a Krispy Kreme.

I checked my phone every two seconds, despite the fact that I had turned the ringtone setting from 'silent' to 'loud' so that there was no way in hell I would not know the very second Callum deigned to reply.

At last it happened.

'Weather rubbish here,' he said. 'Wish I had come with you.'

'Ohmigod, ohmigod, ohmigod.' I danced around the room, flapping my hands.

'Maybe it's just a figure of speech,' said my sister. 'Let's see if he says any more.'

'Should I respond?'

'Do not respond.'

Clare sat on the phone again.

And she was right to do so, because ten minutes later, Callum sent another text and this one really was worth dancing about.

'Bryan says I can still take the rest of this week and the first three days of next week off if I want to, seeing as how I already had it booked. I'm thinking I might come to Majorca after all. Can I meet you there?'

When Clare read that text out to me, I fell backwards onto the sofa as if into a faint, then kicked my legs in the air and sprang straight back up again. I was that excited.

'Ohmigod, ohmigod, ohmigod.'

I grabbed my sister and we danced around the room. Our stupid plan, conceived in such desperation nearly a week before, had worked. I had pretended to be having a wonderful time in Majorca for a week and now Callum wanted to join me there. He wanted me back. There was no doubt about it. Callum Dawes was going to be mine.

Chapter Thirty-Two

Of course, in my ecstatic jubilation at this sudden change in Callum's feelings, I had forgotten one very important point. Callum had said that he wanted to join me on holiday in Majorca, but my sister and I were still very much in my flat in SW11.

'This is a disaster!' I said.

How quickly my mood had changed from joy to despair.

'He's going to find out I never went away.'

'How?' asked Clare.

'Well, I'll have to tell him he can't join me in Majorca because I'm not over there, am I? I'll have to come clean.'

'Not at all. You could just tell him that you don't want him to join you right now. Tell him you want to use the time you have left on the island as thinking time. That should be enough to put him off making the trip and put the fear in him at the same time. He'll start to think he's really lost you so that by the time you do "get back" from your holiday, I wouldn't be surprised if he was waiting on the doorstep with a ring.'

'Do you think so?'

'No, not really. And in any case I'm not convinced you should accept any ring from such a jerk. But it would get him thinking, I'm sure.'

'But your plan means that I'd have to spend another week in this flat!'

'I'd stay with you.'

'That is *not* an option. Anyway, I was going to pretend to fly back tomorrow.'

'Then fly back tomorrow,' said Clare, making quotation marks around the words 'fly back'. 'If you want to lessen the chances of really making an impact that gets you guys back together.'

'You think that would happen?'

Clare nodded.

'Oh.' I screwed up my fists in frustration. Clare probably had a point. If I could stay away for the whole fortnight, then Callum would really begin to worry that he needed to up his game.

She composed the text for me.

'You are welcome to do whatever you like on your holidays,' she wrote on my behalf. 'But please don't come to Majorca to see me. I think what you said to me in London was right. We definitely needed some time apart. I have been enjoying having some thinking time and would like to have another week to myself.'

'That doesn't sound like me,' I complained. 'It sounds too formal.'

'There.' Clare added a 'kiss' to the end of it. 'That makes it a little more friendly. Can I send it now?'

I let her send the text. She was right, I knew. I had to tell Callum not to come. It was the only way to preserve our holiday fantasy. Now was not the time to come clean about our week in Clapham. Especially, as Clare pointed out, once Callum knew the truth, it would be bound to get back to Evan too.

'Evan would never forgive me.'

'Do you think he'd break off the engagement?'

'No,' said Clare. 'I actually don't think he would. He would rather marry me so he can remind me how dishonest and shifty I am every day for the rest of my life.'

That didn't sound like much fun either. Though Clare smiled when she said it, in the light of our previous evening's conversation, I couldn't help being a little worried for her. But mostly right then I was worried for me. Had Clare's formal text done the trick, or had I just frightened Callum into maintaining our split-up status quo? The next hour was Pilates time with added treacle. And then . . . Callum sent another text.

'I understand how you're feeling, but I don't want to have to wait another week to see you. This is too important to me. I'm coming to see you whether you like it or not.'

'Oh, no,' I said. 'He's not giving up. What can I do about this?'

'Don't panic,' said Clare. 'We can still head him off. Does he know where you're supposed to be staying?'

Of course he did. While planning the Majorca trip, I had bombarded Callum with information about our increasingly complicated itinerary. I had sent him the details of our hotel in Puerto Bona by email. I had also printed them out so that he had a hard copy to bring with him on the plane in case our phones didn't work and we couldn't pick up emails when we got to Palma.

A further text followed. Callum had booked his flight for the very next day. He would be arriving in Majorca at around seven in the evening. He'd make his own way to the airport, but would I make sure I was at the hotel to meet him? It was the Hotel Mirabossa, right? How long did I think it would take him to drive there?

I imagined with horror the moment he got to the Hotel Mirabossa and discovered that I wasn't there and never had been.

'This is getting worse and worse! He's going to get all the way to Majorca and find out I'm not out there. He'll decide he was right to break up with me and tell Hannah and Alison and make me look a right prat.'

'Not necessarily,' said Clare. 'I have another plan.'

'Really?'

'I have another plan,' were exactly the words I wanted to hear, but I couldn't for the life of me imagine how my sister was going to get me out of this one.

'How about this? Callum is on the afternoon flight, right? But that isn't the first flight of the day. If you could get on the early morning flight from Gatwick, you could beat him to Palma, get to the hotel and be settled in like you've been there all week by the time he arrives. You've already got your suntan – we can top that up tonight – and thanks to the Internet, you know Puerto Bona pretty well. You've been at the Palacio Blanco every night this week, remember. If only in spirit.'

'You're so crazy.'

'I prefer the term genius,' said Clare. 'I think it's worth a try.'

'I don't know . . .'

'Let's see what we can do.'

Ignoring my naysaying, Clare was soon back online, checking airline websites for a flight that would get us to Spain before an unsuspecting Callum even got to Gatwick.

'There's availability,' Clare told me. 'We could do it!'

'We? What do you mean, "we"? You're meant to be going back home tomorrow.'

'I was thinking perhaps I should come with you.'

'Are you nuts? What about Evan?'

'Evan already thinks I'm in Majorca, doesn't he?'

'But you were only supposed to be with me for five days.'

Clare picked up her phone to text him.

'Don't worry about that. I'm going to tell him I don't think I should leave you on your own. I've told him that now it's getting close to time for me to go home again, you've taken a turn for the worse.'

'You're mad. Don't do it.'

'I've already done it.'

Evan's reply was fairly predictable.

'Why don't you bring her home with you?' he asked.

Clare thought quickly.

'Because she's refusing to come out of the room,' she texted. 'I don't think there's any way I'm going to be able to get her on a plane. Just let me have a few more days to deal with it. And please don't tell Mum about this relapse. I don't want her to worry.'

'Call me,' Evan responded.

'Very little battery,' Clare responded. Then she switched her phone off so that Evan couldn't call her if he wanted to. 'He doesn't really want me to call him,' Clare explained. 'He knows it costs far too much money to use your mobile overseas. Let's book those flights.'

In a week of crazy ideas, this was obviously the craziest idea so far. At such late notice, the flights were bound to be ruinously expensive. And did Clare really think that Evan would be mollified by a few texts? I also didn't much like the idea that she had suggested that I was going mental over my break-up. Not when I thought I was doing particularly well.

'What if Evan tells someone I've lost it? What if it gets back to Callum?'

'Evan won't tell anyone anything. He finds all kinds of emotion acutely embarrassing. He would sooner discuss Mum's gynaecological problems than whether or not you're getting over your break-up. Trust me, he will not be calling our mother to discuss how you're feeling. He never calls anyone except me and that's just to tell me what I'm doing wrong. Now pass me your credit card. I'm up to my limit.'

I refused.

'We're not doing this. I think this is all about to get stupidly out of hand. I don't care if Callum finds out that I'm not really in Majorca. I won't be responsible for Evan dumping you if you don't go back home tomorrow night.'

'He won't dump me. There's no way he wants to put himself through the aggravation of having to find someone to replace me. Do you know how much it costs a guy to start dating a new girl? He'd rather put up with me than have to waste a whole load of money on romantic dinners.'

'Seriously?'

'Not really. But now that I think about it . . . Sophie, Evan will be fine. He's probably already making plans to watch reruns of *Top Gear*.'

When she wanted to be, my sister could be very persuasive and she soon bulldozed through all my reservations.

'Besides, this extra week apart could be just what I need to renew my love for him.'

That sounded more hopeful. How could I argue with that?

'Plus, you do want to get Callum back, don't you?'

Of course I did. Now that I knew there was a real chance that he might change his mind, I wanted to do whatever I could to make that happen.

'Then this is the only way to do it. He has already booked his flights to Majorca. It's too late to stop him turning up at the hotel. You have a choice between telling him you didn't go, thus revealing yourself to be a liar and a flake and exactly the kind of girl who deserves to get dumped, or you follow my instructions and meet him at the hotel tomorrow evening like you've been there all week. Nobody need be any the wiser. What's not to like about that plan? You keep our secret intact *and* get to have a proper holiday after all. And it's your best chance of making things work with Callum. We'll pull it off, I promise. We can do this,' said Clare, as she clicked 'buy' on our flights. And providing there were no flight delays and the hotel had some space, it seemed she was right. We could do this.

'You're not planning on taking all those bags, are you?' I asked when the reality that we were going to Majorca after all finally sank in.

Clare smiled.

'I won't take my knitting,' she said. 'How about that?'

It seemed that luck was on our side. We had our flights. They were expensive but not ridiculously so. I'd be able to pay mine off in just a couple of months, I thought. When I called up the Hotel Mirabossa in Puerto Bona, they told me they had not filled the room Callum and I should have stayed in and we could take it over at once. The exact room. Complete with the sea view I had dreamed of and that Clare had recreated for Mum and Evan with that photo lifted from the website.

We booked transfers from the airport to the coast on the hotel bus. That was easy enough. I already had the currency we needed. I'd ordered that from the post office months ago (before the exchange rate changed in the pound's favour, worse luck). I had all the suntan lotion I could possibly need, having stocked up the moment the new season's supply hit the shops. Not to mention the five bottles Clare had brought. I had the perfect bikini. There was just one question that had yet to be answered.

'What will you do when Callum arrives?' I said. 'I mean, where will you stay all week?'

'Eh? You mean, where will *Callum* stay all week?'

'With me.' That seemed like the obvious answer.

'He's put you through hell, Soph. Don't tell me that you were intending to let him get straight back into your knickers?'

'Well . . .'

The truth was, I had been intending exactly that. I'd missed him desperately. It had been more than a month since we'd last made love. I had pictured him sweeping me into his arms and taking me straight upstairs. I was planning to make our reunion the best night of our relationship so far. I was going to pack my fanciest knickers. Clare, however, had other ideas.

'Callum has to work for your love this time, and part of working for your love will involve fending for himself hotel-wise. You and I will be sharing that room you've just booked. Callum will be allowed to visit during daylight hours only.'

I made to protest, but Clare stopped me with a wag of her finger.

'Oh, no, there are no buts. It's only for a week. He has to make it up to you, Soph. He can't just turn up and expect everything to be as it was. He told you that you were too clingy,' she reminded me. 'He said that you were always following him around. See how he likes a bit more independence, starting with separate rooms. It won't hurt him. And it won't hurt your relationship either. If you two are destined to get back together, then being tough with Callum now will only make your relationship stronger. If he gets fed up at not being in your room and catches the next flight home, then that will only prove he isn't as serious as he should be.'

I grudgingly agreed.

Later that day, Hannah emailed to tell me that she'd heard from Candace that Callum was going to Majorca after all. Alison was incredulous, she said. Probably furious, to boot, I thought.

'What a result. Don't you dare let him winkle his way back into your affections without a fight,' said Hannah. 'You've got to show him you mean business, Sophie. It's the only way you'll ever make him respect you enough to give you a proper commitment of the kind you deserve.'

'See,' said Clare. 'Hannah knows what she's talking about.'

I couldn't imagine many other circumstances under which my sister and my colleague would have agreed with each other.

'I will have my fingers crossed for you,' Hannah added.

'I've got everything crossed for me,' I assured her in return.

So that night we packed our cases for real. Clare took for ever to put her stuff back into her two enormous cases. Though we hadn't left the flat for the past five days – we certainly hadn't been near any shops – the contents of Clare's luggage seemed to have multiplied exponentially so that when she tried to repack it, it was like trying to fit an airbag back into the dashboard panel. No matter how carefully she folded her T-shirts and stuffed bikinis inside shoes, it could not be done.

Eventually, I agreed that she could put some of the lighter items in my bag. I had simply referred to my original packing diagram and packed like a pro, with my shoes (two pairs) in bags and tissue paper around every garment. Two of Clare's evening dresses and a pair of wedge espadrilles fitted easily into the space I had reserved for gifts bought on my travels.

After that, we managed to get Clare's remaining clothes and toiletries into her cases by sitting on the case lids together while we each dragged one end of the two-ended zip towards the middle. The case still looked dangerously full, so I lent Clare one of my luggage straps to make sure it didn't explode in transit.

'Hang on,' said Clare. 'I think you've forgotten something.'

'What?' It wasn't possible that I'd forgotten anything. I had been following my packing diagram. 'What is it?'

'Your Choos,' said Clare. 'Your Jimmy Choos.'

'I don't think—' I began.

'You don't think you should take them on holiday? Why not? What are you saving them for? Don't tell me a special occasion, because what could possibly be more special than your thirtieth-birthday holiday?'

I wasn't convinced.

'Maybe you want to wait until your fortieth birthday, by which time your bunions will be seriously impressive.'

'I don't have bunions,' I said.

'Yet,' my sister replied, 'it's in our genes, you know.'

She was right. Mum had tweeted about her research into bunion ops just that week.

'Take your shoes. And wear them. You can carry them to and from the club and wear flip-flops on the way, but you have to get your money's worth! There's no point keeping anything for best. Remember what happened to Auntie Jan.'

Auntie Jan, my mother's aunt, had died in her eighties. When her children came to empty out her house, they had discovered boxes and boxes of unworn clothes and pristine shoes. The local vintage store was delighted, but my sister and I found the story profoundly sad. The thought of all those dancing shoes that never made it onto the dance floor could still bring tears to my eyes. It was doing so right then.

'Maybe hoarding is the family trait that you've inherited instead of bunions,' Clare mused. That was the last straw.

'OK,' I said. 'I'll take them.'

'Attagirl.'

I decanted the precious Choos into their fluffy lilac dust bag and laid them reverently on top of the neatly folded clothes in my case. Then I took them out again and stuffed them into my hand luggage next to my perfect bikini. I wasn't going to take any chances. Those shoes had cost almost as much as the holiday. They were coming in the aircraft cabin with me.

Things were turning out far better than I could have hoped. I was going to have my birthday holiday abroad after all. I gave Clare a hug.

'I'm so glad you're such a bad influence,' I said.

Chapter Thirty-Three

I didn't get much sleep. I was too excited now it seemed inevitable that Callum and I were going to get back together. Why else would he have decided to come to Majorca and not just book himself a flight somewhere else? He could have gone to Ibiza or Greece. He could have saved his holiday and tagged along with his mates later in the year. Instead, he was coming to Majorca for me. To be *with* me. My heart was almost as light as it had been when Callum and I started going out. I felt wanted. I felt pretty. When I looked into the mirror, even at five o'clock in the morning, unable to sleep with excitement, I was pleased by what I saw. The thought that Callum was coming back to me was a more effective beauty treatment than a week of sleep, a fortnight in the sun or any number of oxygen facials. I radiated happiness again.

I ordered a cab to the airport for six o'clock in the morning. The driver the cab company sent to pick us up was the same guy I had sent away the previous week. He obviously remembered the fare that never was and looked at me curiously.

'Are you really sure you want to go to somewhere this time?'

I assured him that nothing could stop me and that I would be grateful if he put his foot down all the way.

The cabbie got us to Gatwick in plenty of time. Check-in was unusually easy (though Clare had to decant even more of the contents of her bags into mine to beat the weight restrictions), and security was a breeze. With an hour to go before the flight, we were in a Costa Coffee concession drinking skinny lattes and I was genuinely starting to look forward to the week ahead.

'How do my new glasses look?' asked Clare. She'd gone a little nuts in the Sunglass Hut.

'You look a bit like Audrey Hepburn,' I lied. Unfortunately, she looked more like Bono's little sister, but she was not to be persuaded to buy a smaller pair. I did, however, manage to stop her buying a yellow sarong that would not have looked good on anybody and had a destiny as a very expensive duster.

Our luck held for the rest of the journey. Our flight was on time. We crossed France and Spain smoothly and without incident. There was no turbulence. No crying babies. No toddlers kicking the back of the seat. No stag parties in the back of the cabin getting an early start on their drinking. The landing in Palma was gentle, and our luggage was among the first to trundle along the conveyor belt in baggage reclaim. Clare's enormous wheelie case was still held in one piece by the straining luggage strap. So far so good.

Outside the terminal was a perfect summer's day. We shrugged off our jackets and put on our sunglasses as the sunshine wrapped us in glorious Mediterranean warmth.

'That's better,' Clare sighed.

I agreed wholeheartedly.

We boarded the hotel transfer coach with a half-dozen other smiling tourists, eager to swap city life for a week of Balearic ease. Now that Clare and I were really on holiday, I knew what a poor substitute a week in my apartment had been. Just five minutes standing in the sunshine in the airport car park and it was as though the previous seven days had been a bad dream.

The journey to the hotel on the island's north coast didn't take long, but in any case I enjoyed watching the landscape slip by. The centre of the island was largely flat and undistinguished, compared with the mountains I had read about in the guidebook, but all the same it was interesting to see something different. From time to time we caught glimpses of old farmhouses, turned into holiday villas. Their glittering turquoise pools filled us with excitement about an afternoon next to the pool at the Hotel Mirabossa.

'I've been there before,' said a woman sitting across the aisle. 'Best hotel I've ever been to. That's why we've come again this year. We wouldn't normally go back to the same place twice.'

It was a good recommendation.

And so we finally arrived at the hotel where we had supposedly spent the entire week: the Hotel Mirabossa on the outskirts of Puerto Bona. I was strangely surprised to find that it was so much like the hotel I had been describing in my Facebook updates and texts to Hannah.

'I've got déjà vu,' said Clare, summing up the weird sensation we were both feeling as we clambered off the hotel bus and followed our holiday rep into the lobby.

Everything seemed so familiar. The whitewashed

walls. The bougainvillea that tumbled down the front of the building. The tiled courtyard with the tinkling fountain in the centre. Water droplets sparkled like crystals in the mid-morning sun. I couldn't resist slicing my hand through the glittering jets.

Clare squeezed my arm as we waited to be given our room key.

'Isn't this wonderful?'

It was.

Our room – the room I had booked for me and Callum – had a sea view. It wasn't the exact sea view that Clare had photographed from the website, but it was close enough, we decided. If Callum had taken any notice of the photograph that Mum had tweeted, he would have to be pretty geeky to notice that we were slightly further to the right of the pool bar and the geranium planters were marginally smaller.

'We can always say we changed rooms, if he asks,' said Clare.

As I took in the perfect vista from the balcony, Clare set about making the room look lived in. The moment she took the safety strap off her case, it exploded like a jack-in-a-box, spewing clothes all over the floor and giving the room what I thought was an instant 'lived-in' feel. Clare wasn't so convinced. She art-directed the scene as carefully as she had created my birthday beach with Ted and Jason. She draped items of clothing all over the room like bunting. She dampened a bikini in the washbasin and hung it over the rail around the balcony, as though it had been worn and washed the day before. Her attention to detail was quite impressive.

'Let's do the same with your stuff,' she suggested.

I reminded Clare that compared to her I had a reputation for a frightening level of tidiness and organisation. Callum would think it very odd if he saw a single sock of mine on the floor.

'Whatever you say,' said Clare, rearranging a pair of shorts that didn't look quite realistically discarded enough. She arranged her pharmacy's worth of toiletries in the bathroom.

With our unpacking finished, we still had the best part of a day before Callum arrived and we were going to make the most of it. After a week cooped up in my flat, the sea air was the best thing I had ever smelled. Our makeshift beach may have been fun, but it was no substitute for the real beach and the sound of the waves. We decided to take a walk to orient ourselves in our surroundings. I had a small moment of panic when I noticed that the sand on this beach was shingly, rather than the fine sand we'd had in the garden, but Clare assured me that was a detail that Callum would not notice at all.

'You're here in Majorca, large as life. Why should he question whether or not you were really here last week as well? He's not going to think twice about the sand.'

We wandered around the town, matching the real restaurants and shops to the virtual images we had worked with for the past week. There was the tiny bar where we had pretended to stop for lunch. There was the grocery shop where we had stocked up on bottled water when Evan suggested that it might not be safe to drink straight from the taps and it would certainly be too expensive to buy bottled water at the hotel. And there, at last, was the Palacio Blanco, the nightclub we had made our local.

'Looks much smaller in real life,' said Clare. We pressed our faces against the wrought-iron gate that led onto the courtyard full of tables we felt we knew so well. 'I'm looking forward to going there tonight, though.'

I agreed. I could already imagine persuading Callum onto the dance floor, wrapping my arms round his neck and luxuriating in his kisses as we whirled round to some slow tune.

'Shall we go back to the hotel?' Clare asked. 'See if we can't get ourselves a cup of tea?'

'I'm sure you can't get a decent cup of tea in Majorca,' I responded. At last the idea made me smile. And I was right. At least, I was right that you couldn't get a decent cup of tea at our hotel. There's something about tea made with anything but hard old British water that isn't quite proper. The UHT milk didn't help. But I didn't really care. The sunshine more than made up for it.

I was about to upload a real photograph of the pool-side to my Facebook account, but Clare stopped me.

'I think it's for the best that we don't give anyone the opportunity to make comparisons.'

'Good idea.'

After lunch, we settled ourselves by the pool and ordered cocktails. The hotel's sangria was almost as good as Henry and Tabby's lethal brew. It was certainly strong enough to make me feel a little less anxious about the evening ahead, because I was feeling anxious now. After yesterday's flurry of communication, it struck me that Callum hadn't actually texted me since the text he sent to let me know which flight he'd be on.

'What if he was bluffing?' I asked my sister.

'It's one hell of a complicated bluff.'

'Compared to what we did last week? Maybe he knows we were at home all the time and he's been taking the mickey, pretending he's coming to join us. He won't show up.'

'He will show up,' Clare assured me. 'But so what if he doesn't?' she added. 'You're on holiday. You're by the pool. The sun is shining. Everything is right with the world.'

And as if Clare's words had prompted it, Callum chose that moment to text to let me know that he was on his way to the airport and, as far as he could tell from the airline website, the flight was on schedule. My shoulders loosened with relief. He would be by my side in less than six hours.

But then Clare's iPhone buzzed to let her know that she had a message too. She leaned across to pick it out of her beach bag, checked her phone and suddenly her smile disappeared from her face as though someone had switched her happy holiday mood off like a light.

'What is it?' I asked. She suddenly looked so very unhappy that I could only assume the worst. Had we been rumbled? While Clare studied her phone, I looked about us, scanning the crowds at the poolside for a familiar face. Had someone who thought we had already been in Majorca for a week spotted us arriving and sent a text to find out what we were doing? I could see no one I knew, but when I next looked at Clare, she seemed to be struggling to hold back tears.

'Is everything OK?' I asked. Was it news from home?

I wondered aloud. Had something terrible happened while we were in the air or wandering happily around the resort? Had someone died?

Clare shook her head. 'It's worse than that,' she managed at last. 'Evan says he's coming to Majorca too.'

Evidently, Evan had decided that a whole five days without his fiancée was quite long enough. If she really was going to stay in Majorca for another seven days, then he would just have to take a week out of his annual leave, which he had been saving so he could oversee the fitting of their new kitchen in August, and fly out to Majorca to join her.

'As you know,' he said over the course of three lengthy texts, 'I hadn't planned on us taking a holiday at all this year. We've got far too much to do at home, and of course we should be saving for the wedding, but since you insist on staying with your sister for another week, I suppose I will have to come and join you. It isn't right for us to spend so much time apart.'

And that was that. Evan had booked himself on to the same flight as Callum (though he didn't yet know that Callum was flying out too). He would be arriving in Palma that evening. He would get a hire car from the airport (another expense he hadn't planned for) and expect Clare to be waiting for him at the hotel at around nine o'clock.

'Don't go out,' he said. 'I want to see you as soon as I arrive.'

'I can't believe it,' said Clare. 'This is a disaster.'

'It's not so bad,' I said. I had thought, having spoken a little about it on the flight, that Clare was feeling mellower about her relationship that day. 'Evan will be company for you when Callum gets here and—'

Clare interrupted me. 'All I wanted was another week to myself! Just seven more days before I go back to London and a boring summer of DIY, and then next year we get married and I'll never be allowed to go anywhere on my own ever again. But now he's coming here and that means I'll have to spend the week doing what he wants, which will not be the same as the holiday I was planning at all. He won't want to go clubbing. He won't want to eat out except at the very cheapest places. He'll probably insist we go to the local supermarket and buy bread and marg and have sandwiches for dinner every day. And he won't let me read by the pool because he won't have wanted to waste any money on a book of his own, so he'll expect me to talk to him all day long. This is going to be my worst holiday ever.'

'You might be surprised,' I tried.

'When has Evan ever surprised me?'

Clare threw her phone into her beach bag.

'Maybe a holiday together might bring back some of the magic,' I dared to suggest. 'He's bound to relax once he's been here for a couple of days. You've had nice holidays together before.'

'Give it a rest.' Clare fumed beneath her sun hat.

I felt a little guilty that I was still looking forward to the week ahead immensely. I couldn't wait to be reunited with Callum and have at least half the adventures I had been planning before our shocking break-up. While Clare calculated that she had just five hours of freedom left, I was wishing every minute of those hours away. I just wanted to be back with my boyfriend.

'I only wanted to try out a little taste of freedom

again,' Clare continued. 'Just a week. If I miss him, then I'll know that we're right for each other. If I don't . . .'

'Oh, Clare,' I said, 'at least let's try to enjoy this afternoon.'

But as far as Clare was concerned, her dream holiday was already over. She seemed to have decided that she wasn't going to be able to enjoy a single minute more. She didn't want to swim. She didn't want to read. She sat under the sun umbrella with a face like thunder, scowling at her sudden change in fortune. She even turned down my suggestion that we have another cocktail.

'I'd better not have any more,' said Clare. 'Evan hates it when I get tipsy.'

As the afternoon progressed, Clare and I were like the two little people on a weatherhouse. The more excited I became about Callum's impending arrival, the quieter Clare grew. I went up to the room to get a cardigan to throw around my shoulders. When I came back down, I caught her staring off into space with a distinctly sad look on her face.

'What's the matter?'

'Look at the time.'

'The boys' plane will be landing in twenty minutes,' I said. 'How long do you think it will take them to get here?'

'Not long enough.'

'Clare, you've got to try and make the most of Evan being here too. Just think, you could be having a romantic dinner overlooking the sea tonight. How can you fail to have a good time doing that?'

'Yeah,' said Clare, taking another sip of her drink. 'I'd rather have dinner with you.'

That was flattering, but I knew I would rather have dinner with Callum. The next hour and a half couldn't pass quickly enough for me.

Chapter Thirty-Four

When she found out that Callum and Evan would be arriving in Majorca on the same plane, Clare had texted Evan to let him know, since she knew he would be pleased at the possibility of saving a few quid on a shared hire car.

'Good thinking,' he texted back. In the light of her recent unauthorised holiday spending spree, Clare was glad to be able to score at least one brownie point for thrift. Evan confirmed that he had already spotted Callum across the departure lounge and was on his way to let him know that from now on they would be travelling together.

I wasn't so sure that Callum would be pleased with the idea. He and Evan had met before, of course, but though I had hoped that one day the men would be brothers-in-law, they definitely weren't natural buddies. Callum thought Evan was uptight and priggish. A square. Evan thought Callum was an unbearable show-off in his designer jeans and Gucci sunglasses. He disapproved of the amount of booze Callum could sink on a night out. I wondered how they would fare on the drive north together. The disagreements would probably start at the rental-car desk.

I amused myself by imagining the scene at the airport. Evan and Callum would share a hire car, of course. They were both too tight to do anything else.

But who would drive? I knew from the few times we had been out as a foursome that Callum thought Evan drove like an old man. Evan thought Callum was unreasonably reckless and drove too fast. I suppose it would come down to whoever wielded the credit card. That too would be an amusing scene. Whose plastic would they use? Which one of them would buckle first? I tried to engage Clare about it. I suggested we should take bets on who got to pay and who got to go behind the wheel. She didn't care. She said she didn't care about anything any more. My sister was nothing if not a drama queen.

When the boys finally arrived, I could tell at once that Evan had won that battle. He marched in ahead of Callum with a driver's swagger.

Still Evan wasn't pleased with his victory. After giving Clare a perfunctory sort of kiss 'hello', he was off.

'Bloody stupid Micra. I wouldn't be at all surprised if I ended up with deep-vein thrombosis. Ridiculous, the amount of leg room in that thing. Just asking for a clot. If anything goes wrong, I will sue Europcar for my medical treatment.'

'But why did you hire such a small car?' Clare asked him. 'They must have bigger cars than that.'

'Clare,' said Evan with a sigh, 'do I really need to remind you that we're supposed to be saving money, not spending it like water? This trip to Majorca is a major unseen expense, which has thrown out all my calculations for the whole year. That's why I spent the least amount possible on a hire car. That's why I drove all the way across the island in a position that cut off my circulation and has probably caused lasting damage.'

'You could have taken the hotel bus,' said Clare. 'Plenty of leg room on that.'

'What, and put myself in the hands of a driver who probably hasn't even passed his test? Who certainly hasn't passed a *British* test? You don't know what standards, or lack of standards, these local bus drivers are held to. No, thanks. I would rather be in control of my own destiny.'

'And drive us into a ditch all by himself,' Callum commented. It was the first time he had spoken. He had yet to say 'hello' to me.

'That was entirely the other driver's fault,' said Evan. 'She was all over the road.'

'Ah well,' said Clare, trying to avert an argument, 'at least you're both here now. Shall we have a celebratory cocktail?'

Evan picked up the cocktail menu and sucked his teeth at the prices. He shook his head.

'I've got some duty-free brandy in my bag,' he said.

'But I hate brandy,' said Clare. 'And if you want to drink your duty-free, you'll have to do it in the room. You're not allowed to bring your own drinks to the communal areas. Can't we just have a bottle of rosé here by the pool?'

'You can have as many bottles of rosé as you like,' said Evan, 'as long as you don't mind sitting on an old Ikea sofa for the whole of our married life.'

'Christ. OK,' said Clare, 'I get it. I've spent too much money already. Let's go to the bloody room.'

What a great start. Clare and Evan were soon gone. We heard them grumbling their way up the stairs. Callum and I looked at each other and shared a smile.

Still he remained awkwardly on the other side of the table.

'I'm glad you came,' I told him.

And I really was so glad to see him there. For the two hours before he was due to arrive, I had been unable to concentrate on anything but the thought of his arrival. I had ripped a cardboard cocktail mat to shreds in my nervousness. I had not been so nervous to see him since the very early days of our relationship. As I waited, I was reminded of our first proper date. Though by then we had known each other for months through the office, I was sick with nerves as I crossed Covent Garden to the French restaurant he had chosen for our first official rendezvous after the Stockwell Lifts Christmas party. Callum had always had the ability to unnerve me. That first date, I had been convinced he was only doing it for a dare. Likewise, there was still a little part of me that didn't believe this moment was for real.

And he seemed to be looking at my teeth, which didn't help me to feel any more relaxed about the situation. Note to self: a mojito is not a good important-date drink. All those itty-bitty little pieces of mint. I must have looked as though I had been sifting for krill. I stretched my lips over my teeth. The really stupid thing is, I'd only chosen the mojito in the first place because I thought all that mint would give me extra-fresh breath for our first reconciliatory kiss.

When were we going to have that kiss? *Were* we going to have that kiss? Callum still hadn't made any move towards me.

Maybe I would have to be the one to take the first step. I considered just wrapping my arms round him, but nothing about Callum's stance definitively suggested a move like that would be welcome. I suppose it was more understandable in his case. After all, I hadn't seen him for more than a month and the last time we'd spoken, he'd told me that I had to get over him and move on. I had every right to be angry with him and he knew it. Perhaps he was waiting for me to tell him where he could stuff his grand gesture. Or maybe seeing me had been enough to convince him that he had been right to dump me after all.

I don't know how long we stood on opposite sides of the table like that. It was probably only a minute, but it seemed to take for ever. At last I held out my arms. Callum stepped into them, wrapped his own arms round me in a big bear hug and lifted me off my feet. He whirled me round until I had to ask him to stop. My Dutch-courage cocktails were swilling around dangerously inside me.

'Put me down,' I shrieked.

'I never want to put you down again,' said Callum.

But he did. He had to. I'm not that small.

'Shall we have a drink?' I asked while I waited for my head to stop spinning.

Thankfully, Callum was not as tight as Evan and he was never one to refuse a cocktail.

'Let's have two,' he said.

I ordered another mojito. He had a James Bond-style martini.

'I have missed you,' he said, proposing a toast when our drinks arrived. That was exactly what I wanted to hear.

'I can't believe you came on holiday on your own, though. I was convinced you would stay home.'

I felt myself reddening. 'Well, sometimes a girl has to take a risk.'

'I was impressed. Have you been OK without me?'

'I've had Clare here,' I said.

'I can't believe Evan put up with that. Not when they're getting a new kitchen. He wouldn't shut up about it all the way across the island. Shoot me if I ever get like that . . . Here, I brought you this.'

He reached into the rucksack he used for hand luggage and brought out a bottle of perfume: Chanel's Coco. Not something I'd ever worn. It was a jumbo-sized bottle from duty-free. The price tag was still on it, but it is the thought that counts.

'I got this too.' He pulled out a smaller box. My heart skipped. This had to be my *real* thirtieth-birthday present.

No, it wasn't. It was a man's watch.

'I've always wanted one of these,' said Callum, strapping it onto his wrist. I sat on my disappointment. It was presumptuous of me to have expected anything more than the perfectly nice bottle of scent.

Two more cocktails arrived. As we drank, Callum told me what hell he'd been through during his week without me.

'I decided not to take any holiday,' he said. 'I went into work.'

'I did hear something like that,' I told him, trying to play it cool.

'I bet you did. Hannah and Alison never let up in their campaign to make me miserable,' he said. 'Not an hour went by without one of them reminding me that I was at work while you were out here having a fabulous time.'

'Not such a fabulous time,' I tried to reassure him.

'While I had the week from hell. Listening to a running commentary about what a wonderful trip you were having while I was stuck in Stockwell. I tried to keep my head down, but when Alison and Hannah weren't banging on about how good it is over here, Candace was asking if I'd heard from you. She was worried that you were OK.'

'Really?'

Candace was on my Christmas list. Meanwhile, I was feeling a little bad for Callum. It sounded as though he had really suffered stuck there in the office. The girls had not been kidding when they said that they intended to make his life miserable on my behalf.

'Believe me,' I told him, 'whatever Hannah and Alison told me, not an hour went by without me thinking that I'd far rather be here with you than Clare. Great company though she is.'

'She needs to have a good sense of humour,' said Callum. 'God knows what she's doing with that berk. I nearly throttled him on the drive from the airport.'

'Love, eh?'

'Love.'

Callum reached across the table and took my hand. He looked deep into my eyes. I felt as though a live fish was flipping in my stomach. Was he about to tell me that he loved me too? In the eighteen months we had been together, he had never actually used the 'l' word. I let the silence grow between us and waited for him to fill it with the combination of three words I so wanted to hear.

'Anyway, are you going to show me where our room is or what?' Callum broke the moment with an altogether less romantic question than I had hoped for. 'I could do with a shower and some fresh clothes.'

'You want to go to the room?'

'Of course.' Callum's expression changed from dewily romantic to slightly wolfish. I knew what was on his mind. It had been on *my* mind since the moment I found out he had booked a flight to Majorca, but there was no avoiding it now. I had to tell him what Clare and I had planned.

'Well, you can go upstairs and have a quick shower if you like,' I said. 'I'm sure nobody will mind, but you're going to have to find another place to stay overnight. There are no spare rooms at the hotel this week, and Clare and Evan are staying in the room I booked for us.'

'What?'

'Clare and Evan are in our room.'

'They can't be staying there. Tell them to find somewhere else. Why should we have to move out?'

'We aren't moving out,' I said. 'You are. Just you. I'm staying with my sister and Evan, on a camp bed. The hotel provided it.'

'But that's just ridiculous. Come on, Sophie. You booked that room for *us* months and months ago. Tell Clare to sort herself out. Evan earns enough to find them somewhere nice. He spent enough time telling me how successful he is on the drive over here.'

'No,' I said, surprising myself at how firmly it came out. 'I'm not asking Clare to go anywhere. She really put herself out for me this week. I don't know what I would have done without her. And Evan was really good about it too. They're staying where they are. I'll be fine on a put-you-up.'

'But—'

'And,' I continued, 'I think it's better if we take things slowly in any case.'

'What am I supposed to do? Sophie, I have flown to Majorca to be with you.'

'And you can be with me,' I said, mustering as much self-esteem as I had ever found. 'During the day, you can be with me as much as you want, but as far as I am concerned, we are still broken up and we have a lot of talking to do before we decide whether or not to get back together properly.'

Callum clenched his jaw so hard that I could see the muscles twitch. He was not happy. That much was clear. Was he going to accept what I'd told him, or was this going to be it, the moment when we fell apart for good and for ever? It could have gone either way. He looked so annoyed that I would have put money on the probability that he was going to tell me to stuff it.

'Fine,' said Callum at last. 'You've made your point.'

Phew.

'I'll just have to hope there is another empty room in this town. I can't believe you didn't tell me this before I got a flight out here. I might not have . . .'

'Bothered to come?' I finished his sentence for him. 'I didn't ask you to. I told you that I wanted some time to myself. You went ahead and booked the flight anyway.'

'All I'm saying is, I have better things to do than traipse around this town looking for somewhere to sleep. Come on, Soph. Where am I going to go? It's nearly midnight. And I didn't exactly budget for finding myself a room. I've already paid to stay here.' He growled at the injustice of it. 'This is taking the piss.'

'You could always fly back in the morning.'

'Oh, Soph.' Callum suddenly softened and took my hands. 'I'm just frustrated, that's all. I've missed you. It's not only this week I've been missing you. All the time I was up in Newcastle . . . that whole month.'

'Every weekend of which you spent in London,' I reminded him. 'Where I would have been very happy indeed to see you, had you wanted to see me.'

Callum bristled again. 'Don't bring that up. I was confused. Look, why don't you come to another hotel with me? We don't have to do anything except talk. We can keep our clothes on. I'll even sleep on the floor if you want me to. It just seems crazy for me to be on my own while you play gooseberry to the others.'

To be honest, it didn't seem like such a great idea to me either, but I held firm.

'I'm staying with my sister,' I said. 'I'm sure you'll find somewhere good. Ask at reception.'

'Fine,' said Callum, picking up his bag. 'I'll let you know where I end up. Probably on a bench outside the bus station . . .'

Callum knocked back the last of his drink and half of mine before he left. It was hard to watch him go, after having waited so long to see him. I very nearly ran after him and told him I'd changed my mind and would spend the night wherever we could be together. I didn't want to do anything that would make him angry and jeopardise us getting back together.

Upstairs, Clare commiserated a little when I reminded her that it had actually been the best part of five weeks since Callum and I were last in bed together, but she insisted I had done the right thing. She and Evan were more than happy to share the room with me (especially if it meant they didn't have to pay for their accommodation, Evan added). So I stuck with Clare's plan, even when Callum texted to say he had ended up in some fleapit near the dual carriageway, where he would no doubt be attacked on all sides by mosquitoes and bedbugs. There wasn't a single decent room left in town.

'It will do him good. Nobody values something they haven't had to work for, whether it's a free drink, a free car or a relationship,' Clare told me, as she made me a cup of tea using the tea bags that Evan had helpfully secreted in his hand luggage along with a loaf of brown bread and six tomatoes that would have gone off in the time they were going to be away. 'If you make Callum work hard to get you back, he will work hard at keeping you too.'

'Hear, hear,' said Evan, who had mellowed with the brandy and a reviving tomato sandwich. 'I think of you as my little sister too, you know. I don't want you throwing yourself away on someone who doesn't appreciate you. You deserve the best.'

I held that thought close through another sleepless night, though it wasn't my concerns about Callum that kept me awake for once. Clare had not been kidding about Evan's night-time noises. The way he snored really put her horrific nocturnal honking into perspective. Compared with Evan's fog-horn-style exhalations, Clare's hundred-decibel snores were like the snuffles of a newborn kitten. I moved into the vestibule of the room, where the wardrobes were, but I could still hear Evan through a closed door, earplugs and a pillow. No wonder Clare had so enjoyed a week in my flat.

* * *

I got maybe fifteen minutes' worth of decent rest that night, but the adrenaline of having told Callum he had to work to get back into my heart kept me feeling pretty good when I woke. When Callum texted me again at eight in the morning, to tell me that he'd had a sleepless night, I was overjoyed. It wasn't just the dual carriageway outside his window that had kept him awake, he said, but the thought of how much he had missed out on by letting me go away on my own.

Callum's text brought happy tears to my eyes. I told him I had been thinking about him too.

'Can I come over to your hotel now?' was his next text.

Had Clare been awake, she probably would have had me hold out for a little while longer, but I texted to let him know that I was already up and couldn't wait to see him. We agreed to meet by the pool.

I was so excited. The romantic nature of his text, saying he'd been thinking about how much he'd missed, convinced me that we were heading for a breakthrough. Callum and I had never really talked about us with any degree of seriousness before. Sure, I thought that we had, but over our week of being broken up, I had come to realise just how superficial our relationship had been. I'd realised I didn't know Callum's views on so many things and he was in the dark about my opinions too. We hadn't talked about a future beyond this summer holiday. He would change the subject when I talked about the lease on my flat and how much easier it would be to afford somewhere decent if there were two people to pay the rent. It's little wonder I didn't dare raise the really big stuff like marriage and kids.

Right now, that morning, things were going to

change. Since Callum announced that he would come to Majorca after all, I had been receiving a virtual pep talk from Hannah via text. She told me that I had Callum on the run. My going away without him had shown him that he didn't know me as well as he thought and that had hooked him in again. I would probably never find myself in a stronger position where he was concerned and thus I had to take advantage of that fact when setting out my conditions for getting back together.

'Remember,' she wrote, 'Anne Boleyn got Henry the Eighth to change the religion of a whole country by refusing to sleep with him before she got a ring on her finger.'

I didn't want Callum to wage war against the Vatican on my behalf, but I did want him to consider moving our relationship forward properly at last. I wanted to meet his family and I wanted him at least to think about moving in with me as soon as his lease ended (in a couple of months, I knew). After that? Maybe, just maybe our living together would go so well that Callum would start thinking about the sort of steps that involved serious paperwork: mortgages, marriage . . .

I forwarded Callum's text to Hannah. She agreed that it was possible that Callum would agree to everything I suggested, provided I did not sleep with him first.

Oh, that bit was going to be hard. When Callum appeared by the pool that morning, he was wearing my favourite of his shirts, a soft blue number that made him look both gentle and super-masculine at the same time. He was one of very few men who actually look good in shorts. When he sat down beside me, I had a very strong urge to put my hand on his knee, but I

didn't. Instead, I was perfectly polite. I let him kiss me
on the cheek. We ordered coffee and pastries for breakfast. He told me about the hotel he had ended up in,
which was fine apart from its unfortunate location.
There were no bedbugs and the only mosquitoes he
saw were already squashed on the wall.

'I'm sorry you had to go looking for somewhere so
late.'

'It's OK. You were right,' he added. 'I was pissed off
at having to find somewhere else to stay, but when it
comes down to it, I was the one who pulled out of the
holiday at the last minute. There's no reason why you
or your sister should put yourselves out for me.'

He was making me melt all over again.

Later, I applied suntan lotion to his back. Those
muscles. I remembered them so well. It was hard not
to fall upon them with kisses. Just touching them sent
shivers of delight all over my body. When Callum
returned the favour, I felt weak with pleasure. When
we finally did get to spend the night together, it was
going to be one of the best nights of our relationship
so far.

Chapter Thirty-Five

We settled down for a day by the pool. It was everything I had dreamed it would be when Hannah first told me about Puerto Bona. Callum and I picked two sunbeds side by side and lay there all morning in companionable silence. I had decided it would be a good idea to spend some time simply chilling out together before we started to tackle the elephant in the room that was our break-up. From time to time, Callum would reach across the gap between us to grab my hand and give it a squeeze. I'd give him a smile as wide as a melon slice in return. Everything was exactly as it should be.

Evan and Clare joined us briefly at around ten o'clock. They didn't stay long. Evan wanted to see some of the sights that Clare had been texting about that week. For Evan, holidays had to have an element of culture or self-improvement. Topping up a suntan wasn't enough for him. While Evan went back up to the room to get a guidebook, Clare showed me how her beach bag was full of bread rolls and apples that Evan had purloined from the breakfast buffet.

'He's determined not to spend a penny more than we have to.'

I commiserated.

Evan returned with the guidebook and a sunhat. He plonked it on Clare's head.

'You're not burning your nose on my watch,' he said.

Clare rolled her eyes, but I thought it was rather sweet of him to think of it.

While Evan and Clare ate their bread rolls on a bench somewhere, Callum and I had a lovely lunch in the poolside bar. Delicious salad with local ham and a perfectly chilled white wine. In the afternoon, we moved on to cocktails and beer. I drifted into a doze listening to the music from the bar: a series of smoochy summer tunes. I was in heaven.

It was all going perfectly until about three o'clock.

'There's a guy over there keeps staring at you,' said Callum.

'What?'

'That guy. He keeps looking at you.'

'Looking at me?' That sounded improbable. I turned to see who on earth Callum might be talking about.

'Which guy?' I asked.

'That one in the red shirt. I recognise him from somewhere.'

And the guy in the red shirt had definitely recognised *me*. I sat up in surprise. The guy waved.

'He definitely thinks he knows you,' said Callum.

'I don't think so,' I said. 'Perhaps he's got me mixed up with someone else.' This I did not want to have to explain, but Tom the paramedic was already walking round the pool to say 'hello'.

'Sophie!' He looked delighted to see me.

'Er . . .' I clutched my beach towel to my chest.

'I thought it was you,' he said.

My brain went blank at exactly the wrong moment. What should I do? My instinct was to pretend he'd got the wrong girl, but that wasn't going to work. He had already addressed me by name. And now he was standing there grinning, waiting to be introduced to Callum, who was glaring into his beer. It was his third bottle of beer since the bottle of wine we'd finished at lunchtime.

'Oh . . . Tom,' I said. 'What a surprise.'

'You're telling me. I didn't expect you to be here. And . . .' He looked towards Callum expectantly. Callum said nothing. He didn't even meet Tom's eye. He took another swig from his beer bottle.

'This is Tom,' I said. 'This is Callum.'

Callum nodded but didn't look up. Meanwhile, I was very careful not to meet any part of Tom's body with my eyes except for his own steady blue gaze.

'How long are you here for?' Tom asked.

'Until next Wednesday.'

'That's great. Have you signed up for any day trips?'

Oh, no, Tom wasn't taking the hint from Callum's unfriendly body language. He was going to stay.

'I'm going for a swim,' said Callum.

Callum got up walked straight past Tom to the pool, almost but not quite brushing against him. Unmistakably aggressive. I'd seen him like that a couple of times before when we were out clubbing and I got chatted up, but this was just small talk, in broad daylight. I looked after Callum, hoping he would turn back to look so I could reassure him with a smile.

'I'm sorry,' said Tom, watching Callum go. 'He seems a bit upset.'

'No, I'm sorry,' I replied. 'I don't know what's got into him. He's not normally like that.'

Though honestly, now that I came to think about it, Callum was often like that.

Callum jumped into the pool and began to churn the water angrily as he counted out lengths. Tom and I watched him for a moment or two; then Tom turned back to me. His smile this time was wide and genuine. I allowed myself to grin back now that Callum couldn't see me.

'I thought I spotted you this morning, but I convinced myself it wasn't you. You didn't say you were going to be here, when we talked about Puerto Bona last week.'

'I didn't know I would be here,' I said truthfully. 'It was sort of a last-minute thing. After you'd gone, my sister and I said, "Why don't we have a holiday too?" After all that drama with the fire, I felt we deserved one.'

'Good idea,' said Tom.

'So,' I asked, 'are you actually staying here? In this hotel?'

Tom nodded. 'I love it. It's supposed to be the best one in town.'

That was what Hannah had told me. It was the reason I had booked it. The infinity pool. The poolside bar. The restaurant. The view of the mountains behind. Hannah had promised me they were fabulous, and they were.

'I didn't see you yesterday.'

'We were on a day trip to the Caves of Drach. Didn't get back till after dinner.'

'Any good?'

'Quite romantic. We went to a great bar last night, the Palacio Blanco. It was pretty good, apart from all the James Blunt they seemed to play.'

I found myself wondering who made up his 'we'.

'Are you here with your girlfriend?' I asked, trying to make it sound casual.

Tom turned towards the direction he'd come from and I strained to see if there was some stunning girl showing as much disdain for me as Callum had done for Tom. There were a couple of girls in that direction, but they didn't look like the kind of girl I had imagined him with. Neither were they looking back in my direction, as they might have done were they curious, in a girlfriend way, about whom he was talking to. And Tom confirmed, 'I haven't got a girlfriend. I'm here with my mates.'

Given that I had flown to Majorca for the express purpose of saving my relationship, I shouldn't have been interested, let alone slightly pleased to hear that.

'That's nice,' I said.

Tom was looking over my shoulder now, towards the pool again. I glanced in the same direction and caught Callum glaring back. He had finished swimming and was hanging on to the edge of the pool, staring towards us as though he hoped we might turn into stone. This time Tom did take the hint.

'Well, it's great to see you. I'll probably see you around.' Tom nodded and went back to join his pals.

With Tom gone, Callum got out of the pool and sat back down on his sunbed with a harrumph, dripping pool water all over my paperback as he did so.

'Who was that?' he asked.

'Just some guy. I've seen him around the hotel.'

'Really? You've just seen him around,' he said. 'Hannah showed me the photos.'

'What photos?' I asked uselessly.

'The photos of you and that bloke on the beach. Looking very cosy indeed. Looking very touchy-feely.'

'The photos on Facebook?'

'Yeah. I'm surprised you hadn't changed your status to "in an open relationship", you put up photos of so many guys.'

Hadn't I said that Callum would get the wrong idea?

'No wonder he was so pleased to see you,' Callum continued. 'Those photos made me look a right idiot. Do you know how many people emailed me to ask if I'd seen them? Didn't you tell him you had a boyfriend?'

'Of course I did,' I said. Later, I would be disappointed in myself for not having said, 'But last week I didn't have a boyfriend, did I?'

'You didn't introduce me as your boyfriend.'

'I told him you were my boyfriend while you were swimming.'

'Really?'

Callum lay back on his sunbed and draped a towel over his face. The conversation was over.

I rolled onto my side, facing away from him. I would just have to hope that we didn't bump into Tom again. It was entirely possible that having seen how badly Callum had reacted, he would give us a wide berth in any case. It was a shame. I would have liked to have been able to get to know Tom better, but I also wanted to keep Callum in my life. After all, I had gone to such lengths to hang on to him so far. If Tom and Callum got into conversation and the real story behind our acquaintance came out, then that week in hiding would have been for nothing. I would have to warn Clare about Tom's presence in the hotel. I sent her a text.

'Texting your new friend?' Callum snarled.

'No. I . . .' I put my phone in my bag.

*   *   *

Now that I had Callum by my side, I hadn't been half so diligent in keeping track of my email traffic as I had been the week before. Back in London, however, Hannah and Alison wanted to know what was going on. The whole office wanted to know what was going on. Were Callum and I officially back together or not?

The answer was, I wasn't sure. Callum had complained that I hadn't introduced him to Tom as my boyfriend. Did that mean he thought we were together? Had he changed his mind after discovering Tom was staying in the same hotel? Since meeting Tom, Callum had barely grunted in my direction.

Thankfully, at around five o'clock, Callum started speaking to me again and said that he wanted to go upstairs to the room I was sharing with my sister and Evan. Clare had texted to say they had driven to Manacor, in the centre of the island, to visit a cultured-pearl factory. They wouldn't be back for hours. I took Callum to the room.

'Let's have a siesta,' said Callum.

He started undoing the ties on my bikini before we were even through the door. We made love on the roll-up bed. It was every bit as wonderful as I remembered and Callum seemed in a much better mood right afterwards.

'Let's get a hotel room together tonight,' he insisted.

I agreed that we should. Apart from anything else, it would be a relief to spend the night with someone who didn't snore, except when he'd had a great many beers. As luck would have it, the receptionist told us that another room at the hotel had become available for the rest of the week. The couple staying in it had flown back to London after the husband slipped a disc by trying to limbo-dance in one of the clubs. Callum put his credit card down at once and we moved all our luggage into the unfortunate couple's room, so recently vacated, as soon as we were able. We celebrated by making love again. It was even better than before now that Callum seemed more relaxed. I dared to think he had forgotten all about the incident by the pool already. The rest of the holiday would be wonderful, I was sure.

'Callum and I are definitely back together,' I confirmed when I texted Hannah that evening.

'Great news,' said Hannah. 'Though big shame about your Facebook photo friend.' She meant Tom. 'Alison wants to know if he lives in London. If so, could you set her up on a blind date when you get back?'

Chapter Thirty-Six

The following day, Clare and Evan spent the afternoon at a craft market in the old town. Clare had told me she hoped to buy some decent presents to take back to England there, but I wasn't in the least bit surprised when she and Evan returned to the poolside bar empty-handed.

'There were some nice leather goods,' said Clare. 'Some pretty purses and handbags.'

'It was all rubbish,' Evan announced. 'I wouldn't give any of it houseroom. Besides, you've already got hundreds of bags,' he reminded his fiancée. 'They take up the whole of the spare bedroom.'

'I haven't got any bags from Majorca,' Clare protested. 'Anyway, I was only thinking of getting a purse. Just a little thing. Something to remind me of this trip when we're back in grey old London.'

'Isn't your memory good enough?' Evan asked. 'You took enough photos on your iPhone.'

'I know . . . You would have liked those purses,' Clare half whispered to me.

'Why do girls have to buy so much stuff?' Evan asked no one in particular.

Because we were sitting at a table that belonged to the pool bar, a waiter was soon over to see if we wanted to buy a drink and Evan reiterated his view that the drinks at the hotel were way too expensive and he was going upstairs to have a drink in the room.

'Are you coming?' he asked Clare.

That she didn't want to was clear from her face – she was happy in the sun – but Evan was ready to leave. Clare followed a few steps behind. Her shoulders were slumped.

'I don't know what she's doing with that boring schmuck,' said Callum.

At least bitching about my sister's fiancé got Callum off the subject of my new Facebook friend.

I had caught a glimpse of Tom as we entered the breakfast room that morning, but otherwise I had not seen him all day. His group of friends were not in their place by the pool either. Perhaps they had taken another day trip. I tried not to wonder too hard what they might be up to. Callum was far happier that afternoon. He was as attentive and affectionate as he had ever been. So much so that I asked him whether he might like to talk about our relationship and what happened while he was up in Newcastle to make him want to break things off.

'Not now, Soph. Not when we're having such a lovely day.'

I let it slide and the day passed in a mellow haze of sunshine and sangria. Maybe he was right. It didn't seem so important to talk when we were having such a good time. And then Clare and Evan came back downstairs for a swim and our window of privacy was gone.

Clare sulked her way through thirty lengths. Evan and I were briefly left alone while Callum went to the bar.

'Is your sister all right?' Evan asked me. 'I mean, she's been in a right mood this afternoon. Has she said anything to you about worrying about the wedding or the house since she's been out here?'

I didn't know what I could do but reassure him.

'She hasn't said anything to me,' I lied. 'I'm sure that everything is fine. '

'Time of the month?' Evan suggested.

'Never say that to her.'

'Maybe it's because I said she shouldn't buy another bag,' Evan mused.

He asked me to tell her that he was going to the supermarket to buy more water and left the poolside deep in thought.

That evening, the plan was that we would have dinner at a little place on the seafront with Clare and Evan (chosen by Evan for its budget prices) before going to the Palacio Blanco for real, for the very first time. Not that Evan and Callum would know that. As far as they were concerned, we were Palacio Blanco regulars.

Over dinner we four shared two bottles of rosé. Evan, Mr Sensible as always, didn't have much. He wanted to keep a clear head to make sure that we all crossed the road without looking in the wrong direction or something like that. Clare, mindful that Evan might disapprove if she got too drunk without him, also toned down her level of consumption, which meant that both Callum and I probably drank more than we should have done, especially when you took into account the cocktails we'd had while waiting for Clare to finish dressing for the night. Clare took for ever to get ready. I wondered if the sheer volume of luggage she'd brought with her made the task of choosing something to wear more difficult.

When we got there at ten o'clock, the Palacio Blanco was already heaving. Now that we were at the bar for real, I was struck by how much louder and busier it was than I had ever imagined from the tiny slice of it we had watched via the webcam. The décor that had looked slightly tacky in daylight, when Clare and I poked our noses through the gate on the day we arrived in town, was entirely more magical in the glow of fairylights and candles.

I took in our fellow partiers. A new bunch of Brits had arrived that day. You could tell that they were newly arrived because so many of them were as pink and sore as freshly boiled lobsters. Still, they were determined to have a good time. That much was clear. Evan put a protective arm round Clare as they negotiated the crowd together. I followed behind Callum and found myself being separated from him by a determined waiter who cut across my path.

The band was playing James Blunt as we walked in.

'What's with this shitty music?' Callum complained.

Evan gave Callum a stern look. Evan never swore. He'd even managed not to swear when he cut his thumb while fitting the security chain to my front door back in Clapham. Leaving Callum to complain about the music, Evan found a table near the wall. There were only three chairs. Evan gestured that Clare and I should take two of them. Callum slumped down onto the third. By the time Evan had managed to find a chair for himself from the other side of the room, Callum was on to his second beer. He had ordered two at once.

The next hour was tense to say the least. Evan's

disapproval of Callum was obvious to everyone except Callum himself. Clare, sipping a Diet Coke by now, looked as though she would rather be anywhere else. Much as I wanted Callum to think that I was on his side, I had long given up trying to match his drinking. The way he was narrowing his eyes at the swirling crowd made me nervous. There was no conversation. No one even attempted it.

Callum broke the silence by saying, 'Well, this is dull. Whose idea was it to come here?'

'You didn't exactly come up with many alternatives,' said Evan.

'They've been here all week,' said Callum, jerking his thumb at me and my sister. 'I thought they knew where all the action was.'

'I like this place perfectly well,' said Evan, reaching across the table to give Clare's hand a squeeze. 'Good choice, girls.'

It was sweet of Evan to try to defend us, but his efforts only made Callum seem more determined not to enjoy himself.

'I'm having a very good night,' said Evan.

Callum responded, 'The beer's expensive. The band should have retired ten years ago, but then I suppose this music is from your era, right, Evan?'

I wasn't at all surprised when Evan announced that he and Clare were going to have an early night. Clare, for once, didn't disagree with him. She squeezed me lightly on the shoulder as she wriggled out from behind her chair.

'Good luck,' she mouthed.

'I'll be fine,' I assured her, though I had no idea if I would.

'Sophie' – Evan leaned down to whisper in my ear – 'you have my mobile number. Promise me that you won't walk home alone. Call me and I will come and fetch you. Even if we've already gone to bed.'

'I'll be fine,' I insisted. 'Why would I have to walk back to the hotel on my own?'

'I don't like leaving you here alone with Callum when he's so drunk. Make sure you remember to look the right way when you're crossing the road.'

Good old Evan, playing dad. Clare came back to give me a hug.

'I can deal with it,' I said.

Callum didn't see our exchange. He was too busy ordering more alcohol. When it arrived, we sat in silence. I was grateful for the volume of the music, which disguised the fact that we had not exchanged a word for the best part of an hour. This was not exactly how I had imagined my first night at the Palacio Blanco would be. The bar as a whole had a wonderful atmosphere. The live band filled the place with energy, but Callum's mood was creating a black hole in our corner of the room.

Suddenly, Callum straightened up. He puffed out his chest. I had seen that look before and I wasn't very happy to see it back again. The last time Callum had puffed out his chest like that was when he got into an unpleasant altercation over a parking space one afternoon in Brighton. I'd spent the whole time cowering in the car with my face in my hands. Trouble was in the house.

'What's he looking at?' Callum snarled.

'Who?'

'Your mate.'

I followed Callum's gaze to the other side of the room. There stood Tom and his friends. Tom had his back to us. If he had been looking in our direction, he wasn't looking now.

'Shall we go back to the hotel too?' I suggested in an attempt to divert Callum's attention. 'It'd be really nice if we could get a sort of early night so we're all fresh and rested before that coach trip to the Caves of Drach tomorrow morning.'

'I don't want to go on a coach trip,' said Callum. He was still staring at Tom's back. There was a lot of it to stare at. No wonder Callum was twitchy. But surely he wasn't going to make a big deal out of it.

'Where did you meet that dick anyway? How much time did you spend with him before I arrived?'

'Hardly any time at all. It was Clare who got talking to him. We went to a beach party near Magaluf,' I lied. 'It's no big deal. My sister was doing most of the talking,' I tried. 'You know what she's like when she's had a couple of cocktails. Maybe she was trying to do a bit of match-making to cheer me up, but I wasn't interested. I was only thinking about you and now you're here and everything is wonderful and . . .'

Callum wasn't listening to me. His eyes had narrowed. His knuckles, clenched around his beer bottle, were white with tension.

'Callum,' I tried to bring his attention back to me. 'Callum, please.'

He did not respond to his name. It really was as though he couldn't hear me any more. He sank the rest of his beer and got up, pushing his sleeves up his arms as though in preparation for some dirty work. It was the moment I had dreaded. Ordinarily, when Callum got drunk and antsy, at least one of his mates was around to calm him down and keep him from going too far. It had to be one of his male friends, someone who could hold him back without making him feel emasculated. My pleas just did not have the same effect as they might have done coming from one of the guys. Callum wouldn't take any notice of me.

Tom had no idea what, or who, was about to hit him. As far as he was concerned, he had answered an emergency call at my house and stopped by for a drink afterwards. Where was the problem with that? He had no idea that the fantasy holiday Clare and I had been enjoying went any further than our makeshift beach. He didn't know the history of my relationship with Callum and how much depended on keeping the events of the previous week secret. He was simply sipping his beer with his friends, enjoying his holiday, when Callum strode up to him and attempted to land a punch on his jaw.

The punch went nowhere near. Unfortunately for Callum, the strange truth behind my acquaintance with Tom the paramedic meant that I had not got round to telling my boyfriend that Tom's hobby was taekwondo. He stopped Callum's flying fist without even turning to see it coming. At the speed of light, he had Callum's arm twisted up behind his back. Then Callum's knees buckled beneath him and Tom gently deposited him on the floor.

The club bouncers were quickly at the scene of Callum's humiliation. I hung back. Tom was shrugging and expressing confusion. His mates confirmed that Callum's attack had been unprovoked unless . . . One of them pointed across the room towards me. I wanted to sink down to the floor in sympathy with Callum and in embarrassment for myself. What I knew I had to do right then was go to Callum's defence and tell the bouncers that there had been a misunderstanding. There was no need to throw Callum out so bodily. We would leave quietly and never return to the club again. The important thing was to get out of there before Tom mentioned the night of the fire and the Clapham beach club.

'Callum' – I tucked my arm through his – 'let's go.'

But Callum was like a terrier and he would not let it go. As soon as he was back on his feet, he was swinging his fists again.

Tom wasn't very much taller than Callum, but he was definitely wider. He didn't even bother to move away from Callum's punches. They hardly touched him. Callum might as well have been a four-year-old trying to knock out his dad. By now, the bouncers were just looking on in amusement as, at last, Tom caught one of Callum's fists and put him into another lock.

'Give it up. I would knock you into next Tuesday,' he said, 'but your girlfriend deserves better than to have to see that. She deserves better than you.'

Callum strained against Tom's arms until Tom let him go so abruptly that Callum fell to the floor.

'Come on,' I begged Callum as he got back to his feet once more. I was terrified that he was going to square up to Tom again. It was clearly an unequal fight. 'Let's go.'

'I'd do as she says,' a bouncer suggested.

'You haven't seen the last of me.' Callum stabbed a finger at Tom's chest, but for the time being he had to concede defeat and stalked out onto the street with me skittering along behind. He showed no consideration whatsoever for my high-heeled wedges.

'Callum. Wait. Wait!'

As I turned back, I caught Tom's eye. He was looking at me. He wasn't, as I might have expected, crowing about his encounter and accepting the back-slaps of his mates. Instead, he looked concerned.

'Are you OK?' he mouthed after me. 'I'm really sorry.'

'Me too,' I mouthed back. Then I gave a little embarrassed wave and rushed on out after Callum.

Chapter Thirty-Seven

Callum refused to talk to me on the walk back to the hotel. He wouldn't let me hold his arm. When we got to the main road, he dashed out into the traffic ahead of me without looking. When a car screeched to a halt just feet away from him, Callum thumped his fist on the windscreen.

Once at the hotel, while I got ready for bed, he went out onto the balcony and sank another beer from the stash he'd bought at the grocery shop. When I asked him if he wanted to come inside and go to bed, thinking that I could perhaps cuddle him out of his vile temper, he merely growled at me. I had never seen him so angry.

Eventually, I got into bed alone. I didn't know what else to do. There was no talking to him. It was another hour before he crawled in alongside me. He said nothing. He must have thought I was asleep. I thought it best I didn't tell him otherwise. In the morning, he would be in a better mood, I was sure. In the morning, he might even laugh about what had happened that night. I would explain to him that Tom was a martial-arts expert so he shouldn't feel in any way embarrassed for it having been such an unfair fight. Though he should feel embarrassed for having started it . . .

In the small hours, I rolled onto my back and found myself staring at the ceiling. Wide awake. I went over that evening's events. Callum had been short-tempered with my sister and Evan from the moment Evan suggested a budget dinner. He'd drunk too much at the restaurant and the club. He'd tried to bait Evan until Evan decided to leave. He swung the first punch at Tom with no provocation. Looking at it that way, why did I have to try to mollify Callum at all? Shouldn't he be apologising to me?

But I loved him. And that meant that I soon found a way to put the blame on myself again. I should have known that Callum wouldn't like that club. I knew what kind of music they played. And I should have guessed that Tom would be there. He'd told me he liked the place. I could have made sure we had a better night out.

When morning came, it was clear that sleep had not mellowed Callum's mood at all. When I rolled over to kiss him, he pushed me off and my insecurity grew. I had to apologise. Callum wasn't going to.

'I'm sorry about last night,' I said, trying to put my arm round him.

Callum grunted in response. He got out of bed and locked himself in the bathroom.

Obviously unable to follow him in there, I took myself out onto the balcony. There were already people down by the pool, setting up for the day, looking happy and relaxed. Meanwhile, I had rarely felt quite so tense. As I watched my fellow holidaymakers shaking out their beach towels and taking an early dip in the pool, I wrestled with the idea of telling Callum the truth about the previous week's 'holiday'. It was the only way I could explain my knowing Tom in such a way as he wouldn't be jealous or suspect that I'd done anything I shouldn't. On the one hand, it made sense to tell the truth. On the other hand . . . I couldn't. If I told Callum, then Evan would find out too and I had promised Clare on my life that I would keep her secret. I didn't want to be the cause of any break-up. No matter what Clare had said when we were back in Clapham, I liked Evan. He had been so touchingly concerned for me the night before.

Callum remained in the bathroom. Not knowing quite what to do with myself, I checked my email.

I discovered that Hannah had sent me a message, which included an attachment.

'You made page six of the *Sun*.'

Page six of the *Sun*? What on earth was she talking about? I clicked on the link to the attachment and waited impatiently for the thing to download. The wifi coverage at the hotel was spotty and slow, but eventually the newspaper page that Hannah had scanned for me materialised on the screen and became focused.

Oh my God, I really had made page six of the *Sun*. And so had my sister, Clare. There we were together in glorious Technicolor standing in the backyard of my flat. Our feet may have been upon sand, but there was no mistaking the brick wall of a Victorian terraced house behind us.

One of my neighbours must have provided the photograph, which had obviously been taken on the night of the beach party. I read the article that accompanied the picture and, of course, though it was wonderful and entirely complimentary, detailing as it did our rescue of Mrs Kenman, the text immediately gave the lie to our story that we had been in Majorca for the past week. I could not be pleased or proud to read that my sister and I had been nominated for a bravery award, which would be presented by the prime minister's wife at a do in a posh London hotel. I felt red hot with embarrassment. It had never occurred to me that Mrs Kenman's chip-pan fire would be news outside our street, but of course Mrs Kenman's grandson, Paul Kenman, the regional weather forecaster, had alerted the media.

I suppose it was inevitable. Paul Kenman might have just written a letter to thank us, or sent some flowers, but this was an opportunity from him to get *his* name in the papers as well as ours, and for a regional weatherman who was determined to go national before his thirtieth birthday, it was an opportunity not to be missed. Thus the truth came out.

I knew that Hannah's next email would be full of questions, and of course she had tweeted the link so that my mother would be bound to see it the moment she logged on. Worse still, Hannah had forwarded the same link to Callum, copying me in and entitling her email 'Aren't you proud of your brave girlfriend?'

Talk about no good deed going unpunished. Having kept our secret safe by going so far as to fly to Majorca, my sister and I were about to be unmasked by a guiltily grateful weatherman who claimed on his own Twitter feed that he had been beating himself up all week because he had promised to visit his grandmother the night of the fire but was held up at a Met Office conference. His determination to make amends by nominating Clare and me for a bravery award was going to be our downfall. I closed Hannah's email. The only possible option for keeping Callum in the dark just a little longer was to hide his iPhone. If I could just kick it under the bed, it would give me a few minutes to get my story worked out, but as I reached for Callum's iPhone, he came out of the bathroom and saw me.

'What are you doing?'

'Oh. I thought that was my phone,' I blustered. 'I got them mixed up.'

Callum took his own phone back. He immediately checked his mail.

How was I going to get out of this one? If there had been even the slightest chance that Callum might not even have bothered to open the attachment, Hannah made sure that his interest was guaranteed.

'This is so surreal,' Hannah wrote in another email, copying him in and adding yet another helpful link. 'Firstly, because I can't believe you didn't tell us you did something so heroic. Secondly, because I thought you were supposed to be in Majorca last week, not Clapham. What bit did they get wrong? The date of the rescue or your name? Why didn't you tell us that you rescued an old lady? Now that's a Stockwell Lifts PR story I wouldn't have had trouble finding a home for. In fact, can I put it in the monthly newsletter? Makes a change from endless guff about eco-efficiency targets.'

There was no point trying to pretend that the newspaper had got the dates wrong. The reference to the 'hottest day of the year so far' was further evidence that when Clare and I were supposed to be in Majorca, we were rescuing an old lady from a possible inferno in the flat upstairs from mine, in Clapham Old Town.

'What is this?'

Callum scowled at Hannah's message.

There was only one thing for it. I had to tell Callum the truth. But if I had hoped that he would be so impressed by my heroics when faced with the fire that the rest of the story would be irrelevant, I was out of luck. His expression, which was pretty miserable already, only got worse as the tale unfolded.

'You mean to tell me that you rescued an old lady in London and you were only pretending to be in Majorca for the whole of last week?'

'Yes,' I said. 'Talk about Fate. If we'd been out here, Clare wouldn't have seen the smoke . . .' Please be impressed by the rescue, I begged him silently. Please don't focus on the lie.

'So you hid in your flat and then flew out here just eight hours before me?'

'Yes.' I hung my head.

There was a pause while Callum decided what to say next. Unfortunately, it was the lie that he decided to focus on.

'That's so dishonest,' he said at last. 'Why on earth would you pretend to be in Majorca when you were really just at home?'

'I got the idea from you, when you told me that you'd been in London but pretended you were still in Newcastle so you could get some time to yourself,' I reminded him.

'What?'

'You did the same thing. You said you were in one place when really you were hiding out at home.'

'That's different.'

'How is it different?'

'I didn't post about it on Facebook, for a start. I didn't tweet about my whereabouts to all and sundry. I didn't go through some elaborate charade to convince people that I was somewhere I wasn't. I just shut the door and kept quiet. There's a huge difference between my wanting a weekend to myself for once—'

'Three weekends!'

'Three weekends to myself, then. There's still a huge difference between what I did and you lying to everyone about being on holiday. And your sister too. Why did she go along with it?'

'She wanted some time to herself, I suppose.'

'Does Evan know you weren't really in Puerto Bona last week?'

'No.' I shook my head.

'What do you think he's going to say about it when he finds out?'

I could only imagine how the scenario would play out between Clare and Evan. There was no chance that he wouldn't find out. It was a matter of time before someone he knew saw the *Sun* and asked him what had happened. He was unlikely to be any happier than Callum. In fact, he had every reason to be *less* happy, since I had got myself into the situation by default, but Clare had actively lied to him from the start. The only possible silver lining was that Evan would be happy to know Clare had spent less of their savings than he assumed she had.

'Callum, I'm sorry. Of course I wasn't going to pretend to be in Majorca, but Hannah emailed me to say that you thought I had gone and that the idea that I would get a flight on my own had changed your mind about me. She convinced me that if I didn't pretend to go away,' I said, 'I would have lost you for ever.'

As it was, of course by then I knew I had lost him anyway. I could tell from the look in his eyes. All the softness was gone from them. If it had ever come back after the previous evening's embarrassment.

'You're insane. You know you're going to be a total laughing stock when you get back to work. Hannah's probably told everyone in the company by now. You've made me look like an idiot too. I believed you were on holiday. I came out here because Hannah said you had found a new bloke. I saw the pictures of you on the beach. How did you get those?'

'Eight sacks of sand and a little creativity.' I tried to make light of it.

Callum didn't crack a smile. His face was uglier than I had ever seen it. I realised that how things looked was very important to him. He was all about image and me fooling him did not fit his image at all.

'The girls in the office treated me like some kind of pariah for dumping you. Every time I went to make myself a cup of tea, they'd be round the kettle like witches, talking about what a great time you were having in Puerto Bona despite how badly I'd treated you. If only they'd known the truth. At least now they'll know I wasn't wrong to break up with you. They'll know you're insane as well as clingy.' He rattled on.

At no point in the conversation did Callum say that he was proud or impressed or even plain surprised that I had risked my life for the woman who lived upstairs. He was only concerned with how this was going to look to the people we had to work with.

'Pretending to be in Majorca to convince me to take you back. You're touched.' He tapped my forehead with his finger. There was more menace in that gesture than I cared to admit.

'You lied to me,' he continued. 'Then you stripped

off in your backyard with some paramedic for a weirdo fake photo session to keep up the pretence.'

'I had all my clothes on,' I pointed out. Callum wasn't interested.

'If you think I believe that you didn't open your legs for him . . . I hope you at least faked an orgasm too.'

Callum directed that comment at me with such venom he might as well have spat in my face. Now he turned away from me. He pulled his suitcase out of the wardrobe and started to throw his clothes into it. I went into the bathroom and splashed water over my cheeks. He looked like he was getting ready to go. How could I stop him? Did I want to stop him? With him no longer right in my face, I finally gathered the courage to say something in return. I marched back into the bedroom.

'I didn't sleep with Tom. I didn't sleep with anybody. But in any case,' I said at last, 'what business is it of yours? You dumped me. I was technically single. You can't have it both ways.'

'You've embarrassed me,' said Callum quietly.

'I embarrassed you? How do you think I felt last night when you threw that punch? You were drunk and mean and out of control.'

Callum's mouth dropped open. He looked shocked. I'd surprised myself. I'd wanted to say something along those lines for the longest time. Though I had barely admitted it to myself up until then, Callum was at the very least drunk and mean most Saturday nights. I'd put up with it. I'd put up with it because I wanted to be in a relationship and because I could hardly believe my luck that someone as good-looking and popular as Callum could want to be in a relationship with me. I'd willfully ignored his unpleasant traits and the way they made me feel for the sake of not being single. But was this any better? I'd dedicated so much of my energy to make him feel happy and now he was calling me a slut. At last, I had had enough. I told him exactly what I thought about his temper and his selfishness. I told him that I had enjoyed meeting Tom because he was someone with more on his mind than Hugo Boss suits. I hardly drew breath until I'd got it all out there.

'You dumped me right before my birthday,' was my last complaint.

'And now I'm dumping you again,' he said.

'Great,' I responded. 'You do what you like. I'll see you back at work.'

Callum hesitated. He hadn't expected me to say that. Even after I'd told him what I really thought of him, I think he'd expected me to protest his disappearance. I'd moved away from the script.

'I hope you don't have to pay too much to change your ticket,' I added.

'Fuck you.' He picked up his case and left the room, slamming the door behind him.

'Fine,' I said. 'It's really fine. *Bon voyage*.'

I sat down on the bed.

Chapter Thirty-Eight

So I was back at square one. Dumped again.

Callum had left with such determination in his stride that I knew he wasn't kidding. But this time, I decided, I wasn't kidding either. I would not try to change Callum's mind.

For the whole of that week in the flat I had been concentrating on how I could get him back. I had got him back, albeit briefly, and it really hadn't been that much fun. Though he had been superficially sorry for dumping me the week before, he hadn't really given me any explanation for his behaviour. He hadn't made a special effort to make up for missing my birthday. He hadn't really wanted to know how unhappy I'd been and how we could change things going forward. He had been arrogant and foolish when it came to Tom. And rude. Downright vile, in fact.

The Callum I had seen the previous evening at the Palacio Blanco was not one I particularly cared to spend any more time with. The only reason it hadn't kicked off that way before was because his mates were usually there to hold him back and because I had spent the duration of our relationship on eggshells, making sure he had no cause to get into a fight for me.

So, I didn't try to chase him, though I watched him from the balcony as he dragged his case round the pool to the hotel lobby. He didn't look back. I didn't try to call him. I didn't text him. Neither did I text or email Hannah in an attempt to limit the damage to my reputation the story in the news might have caused. The girls at the office would have their chance to laugh at me later on. For now, the most pressing thing on my mind was saving Clare's relationship from the grenade that was that article in the *Sun*.

Perhaps there was still time. I sent Clare a text, asking her to meet me by the pool as soon as possible. I found two empty sunbeds and sat there, picking at my cuticles for what seemed like an age before Clare stepped out into the sun, stretching like a happy cat. She had a big smile on her face. It made me feel bad as I considered the disaster that was about to unfold. Evan was nowhere to be seen.

'How long have we got?' I asked her.

'Oh, ages, I should think. He's sleeping off last night,' she said. 'We were up pretty late.'

'I thought you were going straight home to bed after dinner,' I said.

Clare smiled. 'So did I.'

She settled into her sunbed and waved to attract the attention of a waiter. 'So what's the matter with you?' she asked at last. 'What's with the urgency? Where's the fire?'

'Callum's gone.'

'What?'

'He dumped me again.'

'Oh, Soph.'

She held out her arms to me.

'It's OK. I'm fine about that. The real problem is that he dumped me because he found out our secret.'

Clare didn't yet know about our appearance in the

newspaper. While I opened Hannah's email on my iPhone, I told her why Callum was not with me that day and why I'd probably never see him again outside the confines of Stockwell Lifts.

'Bloody Hannah,' said Clare, as she looked at the incriminating *Sun* article complete with the photograph taken in my backyard.

'I'm sorry,' I said. 'I know this is going to affect things with you and Evan too. Do you think you can stop him from finding out the truth until we work out what to do? You'll have to tell him it was all my fault and I made you do it. I'll never forgive myself if you guys break up because of me.'

Clare shook her head and took my hand. She looked up towards the balcony of the room she and Evan had been sharing that week. As we watched, he shambled out into the sunshine. He was frowning. Was it just a hangover?

'Sophie,' said Clare, 'it's already too late for that.'

'Oh, no.'

This was far worse than being dumped by Callum for a second time. I had so hoped that Clare and Evan would sort things out. I'd been reminded on this trip just how much I liked him, and how much he loved my sister. Was Clare going to use the discovery of our lie as an excuse to get out of the wedding? She seemed strangely calm.

'Last night,' she began, 'as we were walking back to the hotel, Evan took my hand and asked me if I really wanted to go back to the hotel room, since it was still quite early. I told him, honestly for once, that I was actually pissed off to be having another early night when we were supposed to be on holiday. And seeing as how we'd blown half our wedding budget to be in Majorca, we might as well enjoy it. I was expecting him to turn round and tell me that in light of our financial situation, staying out any later would only make things worse, but he said, "You know what, I agree with you. Let's go somewhere nice and have a nightcap." And a nightcap turned into a bottle of champagne to celebrate the one-year anniversary of our engagement. And once he'd had his share of the champagne, I actually persuaded Evan to dance. And once he was dancing, I felt like the guy I fell in love with was back.'

This was terrible. Clare had decided to patch things up and now everything would be destroyed because of me.

Clare sank back into her sunlounger, still looking up at Evan on the balcony. Evan was rubbing his eyes.

'The most important thing is that while we were dancing, he told me he'd known for ages that I was unhappy. He'd been worried stiff about it, but he didn't know how to start turning things round again. He didn't dare say anything to me because he thought it might make things worse. He was scared I was planning to go. I've been a real idiot, assuming that Evan was carrying on in his lunk-headed way, not noticing whether I was happy or sad or about to jump off a cliff.

'Evan asked exactly how unhappy I'd been. He said he really wanted to know how close he had come to losing me. I took a deep breath and told him the truth. I told him that I'd been unhappy enough to spend a week behind closed doors in Clapham. I told him everything. I told him I had a better time confined to your flat than I had done for the rest of the year. He knows about the beach. He knows about the fire, Soph. He even knows about Jason.'

'That you kissed him?'

'That he tried to kiss *me*, but I resisted,' said Clare.

'OK.'

She knew I would keep her secret.

'Anyway, I had to make him realise how serious the situation was, and it seemed that telling him the whole truth really was the only way. I couldn't risk letting another month go by just hoping that something would change. It was all or nothing. Either Evan would understand and prove he was the man I fell in love with or he would freak out and we'd come to the end of the road. He said he understood. I apologised. He apologised too. What he told me last night made me know for sure that he's a good man and he wants us both to be happy. That's all he's ever wanted. We've promised to try to make things better. He knows he's been stressed stupid about money and that all the budgeting has been driving me insane. So I've said I'll scale back my wedding plans and he's sworn that we'll never go without a holiday for so long again.'

'I'm so relieved. I thought that week in my flat was going to be the end of everything for both of us.'

'Our holiday in your flat brought me and Evan back together . . . Hey, gorgeous!' Clare shouted up to Evan on the balcony. He stopped rubbing his eyes and looked down at us. When he saw his darling fiancée, he smiled as though he'd been given the universe.

So Clare and Evan were happy again. Thank God. With Clare gone back inside to help Evan put his suncream on – he believed in getting covered before he even stepped outside – I could concentrate on my own disaster.

But was it such a disaster? Callum had gone, but I was nowhere near as unhappy as I had been a week earlier, when he refused to come on holiday at all. I settled down for another day by the pool, but this time it was going to be a day of not having to worry whether Tom would pitch up across the cool blue water. In fact, I would have been glad to see him. When, a little later, I thought I might have felt a tear coming on, I raised my face towards the sunshine and its golden warmth chased the prospect of salt water away. Forget Callum. Forget the girls at work having a laugh at my expense. Sunshine makes everything better.

The morning progressed. I ordered a tall fruit smoothie and ate ice cream for elevenses. I read my book without interruption. I let the emails pile up on my iPhone. I did not even let Mum's hysterical email entitled 'You could have been killed!!!' spoil my peace.

'I am back in London,' Callum texted at around three o'clock.

'Good,' I texted back. 'I'm glad you had a safe flight.' But that was it. I had no desire to know what he planned to do next. I wasn't going to prolong that morning's discussion. I certainly wasn't going to beg his forgiveness for the holiday charade. I was going to enjoy the rest of my real holiday without him.

'You know what,' I said to Clare as we ordered aperitifs in the pool bar. 'I don't think I'm going to miss him at all.'

When Evan joined us, he ordered a couple of cocktails to help me celebrate my sudden weight loss.

'Weight loss?' I was confused.

'Yep, you've just lost eleven stone of useless fat-headed boyfriend.'

It was the first time in a while I'd heard Evan make a joke. Maybe Clare's dream of an altogether lighter, more fun-filled future could be a reality after all. Indeed, it was Evan who suggested that we go to the Palacio Blanco that night. When he and Clare came downstairs after changing, I was surprised to see she had got her own way on what he was wearing too. His usual buttoned-up polo shirt was gone, replaced by an altogether more continental-looking linen shirt. A pink linen shirt. Slightly creased.

'I pointed it out in the hotel's boutique,' Clare whispered to me as Evan walked in front of us. 'And he went ahead and bought it. He didn't quibble about the colour or the creased look, and I didn't even have to tell him that it would last for ages to make sure he got his money's worth. And look at this.' Clare showed me her new leather handbag, decorated with pretty punched flowers. 'Evan went back to the market and bought this for me while I was sulking in the pool.'

Guessing that we were talking about him, Evan turned round. Clare smiled at him with an expression that could definitely be described as love. Maybe Puerto Bona was as magical as Hannah had suggested all those months ago.

Chapter Thirty-Nine

So we went to the Palacio Blanco. The band was playing as we arrived. The bouncer on the door gave me a knowing nod as we walked in. I had been just a little worried that he wouldn't let me in. I was relieved that I didn't seem to have been barred along with Callum.

Evan found us a table near to the dance floor. We ordered a huge pile of tapas, a big jug of sangria and settled down for the evening. It was wonderful to be in the company of my sister and Evan that night. They seemed completely different people from the couple who had come out the night before. I wondered if Callum's absence had anything to do with the increased level of bonhomie.

Though I was happy that my sister and Evan were so obviously in love again, I was perhaps a little more reflective now that we were in the club. I couldn't help thinking back to the previous evening and how angry Callum had looked when he caught Tom looking at me from across the dance floor. If only Tom were looking at me now that I didn't have to worry about my jealous ex. I scanned the crowd.

'Looking for someone in particular?' my sister asked. Of course she had guessed who. That afternoon, I had told her how flattered I had felt when Tom told Callum that he didn't deserve me. Even when I should have been worried that Tom was going to knock Callum into next Christmas.

'I told you Tom fancied you,' said Clare. This time, I was pleased to hear her say it and asked her to tell me in great detail why she thought that was. What were the signs?

And suddenly there he was. Tom and his friends arrived at a little after nine o'clock. Tom was dressed in a white shirt that made the most of his holiday tan. As he walked in, he seemed to be scanning the room too, and when his eyes fell on me, he smiled. I blushed to the roots of my hair and concentrated on the ice in my margarita.

'Looks like he's arrived,' said Clare.

'We'll stop cramping your style,' said Evan. 'Why don't you stay here and look after our drinks while Clare and I take a turn round the floor?'

'Dance? To this song?' my sister protested. The band was taking a breather and the DJ had put on that summer's biggest dance hit, sung by two Eastern European girls whose dance moves were better than their singing voices. In resorts all over the Med, the song had sparked a new dance craze that looked like mass morris dancing. Already, a group of excited teenagers were on the floor and going through the routine, which started with a movement like brushing your teeth and followed with several knee bends guaranteed to sort the young from the old. 'We can't dance to this,' Clare complained. 'I don't know the moves for a start.'

'Come on,' said Evan, dragging her to her feet.

And so Clare and Evan stepped out onto the dance floor together and pretty soon Clare was laughing her head off while Evan tried to keep up with the teenaged girls who surrounded him. And while they were dancing, Tom made his move. He was smiling broadly as he approached my table. I couldn't help but be embarrassed. The last time I'd seen Tom, he'd been wrestling Callum to the floor.

'Where's your boyfriend?' Tom asked. 'I don't want to risk getting my nose broken.'

'I am so sorry about that.' I blushed to the roots of my hair again. 'He's actually gone back to England.'

'Really?'

'Really. He flew out this morning. I think he felt embarrassed having picked a fight with someone out of his league. I don't know why he did it,' I continued. 'Well, I do know, but it's all really silly. I think he thought you fancied me.' I added a comedic grimace to show that I thought that was a stupid idea.

'What's silly about that?' Tom asked.

I was about to tell him exactly what was silly about that, but I was distracted by the way he was suddenly looking at me. He was completely straight-faced.

'I do fancy you,' Tom admitted. 'I fancied you the moment you opened the door to let me into Mrs Kenman's flat.'

'You did?'

'Yeah. Though obviously I didn't have time to do anything about it at that point. And I fancied you even more when I came back later that night. I don't make a habit of mixing work with pleasure, but you seemed like someone worth getting to know.'

'But you must have thought I was a crazy woman – all that sand in the backyard.'

'It was an odd sort of thing to do, but it didn't stop me thinking about how pretty you are. I was dead nervous about coming back to your flat for that party. And then I got really drunk. I would have tried to kiss you there and then if you hadn't seemed a bit preoccupied.'

'Oh. Gosh.' I sounded like something out of the 1920s. I was still blushing so hard that the temperature must have been five degrees higher in my immediate vicinity.

'Do you want to dance?' Tom asked.

The band had struck up James Blunt's 'You're Beautiful'. It wasn't exactly a George Michael disco classic. There's only one way to dance to James Blunt's most croonful tune. I wasn't sure I was ready for it, but Tom took me by the hand and led me to the middle of the floor and pretty soon I had a feeling that I was about to embark on a holiday romance.

Epilogue

And so my two-week holiday drew to a close. It certainly hadn't been the holiday I was expecting when I left the office that Tuesday night fourteen days earlier. I wasn't sure the carpet would ever recover from Clare's impromptu beach party, but I felt as though I had had one of the best holidays ever. I returned to my scruffy, sandy little flat full of energy and optimism about the future. It helped that I had Tom's phone number saved on my iPhone.

Of course there was lots of explaining to be done. Though she claimed to have been furious when she discovered that Clare and I had faked half our time in Majorca, by the time we got back from our real trip abroad, Mum had forgotten about her anger at our lies and was instead utterly thrilled to have two daughters on the shortlist for a national bravery award. She was over the moon when I told her that, since Callum would no longer be my plus one, she could be my guest for the star-studded ceremony, where the awards would be presented by one of her favourite actors. She told all her friends, sparing no detail of the story, including my being dumped and deciding to hide at home.

'You can be a very silly girl,' my mother told me. Never mind that I was thirty! 'But I think it was Fate that meant you were in your backyard that afternoon.

If you had been where you were supposed to be, poor Mrs Kenman would be dead.'

Evan too had shelved any disappointment in Clare's sneakiness and decided to concentrate on what a bright and brave woman his future wife was. He had also switched his focus from hard-core budget management to making sure that he and Clare enjoyed their lives together more. He started his new regime by diverting some of the money saved for new decking in their back-yard to booking another holiday in the sun. He also agreed that Clare and I should make our five-day 'break from reality' (as we now called it) an annual tradition.

'Perhaps you should recreate your five days in Sophie's flat every year,' he suggested, hoping to save a little money on flights.

I was pleased to see that as well as agreeing that holidays were an important part of any household budget, Evan had been far more open to Clare's dreams of retraining as an artist than she had hoped. In fact, he was entirely encouraging, having learned that her happiness made life much better for them both.

Clare did use her photographs of our urban beach in her application to art school. When she showed me the testimony she had written to support the work, I couldn't help but be reminded of the imaginary Disney holiday she had invented all those years before. My sister had a truly creative mind. I was very proud when she announced that she had been accepted on a foundation art course.

My sister and I definitely had a new appreciation of each other as a result of our little adventure. Of course, we can't choose our sisters, but I knew for certain now that I would have chosen Clare as a friend had we not spent thirty years of our lives together. She had helped me survive what could have been one of the most horrible times in my life. She said that I had done the same for her, helping her realise at exactly the right time that what she had with Evan was worth keeping. Clare truly was my best friend.

I dreaded my first morning back at work, but the girls in the office were a great deal more sympathetic than I had expected. Callum's indignation cut no ice with them. They were much more interested in hearing exactly how I had pulled the wool over everyone's eyes. They pored over the Facebook photos, unable to believe that they really had been fooled by a picture taken in my back garden.

'Eight sacks of sand from a builder's yard,' breathed Alison in something approaching admiration.

'I should have known it wasn't Puerto Bona,' said Hannah. 'They don't have sand like that.'

And then, of course, the girls wanted to know about my very real holiday romance.

Tom and I spent quite a bit of time together before I had to fly back to London. He had another week of holiday to go after Clare and I left the resort. He texted every day and assured me that he wished I was still there. We had our first proper date about two weeks after I got back from Majorca. We went to a tapas bar in Stockwell. We had been unable to get together sooner because of his shift patterns and when we at last got the chance to catch up, I was incredibly excited. Clare lent me a red dress with just a hint of flamenco in its ruffled hem. With it, I wore my birthday Jimmy Choos, of course.

It was a wonderful evening and I think we both knew that it would be the first of many. The English summer had reverted to type with endless grey days and blustery showers, but somehow, seeing Tom again made me feel as though the sun had come out and brought that holiday feeling rushing back. It was either that or the sangria, with its sunburst notes of orange and lemon. Whatever it was, I was only too happy to agree when, as Tom walked me home, he suggested that he show me some first-aid techniques. I told him that I wanted to know everything there was to know. Especially when it came to mouth-to-mouth skills . . .

CHRISSIE MANBY

Thirty-nine-year-old Kate had almost given up on love when she met her fiancé. Now she's planning for the wedding she never dreamed she'd have. But things seem to be slipping out of her control.

Diana, born on the day of the 1981 Royal Wedding, never doubted that one day she would find her prince. Newly engaged, and with daddy's credit card in her grasp, she's in full Bridezilla mode.

But will each bride get her perfect day? Or will it all become a right royal fiasco?

Available in Hodder paperback

HODDER

CHRISSIE MANBY

Have you ever had your heart broken? How did you get over it? Did a tub of ice cream cheer you up? Did you delete his number and start again? Are you now friends with your ex? Perhaps you're godmother to his children?

In which case, you're a weirdo and this book is not for you.

But if you reacted with denial, begging or a spot of casual witchcraft, then you've come to the right place. This is one woman's journey from love to lunacy and back again . . .

Available in Hodder paperback

HODDER

We love a happy ending. But, almost more than that, we love the promise of a new beginning.

Join us at www.hodder.co.uk, or follow us on Twitter @hodderbooks, and be part of a community of escapists who enjoy nothing more than curling up with a good book.

Whether you want to find out more about this book, or a particular author, watch trailers and interviews, have the chance to win early limited editions, or simply browse our expert readers' selection of the very best books, we think you'll find what you're looking for.

And if you don't, that's the place to tell us what's missing.

We love what we do, and we'd love you to be part of it.

www.hodder.co.uk

@hodderbooks

HodderBooks

HodderBooks